PAGES
OF
DEATH

HOWARD
SHAW

OFFA

© Offa Press 2000

Published by Offa Press
2 Leigh Court, Byron Hill Road
Harrow on the Hill
Middlesex HA2 0HZ

I.S.B.N. 0-9539521-0-X

Merchet School does not exist, neither does the village of Merchet Farthing. They are products of the winding stair of imagination which places them somewhere in the Sussex downland beloved of the Bloomsbury set at Charleston and Rodmell, probably not too far from Glyndebourne. The origins of the name Merchet are obscure. Merchet was a fee paid by a villein to his lord in the Middle Ages for the right to give his daughter in marriage and it is believed to be related to this. The storyline is pure fantasy: in my experience housemasters' wives are not nymphomaniacs, nor do they seduce the boys in their charge. The names of real places and real schools have been used to give verisimilitude to the narrative, but no reference is intended to any person living or dead.

Printed and Bound in England by
MPG Books Limited, Victoria Square, Bodmin, Cornwall PL31 1EG.

For Ann

Prologue

But the merriest was this Shore's wife, in whom the king therefore took special pleasure. For many he had, but her he loved, whose favour to say truth...she never abused to any man's hurt.

SIR THOMAS MORE

Legend has it that Eton College, founded by the Lancastrian Henry VI, was saved from extinction under his Yorkist successor, Edward IV, by the intervention of his mistress, Jane Shore. Sadly – for nothing is so agreeable to a respectable institution as the whiff of ancient scandal – the tale cannot be substantiated and Eton lacks the blessing of a bend sinister on its escutcheon.

It is less well known that this same Jane Shore, a delightful companion by all accounts, persuaded her royal lover to endow a school at the Benedictine abbey of Merchet after they had spent a memorable night together in the abbey guest house, thus creating the only educational foundation with which this virile and profligate monarch is credited. Less well known, but much better documented, for the Croyland Chronicler not only gives details of the royal benefaction, but also expresses moral disapproval of the *union de flammes* that gave rise to it.

The school survived the dissolution of its mother abbey under the Tudors and Merchet is now one of the great schools of England. For years its standing was modest, a grammar school for the sons of local Sussex folk, but its reputation was made in the nineteenth century by a headmaster whose flagellant prowess rivalled even the notorious Keate of Eton. Such an ardent panderer to *le vice anglais* was bound to attract the aristocracy and by the end of Victoria's reign the fortunes of the school and, indeed, the country were judged by the number of Old Merchets in the Cabinet.

Built largely of mellow brick, Merchet moulds itself into a fold of the South Downs. From the south it is invisible, unless one climbs

4

the slope of Gallow Down; from the east and west it is hidden by woodland, the last vestiges of the ancient Andredesweald, the forest once covering most of Sussex; only from the north, where the main road passes the entrance gates, is one aware of the abbey tower, the huddle of buildings housing more than seven hundred boys, and the adjacent village of Merchet Farthing, most of whose inhabitants earn their livelihood at the school.

Such retiring modesty was once characteristic of the great schools. Eton, Harrow, Winchester, Merchet – they did not need publicity and they did not seek it. Secure in their history, they relaxed in an atmosphere of cloistered confidence – some might say complacency – where traditional standards were maintained and understatement was the order of the day. For them, as for Pangloss, all was for the best in the best of all possible worlds, and they adapted imperceptibly to the tides around them, self-effacing landmarks amidst the ebb and flow of changing educational fashion.

Today things have changed. We live in the age of self-advertisement where the glossy brochure and trumpeting of scholastic and athletic achievement are essential for all if they are to survive in a competitive world. The older schools still contrive a degree of stylish understatement and one detects a reluctance to commit themselves to the cruder aspects of the market-place; but the fact remains that it *is* a market-place and trumpets must be blown, albeit discreetly.

Just occasionally, however, an opportunity presents itself which even the most dignified of institutions cannot resist. The quincentenary of the granting of Merchet's charter by Edward IV was such an occasion. Merchet prepared to celebrate and blazon forth its survival to the world.

Christmas

Chapter 1

Thinking about it later, Tristan knew the exact moment the idea of the pageant came to him. It was at the beginning of the carol service on the last night of the Christmas term. He was sitting in the senior masters' stalls, watching the choir process from the cloister into the warmth of the abbey. It was the draught at the open door that did it. He found himself thinking not of well-fed schoolboys, bright-eyed at the prospect of the Christmas holidays, but of the monks whose abbey it had been in the Middle Ages. The sudden gust of cold air swept over him and, looking down the nave towards the cloister, he saw in imagination a line of gaunt, black-cowled men shuffling across the flagstones between the guttering candles.

The choir, singing cheerfully, reached the chancel. The chaplain, Alastair Munro, a bearded Scotsman nicknamed The Ayatollah by the boys, led the bidding prayer; of austere appearance and opinions, he had a flinty voice that easily reached the remoter regions of the abbey. The Usher closed the door; the draught was cut off and the heating reasserted itself. The moment had come and gone, but for the rest of the service Tristan St. Leger, second master and head of history at Merchet, allowed himself the luxury of a wandering imagination.

Choir and congregation launched into *See amid the winter snow...* Beside him his wife Melanie caught his eye and smiled; her blonde hair curled out from beneath an elegant fur hat and Tristan felt a glow of affection as he sensed her move closer. In the stalls opposite other masters and wives sang with the enthusiasm of those who know they are on show.

He saw the monks outside now, a melancholy group in a Breughel snowscape; behind, the ruins of their abbey, before them the unhedged fields, a wide grey sky, and the uncertainties of the world they were forced to face by Henry VIII's Dissolution. The picture formed and reformed. The stark outline of a gallows on the Down; the gloom of a January morning as old Abbot Greenfield prepared to meet his maker for defying the King's commissioners. His final words, 'I acknowledge no Lord but God', had become by tradition the text for the visiting preacher every Founder's Day, a nice irony when, as was often the case, he was an ambitious Old Merchet whose climb into the ecclesiastical hierarchy had involved a studied compromise with Mammon.

A new boy read of the birth of Christ from St. Luke, his hands gripping the wings of the lectern eagle; the congregation sang *While shepherds watched their flocks by night;* the shadowy ranks of the School, white faces illuminated by the candlelight, ranged backwards into the depths of the nave and transepts.

St. Leger looked up at the window above the altar where the tracery showed signs of transition from Decorated to Perpendicular, the last alteration made by the Benedictines before their expulsion. Yes, a pageant was the obvious answer. For six months the head man had been agitating about ideas for the quincentenary, but precious little had been decided. A royal personage had agreed to open the new Sixth Form Centre, but apart from a proposed dinner for Old Merchets in the House of Lords nothing else had materialised. A building appeal had been mooted then promptly quashed because Old Merchets were only two years into their covenants on the last one. Paul Rathbone, who ran the Corps, had suggested a tattoo – an idea still running – but the headmaster was not anxious to saddle Merchet with a military image, while Rathbone's colleagues were suspicious that a pyrotechnical display by the Combined Cadet Force might be no more than an ego-trip for its commander. Besides, the Corps would fit into the pageant. There were distinguished Merchets in both world wars and it would be easy to work in a military showpiece; and going further back there was bound to have been someone involved in the Boer War or the Crimean shambles. What about Waterloo? Eton had hogged the limelight there, but a little research would no doubt reveal the Merchet touch not far beneath the surface. He warmed to his theme. Blenheim? Ramillies? No, Marlborough had not been to Merchet. But there was good material in the Civil War. There had been a skirmish on the Downs and Prince Rupert's troopers had raped half the village while ostensibly resting afterwards. Yes, there were plenty of possibilities for the Corps.

The head of school, a confident young man named Pomeroy, made a stately progress to the lectern and read of the journey of the Magi. The choir, conducted by Jasper Hillyard, head of music, sang a modern arrangement of the Coventry Carol; the crimson of Hillyard's Oxford hood fitted the festive mood, reflecting the red ribbon used to tie the holly decoration all round the abbey. Musically philistine though much of it was, the School listened in hushed appreciation.

St. Leger looked across the aisle at John Pilgrim and his wife, Rachel. If the pageant came off – he was so enthused by the prospect the conditional seemed superfluous – then Pilgrim would have to produce it. Tristan was prepared to write it, but it would need Pilgrim's rare skills in dramatic production to make it a success. Pilgrim was listening to the carol, his head, grizzled, groomed with studied nonchalance, held at an angle, giving the impression he was weighing every note and nuance. In the school at large he was respected for his academic ability; those who tried to get to know him personally suspected a certain hollowness of character. Beside him was his wife, mousy-haired, small-featured, reflecting something of her husband's approach to life but lacking his intellectual capacity. She looked permanently bad-tempered.

He didn't anticipate much difficulty in persuading Pilgrim. Just as long as it was clear that Pilgrim was in charge and that he, Tristan, was willing to adapt the script to the whims of the producer all would be well. He didn't want to take overall responsibility himself anyway; well aware of his own administrative shortcomings, he would not put forward the idea at all if he did not think Pilgrim would produce it.

He would need to get most of the masters' room involved, of course. His eyes moved to Sylvester Ford, head of art, whose department normally provided scenery for drama productions. He was a notable artist in his own right who seemed strangely unaware of the incongruity of the wispy beard he had grown on his moonlike face; beneath the beard was his inevitable bow tie. Beside him was Matthew Tawney, tall and spare, a young linguist coming to the end of his first term. Beyond these two sat the only two women on the staff: Jane Osgood, trim, fair and pretty in a rather obvious way; and Pamela Baskerville, untidy, dark and brooding, a brilliant physicist whose brief career at Merchet had been marked by aggressive feminism: as a humanist she regarded the carol service with contempt, but had decided to attend as she wanted to mark her presence at all school 'occasions'. To her male colleagues, who found her a disturbing influence in a world they had always dominated, she was known as 'Mad Millie'. She would have to be included in the

10

pageant, St. Leger decided.

To his right a candle flickered perilously. For an instant it seemed about to go out, then it recovered, burning with a stronger flame than before.

The service followed its traditional course. *Hark, the herald angels* reverberated around the groined roof, the masculine weight of the congregation sweeping all subtlety before it. Bruce Irving, the headmaster, went to the lectern and read the mystical opening of St. John's Gospel: 'In the beginning was the Word. And the Word was with God. And the Word was God...'

Irving was an administrator rather than a scholar, but he knew how to read and his well-modulated tones made the most of the passage. He was, thought St. Leger, a successful headmaster who had never managed to make himself popular. Physically, he was impressive: tall, broad-shouldered, with a high forehead and faintly aquiline nose, his sheer bulk earned respect, as did the fact that he had once rowed in a winning Cambridge boat; his eyes, pale blue and alert, could on occasion freeze masters and boys alike. His success as a headmaster lay not in his apparent interest in individuals, widely suspected to be spurious, but in his ability to choose good subordinates and then leave them to get on with it. Imagination was not his strength, but he could appreciate it in others. As he put it at one masters' meeting: 'The boys have more than enough imagination for all of us. Our duty is to keep it under control'. The comment was seen by those present to be mildly funny and a chuckle had gone round the room. Irving had not understood. His failure to gain popularity sprang in large part from his complete lack of a sense of humour.

St. Leger knew Irving would approve the pageant if he presented the idea properly. He disliked untidiness, projects not thought through, but once he saw a good scheme he would lend it his authority; put simply, he saw his role as separating the efficient from the inefficient. Yes, he would approve it and he would give public support, at least to begin with; but once the snags appeared – and there were bound to be snags – he would stand back and let the instigator carry the heat of the day. An enterprise like the pageant would inevitably upset vested interests. Rehearsals would clash with games, music practice, preparation for confirmation – the list was endless. And here and there the awkward squad would dig in its heels. Certain things could not be done because they had never been done before,

11

because they interfered with prep or prayers, or some sacrosanct institution on the Merchet calendar : there would be plenty of obstruction.

From Moncrieff, for instance. Tristan looked across at the senior housemaster, sitting in what had become over nearly forty years his private pew. He was a reactionary bachelor who resented any change; his record of obstruction was massive and within the decentralised power structure of the school it only needed inertia at one critical housemastering point to clog up the whole works. He sat there now, curiously Pickwickian, yet clearly anything but ingenuous. Why did Moncrieff survive, a feudal relic at the end of the twentieth century? He survived, indeed he flourished, because he had style and arrogance. His dress, a cross between that of an Edwardian squire and a forgetful Oxford don, was eccentric; he gave outrageous dinner parties at which one might meet a cabinet minister or an adulterous film star, both at the same time if one brought the other; he took his senior boys boating on the river on summer evenings, introducing them to the delights of strawberries and Château d'Yquem; his impossible snobbery was so absurd as to be disarming to all but the most critical. In short, he was an anachronism, the last remains of a Merchet in which social cachet had taken precedence over educational excellence.

The choir was singing again: Byrd's *Christus natus est*. Pilgrim had altered the angle of his head, pondering perhaps the wisdom of the protestant Elizabethan regime which allowed a talented catholic to compose for it.

But if Moncrieff obstructed, others would lend support. He looked along the crowded pews at the nine other housemasters. Wentworth, for example, would want everyone in Theobalds to take part. He worked on the Wesleyan principle that the Devil finds work for idle hands, so every boy should be fully occupied. Calverley would help, too. He believed Merchet still spent too much time on sport and that anything encroaching on the gamesfield must, *ipso facto*, be a good thing. And Trevelyan and Scott...

The service was coming to an end. Munro read a collect and gave the blessing. Choir and congregation stood to sing the final hymn, *Adeste fideles*, sung in Latin by boys only dimly aware of its meaning. In the final verse the trebles, heavily outnumbered, rose thinly in descant above the massed voices round them.

The Usher opened the great double doors at the end of the nave and the chill of the winter night re-entered; all through the abbey the candles flickered, casting wild shadows on the high Gothic arches. For the last time St. Leger was taken back to the dispossessed Benedictines.

There would be a pageant.

Chapter 2

If the seeds of tragedy were unwittingly sown in the carol service, they were at least partly germinated at Drydens the same evening.

The last night of term is an uneasy one for housemasters at boarding schools. With the boys aware that the normal discipline structure has only a few hours to run, tensions are inevitable. Accordingly, official policy is to occupy the boys as fully as possible and keep known troublemakers under surveillance. The carol service over, the whole school went to the great hall for a Christmas dinner and after that housemasters made individual arrangements in their houses. Most housemasters invited one or two parents to the dinner and back to their houses afterwards for a drink. At Drydens on this occasion Mark Calverley had encouraged the acting fraternity – always keen to show off – to put on a short review. To leaven the excitable boy audience with adults and to ensure a measure of decorum, he had invited the parents of his head of house, a Mr and Mrs Sandbach, the St. Legers, always good value at Merchet social occasions because they were prepared to talk to boys, Alastair Munro, Hugo Charteris and his wife, and Henry Korn, an historian with radical views. He had also asked Matthew Tawney and Jane Osgood; Tawney had earned himself a promising reputation in his first term and Jane could always be relied upon to mix well. Calverley had studiously avoided Pamela Baskerville and had persuaded one of his colleagues it was his turn to have her. While anxious to ensure the two women were always included, it was invariably Pamela who had to be fitted in at the last moment by an unenthusiastic host.

While the performers were getting themselves organised, Calverley took his guests to the drawing-room, a gracious, high-ceilinged room with a crackling log fire and gold velvet curtains. A First in Greats, with several learned monographs to his name, Calverley scorned the vagueness and untidiness traditionally associated with intellectuals and was considered the warmest and most stylish host at Merchet. A fifty-year-old who looked nearer forty, tall, with an air of distinction envied by his colleagues, he had the knack of getting on with people at all levels in the school hierarchy. Now he effected introductions and dispensed drinks, while his wife, Mary, a plain no-nonsense woman wearing a simple red dress, fetched coffee.

The St. Legers were already talking to three of Calverley's senior boys who had also been asked in for a drink, one of whom was the Sandbach's son. 'Enjoy the service?' Melanie asked brightly.

'My favourite service of the year,' said Sandbach. 'It means the end of term,' he added with a smile.

'Most of the boys enjoy it,' said one of the others. 'Which is more than can be said for the normal weekday services.' He looked carefully over his shoulder to make sure the chaplain was out of earshot. 'Compulsory religion is out of date these days. There's a lot of feeling among the sixth-formers.'

'We're a religious foundation,' countered St. Leger quietly, well aware this was a tricky subject. Even as he spoke his mind was going back to the Benedictines and the idea of the pageant.

'All a long time ago, sir,' said the third boy, an intelligent scientist with a safe place at Cambridge. 'I'm an atheist anyway, sir,' he said challengingly. 'I don't think I should have to go.'

St. Leger had had this conversation many times in his career at Merchet and he knew how to avoid confrontation. 'It's all good for your education, Johnny. You don't want to be an *ignorant* atheist, do you?' He smiled encouragingly and changed the subject: 'You'll have a beer, won't you? Your housemaster's slow with the liquid entertainment this evening.'

Calverley was getting a drink for the Sandbach parents. 'I hope your turkey wasn't too cold, Julia,' he said. Christian names were usual with parents of long standing and the Sandbachs had had two sons in Drydens. 'Chef tries hard, but the food has a long way to come from the kitchens. One of the snags of being a medieval school.'

'Well, I won't say it was hot!' Julia Sandbach laughed attractively. 'But I enjoyed myself. I hadn't dined in the great hall before and I tried to imagine sitting there with the monks in the old days. Quite exciting with all those celibates.'

'Not as celibate as all that if the record of the Cromwellian visitation is to be believed. There was plenty of talk of loose women from the village.' Calverley was never slow to respond in kind to the flirtatious tone set by a pretty woman.

'Even more exciting. Not too much, Mark' – she waved an admonishing finger at the brandy bottle he was holding – 'I'm driving, so that John can enjoy himself. After all, we're beginning to celebrate. When Paul leaves in the summer, that will be the end of school fees.'

'Thank God! The treadmill's been running a long time', said her husband, an ex-soldier, now farming, with a terse but genial manner. The brood's done its best to ruin me.'

'If Paul were going on to university, you'd still have a lot to find.' Alastair Munro joined the conversation. He was relaxing after the carol service and had already drunk a good deal.

'Too many people go to university,' opined Sandbach. 'Too many universities and too few brains. Most young people would be better getting a job. Paul's going into the army for a few years. That will train him for life better than any university.'

'Our first boy went to Oxford, you know,' said his wife, who sensed her husband mounting a hobbyhorse not tastefully ridden in Merchet surroundings. 'Read Oriental Languages because it was the only way he could get in. Now he's forgotten the lot, but he made hundreds of useful contacts and wouldn't have missed Oxford for anything.'

Julia Sandbach's crude appreciation of an Oxford education pushed Calverley away but pulled Hugo Charteris nearer. He was a big florid man, with all the confidence of one who has been laying down mandarin law for twenty years. He said: 'I remember teaching him, Mrs Sandbach. What was his name?'

'Rawdon.'

'Ah, yes.' Charteris nodded vaguely. For most schoolmasters the names of past pupils are a perpetual hazard; he remembered the face of a boy called Sandbach, but the Christian name meant nothing.

Calverley handed Matthew Tawney a whisky and pulled him towards the group round Julia Sandbach. 'You'd just been reading *Vanity Fair*, hadn't you, Julia?'

'I took it into the nursing home with me. John didn't know what I was talking about when I suggested it, but in those days he humoured me.' As a parent of long standing she smiled encouragingly, almost patronisingly, at the young master.

'The trouble with a name like Rawdon is that it suggests a certain type of character. Has he lived up to it?' said Tawney.

'Hardly. He's an accountant living in Epsom. Model husband and father, and conscientious with his mortgage. Not the Rawdon I had in mind.'

'You're a romantic, Julia.' Calverley interrupted his drink dispensing duties. 'Now if you moved in the Merchet circle you'd be a cynic like Hugo here.'

'We're not as cynical as the boys,' said Charteris.

'I agree.' Andrew Korn spoke for the first time. He disliked Merchet social occasions and Calverley had not expected him to come. 'It's not surprising considering the materialism of the homes they come from.'

Sandbach, himself used to blunt speaking, clearly resented this tactless criticism of Merchet parents. His wife anticipated him: 'Oh come, Mr Korn, there are plenty of boys here who bring ideals from home. You can't get away with that.' The hint of humour in her voice could not wholly mask the steely intent.

Korn adjusted his heavy horn-rimmed spectacles; his wiry black hair stuck out aggressively; he spoke as though making a formal speech. 'Mrs Sandbach, I cast no aspersions on your son, of course. I'm sure he has every advantage at home. But he's the exception rather than the rule. The average Merchet boy has a head full of prejudices, most of them based on crude materialism. I spend half my time trying to get them to think for themselves, to question a world that measures success by the cash in the bank account or the number of cars in the garage. What do most boys want to do when they leave? Make money. I haven't found much home-grown idealism, I can assure you.'

The strength of feeling in his tone brought silence. Korn looked for support in an unexpected quarter. He turned to Munro. 'Why do most boys get confirmed, Alastair? Usually because parents want it for conventional reasons and loaded god-parents offer a substantial cash inducement. Isn't that so?'

Munro, who didn't like Korn – an aggressive agnostic at the best of times – felt his office as well as the attitude of the boys under attack. 'One or two perhaps' – honesty dictated a strategic withdrawal – 'but in the main it's personal conviction. I don't let them go through with it unless I'm sure of their motives.'

'They fool you, Alastair.'

'Not a bit of it. You're the one with the preconceived ideas, Andrew. My impression is that we have a very idealistic generation

17

on our hands, and we should give the parents much of the credit. Look at the numbers who went in for the sponsored charity run this term.'

'There was a crate of beer waiting for them at the finish. And plenty of kudos in the eyes of the School because it involved athleticism. Look at the way it confirmed young Treece's heroic status. He'd already got his rugby and cricket colours before he won it.'

'Who's the cynic now?' broke in Calverley. He disliked tension on social occasions and deplored Korn's insensitivity. I'm bound to say that my impression is that boys think about important issues more than we did in my day. They're...What on earth...?'

Calverley's calming interjection was interrupted by a wild outburst of dogs barking in the hall outside. He rushed out to investigate. For a few moments there was a frenzy of noise: Calverley shouting, dogs barking, the crash of breaking china. This last took Mary Calverley out to join her husband. Eventually order was apparently restored and Calverley reappeared.

'Panic over,' he said. 'Sorry about that. Our wretched dog has been out and brought back one of his friends – the Wentworth's alsation. They're usually amicable but ours turned nasty when the visitor went for his food. Understandable really. Just like the boys in hall. Their manners can be appalling.'

'What broke?' asked Tristan St. Leger.

'That's the real casualty. One of Mary's Chinese pots. It's been in her family for years. If you'll excuse me, I'll just take the Wentworth's dog over to Theobalds and by the time I get back the boys should be ready for us. Mary will get you another drink while I'm away.'

The rest of the evening followed the usual pattern. The boys produced a light-hearted review marked by a good deal of over-acting and a little modest talent. The jokes were about parochial house or school matters and hence mystifying to the guests. Several masters were satirised, notably Stephen Higham, who was not present but whose camp characteristics made him fair game on any Merchet occasion, as well as the housemaster, whose good nature and sense of humour could be relied upon. Andrew Korn, who had withstood many such evenings, was bored to tears and left early; the Sandbachs left as soon as they decently could, and the others left shortly before midnight, Tawney feeling gauche and new and puzzled by the whole occasion. On the boys' side the excitement generated by the review gradually died away and soon all lights were out except those of the monitors.

Mark Calverley poured himself a nightcap and put the guard in front of the dying fire; overhead he heard his wife moving about in their bedroom. He looked at the pile of house reports on his desk he had barely started; he thought back over the evening and looked forward with anticipation to the sense of relief he knew he would feel when the last boy had gone home in the morning. Then, vaguely at first, but with increasing recognition of a conscious drift, he thought back to his visit to Theobalds with the errant dog and his meeting with its owner, Jennifer Wentworth. There had been a moment on the Theobalds doorstep which he had found disturbing, a moment when he had recognised a truth about himself he did not really want to face.

'Your dog,' he had said laughingly.'He's broken one of Mary's pots.'

'Oh Mark, I'm so sorry. He shouldn't have been out at all. Won't you come in? James will be messing about in the house until midnight, and probably later if he suspects they're up to something. I could do with some company.'

She held her dog by the collar and was leaning forward; the rich auburn hair falling round her face framed a smile of genuine welcome. An expression passed across her face so imperceptibly that a casual observer would not have seen it.'Please,' she said.

'Sorry, Jenny, I can't stop. I've got a drawing-room full of guests, and then the boys are doing something or other. Haven't you got anyone in?'

'No, thank God. Our parents wanted to go straight after dinner and James decided to make the boys spend the evening cleaning the house up. They left it filthy at the end of last term and our dailies nearly went on strike the next morning. I'm on my own now. That's why I've got my shoes off.' She wriggled her stockinged toes and pushed her dog into the house.'Perhaps another time, Mark?'Again Calverley registered an expression he had never seen before as their eyes met.

He went back to Drydens and watched the exhibitionism of the boys' entertainment with his mind only partly engaged. Now, relaxing on his own for the first time in the day, he thought about Jennifer Wentworth and wondered how many of the things he had heard about her were really true.

* * * * * *

That same night, at about 11 p.m., an old man living alone in a brick and flint cottage near the village of Monks Risborough in Buckinghamshire made a telephone call. He had been putting off the decision for days – one might say years – but he could do so no longer. At eighty-three he had hardly had a day's illness in his life and he had a hearty contempt for those of his surviving contemporaries who constantly pestered the medical profession. But certain symptoms could no longer be ignored and a visit to the doctor earlier in the week had sounded alarm bells. Optimist he might be, but he was also a realist. The time had come to communicate.

Strange. It stirred the embers. As a classical scholar he recalled the Virgilian phrase *Veteris vestigia flammae* – 'Ashes of an old flame'. Yes, it would be a relief to talk after all this time.

But what about the gun? That *was* a problem.

The telephone rang in Theobalds and Jennifer Wentworth picked it up.

Chapter 3

The following day the Christmas term ended. A few boys given special leave to catch trains or planes to exotic places ordered early taxis and left before breakfast. The majority tidied their rooms, attended a final call-over, then either waited for parents to appear in cars or caught specially chartered coaches to Brighton station. By noon, apart from the odd boy still standing disconsolately by his house waiting for a dilatory parent, Merchet was silent.

Matthew Tawney stood at the window of his flat in the Abbot's House and watched the final cars vanish into the surrounding woodland. He had dark, short-cropped hair and a face which, though young in age, was of the type whose firm outline already hints at its future appearance in later years. He felt a sense of relief that the term was over; at the same time he was trying to analyse his feelings about Merchet. He himself had been to a grammar school in the north of England and had been apprehensive about teaching in a public school, particularly one as well known as Merchet. Not, he told himself, because it was likely to be better in any way, but because it represented the unknown.

The first surprise had been a pleasant one: the sense of community, and a welcoming one at that. He had expected things to be different, even odd – and they were – but he had not been prepared for the genuine warmth awaiting the newcomer. Drinks before lunch or dinner, friendly family suppers, formal dinner parties – the invitations had flooded in and whatever difficulties he might have had, they did not stem from lack of hospitality. Why, then, this sense of relief ? The work was strenuous, of course, but he had expected a boarding school would require greater commitment from its staff than a day school, indeed that was one of its attractions. The actual teaching was easy. As an Oxford First he got most pleasure teaching the more academic boys, but, slightly to his surprise, he had also enjoyed coping with the dullards. It was, he had discovered, a question of ingenuity and imagination, of presenting the daily diet in novel ways. He recalled the day he had walked into his form-room singing *The*

Vicar of Bray. He'd got across more ideas on literature, religion and history than in any other period of the term; when the bell rang, they all left singing it in unison. Unknown to him, one or two senior colleagues remarked privately that he was a born schoolmaster.

No, the strain did not lie in the work. It lay mainly in the social adjustment, the need to come to terms with the customs of an institution that did things in its unique way. It was not that anyone was overtly snobbish, with the exception of Moncrieff; but there could be no doubt that five hundred years of history weighed heavily on daily practice and everyone expected you to know. So far from being excluded as an outsider, it was assumed he had always been privy to Merchet's curious ways. It had not taken him long to realise that no-one actually told you anything; the expectation was that the strange local vocabulary of Merchet, together with its arcane social habits, were somehow absorbed by newcomers with the air they breathed.

The hurdles presented to the uninitiated were legion. No-one had told him, for example, that masters and boys wore black ties on Remembrance Sunday and he had spent the whole of the morning service in the abbey unsuccessfully trying to conceal a nice little number with bright red and white stripes he had found in a Brighton charity shop. Nor had it been revealed that the head of school's extensive privileges included the right to leave the abbey straight after the headmaster and it had been mere chance he had not mown him down by stepping into the aisle at an inappropriate time. He had been told a suit was required dress for teaching, but no-one had thought to explain that while his chalk pinstripe was wholly acceptable for an ordinary weekday it would look out of place on a Saturday when, for reasons presumably connected with the sporting activities of the afternoon, it was customary to relax into tweeds and Prince of Wales checks.

None of these things mattered greatly in themselves, he knew that; but somehow the dress issue focused the problem of settling down at Merchet. His background had not prepared him for the formality that was treated as normal. At his own school the staff dressed in motley, with a preference for sweaters, nondescript sports jackets and, out of doors, anoraks made of nylon. The idea of wearing a gown, a daily requirement at Merchet, would have seemed comical to them. So his term had been spent adjusting, modifying, conforming, trying to fade into the scenery. He had just discovered that a dinner jacket was *de rigueur* for certain functions, notably dining with housemasters, when he was invited to Freddie Tichbourne's house, Muchelney; there he found – too late, of course – that Tichbourne had radical views on virtually everything, including dinner jackets, and once again he was the odd man out.

Tawney turned away from the window and went into the kitchen. Time for coffee. He put on a kettle.

It was partly a question of how much he should conform. He was not a weak character anxious to bend with every breeze and he wanted to be accepted for what he was, a straightforward Northerner who spoke as he thought. But he did want to be accepted and he could see no virtue in emphasizing his provincialism, just as long as his conformity did not appear to be the plastic compromise of the social climber.

And there was something else. He was lonely. At Oxford he had not made friends easily, but by his second year had acquired a small circle within which he moved confidently. Here he was starting from scratch again and he had not found anyone of his own age to whom he was particularly drawn. He helped with the Junior Colts rugby – or rugger, as he had learned to call it – but he was not a natural games player and did not gravitate towards the hearties, whose academic aspirations were, at best, modest. Among recent appointments only one was a genuine intellectual and he was an oddball who found it difficult to communicate with colleagues or boys. Besides, he could not keep order and that was the main test at Merchet. Tawney, whose own discipline was firm but friendly, shrewdly judged he would not survive beyond the probationary year.

As a community Merchet was warm in its hospitality, but however generous the spirit, married couples closed their doors when the guests had gone and the bachelors were already arranged in groups with which he felt no particular affinity. There was a group of aesthetes centred on Sylvester Ford with whom he might have identified, but although outwardly friendly there was a certain cliquishness about them he did not find attractive. Gossip, sometimes malicious gossip, was their stock in trade and Tawney saw that this little coterie had to some extent isolated itself. Besides, Stephen Higham, known as 'Stephanie' by the boys, was a key figure and this was offputting. If there was a particular grouping to which he felt drawn, it was that

23

comprising a few masters with evangelical leanings who held regular religious discussions with the boys; they were of all ages and affectionately known as 'The Hotgospellers'. Tawney approved their enthusiasm, their clear-cut moral stance on all issues, and deplored the ribald wit of the games players at their expense. But however welcoming they might be, he could not expect to live in their pockets and after going to several houses for informal suppers early in the term he realised he had to start standing on his own feet.

What he really wanted was a girl friend. After a sheltered upbringing he found it difficult to make close relationships with women and although he numbered one or two girls among his Oxford friends they had all been on an intellectual level. He reluctantly admitted envy of the easy charm of the hearties, who pursued pretty but brainless girls in their sports cars, even though he had an idealistic view of women and a strictly moral attitude to marriage.

A term's observation at Merchet might have done something to dent his idealism for several of the marriages there had been tarnished by time, but he had noticed nothing of this, seeing only the comfort of apparently stable relationships. The St. Legers, literary and cultured, their home a treasure-house of antiques; the Tichbournes, easygoing and untidy, a cultivated affront to the Merchet style, yet happily encompassed within it; the Pilgrims, shrewd and worldlywise, standing together in their critical assessment of events around them; even Bruce Irving and his wife, he commanding and confident, yet clearly dependent on support at home. And the Wentworths...

Why had he stopped at the Wentworths? Was it because he felt sorry for Wentworth suspecting a basic discipline problem in his house? Was it his suspicion, in spite of his ingenuousness, of flaws within the marriage? Or was it – and he was barely able to articulate the thought – that he found Jennifer Wentworth so physically attractive he did not want to admit the strength of the carnal side of his nature?

He made his coffee and took it into the sitting-room. Through the open window he watched a boy, an unpleasantly arrogant boy called Hawkins-Manville, packing himself and his belongings into an opulent limousine. 'By their cars shall ye know them,' he murmured.

The prospect of Christmas with his parents in Rochdale did not excite him. It was time to cheer himself up. He put Mozart's *Jupiter* symphony on the CD player and picked up the Thurber anthology he kept for such moments.

* * * * * *

Jennifer Wentworth had not slept well. Two problems had revolved in her mind. First, she was aware that Mark Calverley, for whom she had long nursed a secret but unexpressed desire, might after all be susceptible to her attractions: that was encouraging, though it would add a dimension to an emotional life already byzantine in its complexity. The second problem was more puzzling and more immediate. What did the old man want?

The late telephone call the previous night had been brief but peremptory. Her grandfather, whom she had not seen since the summer, wanted her to come immediately. She had suggested several possibilities more convenient to herself, but he had been adamant: she must go at once. Accordingly she had spoken to her husband and by ten o'clock the next morning was heading north for the Chiltern village of Monks Risborough.

Jennifer and her grandfather did not see each other more than three or four times a year, but when they did the relationship was warm and close. She was his only grandchild and since her parents' death in a car crash some years ago his only relation. She had always said that if he wanted anything he had only to ring and say. Normally he was massively independent and self-contained, seemingly needing nothing, but now he wanted her and when she asked why he had been bafflingly cryptic.

She assumed he must be ill, but he had denied it. He had, he said, something to tell her.

There was only one way to find out. North of Horsham she put her foot down and accelerated towards the M25.

Chapter 4

The Duke of Cambridge in Merchet Farthing had not yet been discovered by tourists and retained the spartan simplicity of a simple country pub. No piped music, no frozen scampi either in or out of the basket, no fruit machine; the furniture was dark oak, there was a dart board and a log fire that smoked. The landlord and his wife – he a onetime groundsman at Merchet – had been there for years; they looked vaguely like each other and both bore a resemblance to the elderly collie who, tired and dispirited, lay in front of the fire, viewing the world through rheumy eyes.

Assembled at the bar were several Merchet masters enjoying the most satisfying drink of the term. Hugo Charteris was there, as always, his high colour already enhanced by his first pint; an Oxford rugby blue who taught geography, he was now grotesquely unfit and took perverse pride in his developing waistline. On a stool opposite sat Roger Halstead, a physicist who was prematurely bald; he was not a sportsman, but always hovered on the fringe of the games-playing set. Between them stood Jim Clode, who ran the cricket and taught history; curly-haired, with a ready smile and humorous creases round the eyes, he viewed the world as a whimsical place and never took anything very seriously. Several younger masters were centred on the doyen of the Duke of Cambridge drinking school, George Spooner, a mathematician and erstwhile England three-quarter. For some obscure reason he was known only by his surname; he was due to retire at the end of the year.

'Two terms to go, Spooner,' said Clode.

'Thank God!'

'You don't mean that' This from Halstead.

'I do, you know.' Spooner pulled at the yellow silk handkerchief in his top pocket, allowing even more of it to hang out. 'I'm too old a dog to learn new tricks. All this GCSE course-work nonsense is driving me up the wall. And now Irving's starting this appraisal business. Besides, my patience is running out. I nearly clouted Beaver the other day. When that happens, it's time to go.'

'You can spend all day in The Duke, lining them up for us,' said Clode. 'I'll come and see you in my free periods.'

'Not a chance. I'm retiring to King's Lynn. Far from this particular madding crowd. There won't be any Old Merchets up there.'

'I shouldn't bank on that. The head man went fishing in Greenland last year and found two of them sitting on an ice-floe.'

'I expect he was pleased to see them. I don't think that man ever relaxes. And he's had a sense of humour bypass.'

'It's difficult to be human as a headmaster. Someone's bound to take advantage.'

'For a successful man, Irving's remarkably unpopular,' interposed Charteris. 'He's too concerned with his image. No-one sees through that more rapidly than the boys.'

'He's worried about drugs,' said Clode.

'Aren't we all?'

'Yes, but I don't think he minds what goes on as long as we don't have a public scandal. Image again.'

'There are bound to be drugs here somewhere. Every other big school's had them and there's no reason why we should be immune. You can't isolate schools from society at large.'

'Mark Calverley told me that Irving hardly talks about anything else in housemasters' meetings. We'll all have to keep our fingers crossed nothing breaks during the quincentenary year.'

'Irving will revel in the quincentenary,' said Charteris. 'Just the chance to show Merchet is up to date in spite of its history.'

'Is it?' Jim Clode raised a quizzical eyebrow.

'Stop being an iconoclast, Jim,' said Spooner. 'When you've been here as long as I have and your pension's in sight, you give thanks for stability.'

'Look at the form-rooms next to the cloisters,' said Clode. 'Cold, damp and downright unhealthy. They wouldn't last a week in a state school. And we show them off to tourists!'

'The state always spends its money on the wrong things. They modernise buildings before they buy books. Comforts don't matter, books do.'

'You're out of date, Spooner. The days of discipline through draughts is over – just like cold baths before breakfast. The modern mother looks for something softer these days. Did you hear about the parents Freddie Tichbourne was showing round Muchelney? Quite blind to the beauties of the hammer-beam roof in the junior dormitory and kept asking where the baths were. They almost took their son's name off his list when they found the wretched boy would have to sprint across to the Old Buttery to find running water.'

'Almost – but not quite. The name of Merchet still means something,' responded Spooner. 'There's too much building going on here anyway. Show before substance again. Skips all over the place and you can't move without tripping over a pile of bricks. God save us from the vandals.'

'Did you hear that Moncrieff refused to let the governors modernise Ryders? Said they could do what they like when he retires at the end of the year, but a builder won't cross the threshold while he's in residence.' Charteris spoke with obvious approval.

'It's time he went,' said Paul Rathbone, who had just come in and always liked to make his mark. 'The Merchet he wants to preserve is no good for anyone, least of all us. He's the sort of man who justifies the case for abolition.'

'The boys like him,' said Clode.

'The boys like eccentrics. He's just a snob, pure and simple.'

'To borrow from Wilde, snobs are rarely pure and never simple,' said Clode. 'He's a clever man who's filled his house with blue blood and money and can freeload in half the country houses in the kingdom, not to mention his links with the City mafia who handle his stocks and shares. Besides, I've a vested interest in Moncrieff. He always produces at least two top-class cricketers for the Eleven, sometimes more. If a boy comes as a cricketer from his prep school, he sticks with it in Ryders. No messing about with tennis or sailing or any other nonsense. I wish the other housemasters took the same tough line. Some of them positively discourage the game. Look at Freddie Tichbourne. He banned Fisher-Cooke from the Winchester match last year simply because it was a two-day game and looked as though it might handicap what was already a dodgy Maths GCSE. He's the best leg-spinner we've had for years.'

'Like Moncrieff, leg-spinners are a dying breed,' said Charteris. 'They'll never come back while the professional game relies on the medium-pace trundler. Who's ready for the next round?'

'I am,' said Spooner. 'And I'll join the dying breed. The trouble is that the professionals are taking over everywhere. Moncrieff and I go into retirement together – the last of the amateurs. No-one ever taught me to teach. I just got on with it. Made a mess of it for the first couple of years, too. But we all got through. Nowadays everyone who comes into the profession is so bloody serious. In my day it was just a question of whether you could keep the little buggers quiet.'

'Tawney's O.K.,' said Clode.

'Right. But not because he's got a fancy bit of paper. Schoolmasters are born, not made. At bottom it's a question of character. He's got it.'

'He's an asset,' said Rathbone. 'A genuine academic with a good dose of commonsense. That's a rare combination. I like him. One of Irving's best appointments.'

'Northern realism,' said Halstead. 'Calls a spade a spade. But reserved. He never comes down here.'

'We've never asked him,' pointed out Clode.

'Yes, our fault,' said Spooner. 'We'll get him down next term. He'll probably do some cricket for you in the summer, Jim. You still need another man with the Yearlings.'

'Another sign of the times,' said Charteris, pushing his upper lip into the froth of a new pint. 'When I first came you didn't get appointed if you didn't know what you were doing on the games field. And now we've got these two women – and there'll be more. They can't coach rugger or cricket and they don't even see how important they are at a place like Merchet. Mad Millie doesn't do anything at all outside the form-room except criticise us and the system.'

'Equal opportunities,' said a young man hovering on the fringe of the conversation. 'We can't keep them out. Besides, if they're as pretty as Jane Osgood, I don't want to.'

'The place is changing,' said Clode. 'We can laugh at Mad Millie and ogle Jane's legs, but we can't keep Merchet in the nineteenth century for ever. We should ask them down as well.'

Spooner snorted. Rathbone changed the subject abruptly. 'Theobalds has had a bad term. Wentworth's losing his grip. You can see it in the boys' dress. It always shows there first.'

'Did he ever have a grip?' asked Spooner. He spends his time chasing round after everybody but misses the obvious. He believes everything the boys tell him. Do you know he let Slade, O'Reilly and Orchard go to London to see the Monet exhibition? They never went near it. Spent most of the time having a booze-up at Slade's flat in Kensington and then went on to some dive in the King's Road. Totally predictable. I wouldn't let that trio go to church on their own.'

'He's an idealist,' said Clode. 'They're his boys, so he believes them.'

'You can believe most boys,' said Halstead. 'But housemasters can't afford to take risks.'

'Healthy scepticism is the first duty of the historian and the housemaster. There's a *bon mot* for the end of term,' said Clode, looking pleased with himself.

'Wentworth could start by being sceptical about his wife.' Rathbone spoke bluntly, then realised he might have spoken out of turn and looked round to see if his words had gone beyond his immediate audience. They had not, but he had induced an embarrassed silence. 'All right,' he said. 'Tactless, but true. Jennifer's James's real problem.'

No-one responded and Rathbone saw he had raised an issue of gossip before too large a group. What might have been discussed privately with one or two was plainly out of order in more numerous company. He eased himself off his stool and stretched for his beer. 'O.K. No discussion of ladies in the mess. Who's coming to Brighton for lunch? I fancy something Italian.'

Rathbone made for the door, followed by two or three young masters. Reaching it, he remembered something. 'I met Tristan this morning. He sounded me out about helping him with a pageant for the quincentenary next summer. He's put the idea up to the head man. I told him the Corps would take part. What do you think?'

As he spoke Charles Moncrieff came into the pub. He was wearing tweeds and a bow tie he always put on at the end of term. 'You could start by shooting Mad Millie,' he said.

Moncrieff had opposed the appointment of women to Merchet from the start and his misogyny was something of a joke. Pamela Baskerville's unrestrained feminism had confirmed his worst fears and he now regarded her with great loathing.

30

Chapter 5

The day the boys go is a curious no-man's land in the life of a public school. One moment the place is humming with action and its associated problems, the next silence descends and the sense of urgency that characterises the term vanishes. Quite suddenly the tempo changes. At the top the headmaster and housemasters know they can get on with their reports without the constant interruption of colleagues or boys; even the debris of end of term crises can be dealt with in leisurely fashion. Ordinary masters, relieved of teaching, marking, games, private tutorials and the hundred and one duties of the daily round, relax into unaccustomed calm; a few of the younger ones are away to foreign holidays as rapidly as the boys.

Bruce Irving sat at his desk and relished the lightening of responsibility represented by the withdrawal of the boys. He had had to deal with a couple of miscreants from Theobalds found drinking and smoking by Wentworth the previous night, but with lunch not far off he did not anticipate any further disciplinary left-overs from the term. Indeed, as last nights of term go it had been peaceful. He remembered a time shortly after his appointment when there had always been a line of defaulters outside his study on the final morning.

Now he had more than seven hundred reports to write and that was not a thrilling prospect. He got up and poured himself a gin and tonic, a relaxation he would never contemplate at lunch-time during the term. Out of the window he saw Alastair Munro and John Pilgrim crossing the quad after a game of squash. Momentarily he felt a twinge of envy that they could shrug off the term so rapidly, and just for an instant he wondered if he was losing his enthusiasm.

Normally Irving had no doubts about himself or anything else. He was a solid professional and confident he was good at his job. Doubts were for lesser men who could not make up their minds; unkind critics said he simply lacked imagination. Irving was not unaware of such criticism, but twenty-five years of headmastering, nine of them at Merchet, had hardened him and he knew he could not please everybody. Once, letting his hair down at the Head Masters' Conference, he had unwisely delivered himself of the truism known to all headmasters: 'The staff are always more trouble than the boys'. His embarrassment in the masters' room had been comprehensive when he found his supposedly off-the-record comment reported in *The Times*.

He picked up the note he had received that morning from Tristan St. Leger suggesting a pageant as a focus for the festivities in the summer. It appealed to him. For some time the governors had been asking what he planned to do and up till now he had stalled, saying the examination needs of the current generation had to take priority and should not be jeopardised by untoward celebrations. But St. Leger's proposal satisfied several of the criteria he had set, albeit subconsciously. First, it used Merchet's history, the one thing making the school unique; second, he would be able to harness support from the masters' room by pointing out that it was an idea emanating from one of their own and could take place when most public examinations were over; third, it would give scope to Pilgrim's acknowledged skills as a producer, at the same time removing him as a source of criticism, for he was notoriously hostile to any school activity in which he was not involved; and last, but by no means least, it would provide a show for the parents with a maximum of their progeny on display.

There would be problems, of course. Cricketers would complain about the invasion of their term; one or two heads of department would moan about the demands of rehearsals and ask how Merchet could expect to be taken seriously in the academic world if it put play-acting before examination league tables. Moncrieff might be awkward. In his last year, with thirty-eight years behind him, he was a powerful figure whose idiosyncracies had become increasingly irritating. He realised he disliked the man intensely and would be relieved when he had gone.

On the positive side sectional interests could be incorporated, as St. Leger's note pointed out. Hillyard and the musicians, Rathbone and the Corps, Pilgrim and the actors, Sylvester and his artists; even the new Technology Centre, widely believed to be a white elephant masquerading as Merchet's arrival in the twentieth century, could at last be put to use, designing and making practical odds and ends for the production.

The bursar's views would have to be taken into account, of course, and he would find plenty of objections, most of them revolving round the fact that the works department was permanently overstretched and any extra load would be impossible. But this happened once a term anyway, and the necessary elasticity was usually found, either by impressing old retainers who imagined they had retired some time ago but found school arguments persuasive because they still lived in tied cottages, or by discovering a section of the workforce that drew its wages regularly but because of the haphazard nature of bursarial supervision managed a life of some comfort and modest industry in one of the more peaceful areas of the estate. Irving remembered the day he had surprised a plumber, a carpenter, and three painters playing pontoon in the cricket pavilion during one of his afternoon walks. Somehow a lunch break started at noon had merged with a tea-break at 3 pm and it was clearly intended it should continue until 'work' finally stopped at 5pm. Yes, there was always some slack to be taken up; he need not worry too much about opposition in that quarter.

It would be wrong to say that Irving was fired with enthusiasm for St. Leger's idea. As a tidy-minded administrator he deplored anything likely to upset the tenor of daily routine. But something had to be done. A pity, but there it was. Just his luck the quincentenary had fallen during his term of office.

He picked up another letter from his desk. This was from Killigrew, his head of modern languages, asking for the appointment of a French *assistante* to improve the boys' spoken French. He made a good case and in his relaxed mood Irving decided to agree. With the school full there should not be too much of a problem persuading the governors to provide the funds.

His mind flicked back to the pageant, more positively this time. The upset to routine could not be helped. St. Leger would undoubtedly write a good script and Pilgrim's productions were invariably successful. Perhaps the quincentenary could be seen as a fitting climax to his own career. The school would certainly be spending a year in the full glare of publicity.

Inevitably a shadow passed across his thought processes: 'Just as long as there are no drugs.'

* * * * * *

Sylvester Ford never went to the Duke of Cambridge. He and his coterie despised athleticism and always distanced themselves from

33

those who took games. A talented artist in his own right, he had developed a highly respected department and the boys' art was displayed to acclaim throughout the school. Pilgrim, who as registrar often showed prospective parents round the premises, had recently introduced a new line: 'I'd rather spend good money on some of the boys' work than anything I saw in the Academy's summer exhibition this year.'

The moment the boys left Ford got out his own work. He went up to his private studio at the top of the art school and set up two easels: the large one held a self-portrait in oils; to its right a smaller one supported a watercolour. The portrait was well-advanced; it had successfully captured the pale round face with its high forehead and greying straggle of beard. He was less happy with the eyes; they were too narrow, too cunning. Artistic truth clashed with *amour propre;* he would have to do something about them. He had barely started the watercolour, but he wanted to make progress this morning. When he had dealt with the eyes.

He crossed to the door and locked it. He did not want to be disturbed.

Tomorrow he would go to London. He sniffed, took out his handkerchief and blew his nose. He looked at the small plastic bag he had placed next to his palette. He needed more supplies; and more money to pay for them.

* * * * * *

Jennifer Wentworth turned off the M25 and joined the M40. At Denham she switched to the road for Amersham and was soon driving up the Misbourne valley. Near Great Missenden it started to rain, but the sun was still shining and a rainbow arced across the darkened sky and down to the Chiltern beechwoods. By the time she turned to cross the ridge towards Whiteleaf the cloud was thicker, the sun had disappeared and it was raining hard.

Her grandfather's cottage stood back from the road at the end of a short muddy lane. In summer its small garden, full of roses, holly-hocks, and other traditional cottage flowers, created an idyllic impression; in winter, as now, with the dripping woods closing in, it was dark and dismal.

Jennifer parked her car and picked her way carefully between the puddles and patches of mud to the front door. Her grandfather had heard her arrive and opened the door before she reached it. He was a solid, well-built man, wearing a fawn roll-neck sweater; only the lines on his face, notably those which pushed his eyes into deep hollows, and a certain stiffness of movement, indicated a man in his eighties.

'Bonjour, ma petite,' he said, holding Jennifer in a warm bear-hug. 'Come in, come in. I've got a good fire going.'

'Hullo, Grandpa. It's good to see you.'

'Cup of tea?' He helped her off with her coat.

'Lovely.'

The old man went into the kitchen while Jennifer sat down by the log fire. It was a comfortable room, with black sixteenth-century beams and walls lined with books. A Haydn string quartet played softly from two speakers.

'Thanks for coming so promptly.' This was shouted from the kitchen.

'You knew I'd come.' She was almost coquettish; she had taken off her shoes and was warming her stockinged feet before the fire. 'But what's the mystery? Why couldn't you tell me over the 'phone?'

'Be patient. I'll tell you in a couple of minutes. Just wait for the kettle. Cake?'

'No thanks. I've reached the age when every pound shows.'

'Nonsense. You've still got them eating out of your hand.' There had always been great honesty between them and he knew a good deal about her erratic emotional life. He had always listened, never condemned.

He came in with the tea and sat down opposite her. 'I'm having cake, anyway. It's Mrs Finch's – a trial run for Christmas. You can taste the brandy. I expect you'll change your mind and have some. I've never known you resist temptation.' He laughed affectionately.

'You know me too well. Now come on, Grandpa, what's this all about?'

Her grandfather poured the tea methodically, then sat back in his chair. Although it was only mid-afternoon, the lights were on and the lamp on the bookshelf beside him threw the lines on his face into relief, making him look his true age.

'All right, Jenny. I'll come clean. I wasn't strictly honest on the 'phone. I went to the doctor yesterday and I've got a heart problem. He's sending me for tests and so on and he makes optimistic noises.

But I'm not daft and as it's something I've ignored for a long time, I think it's time to get one or two things sorted out.'

Jennifer leaned forward and took hold of his hand. 'Do you want to come down to Merchet? You know I've always said there is a home for you there if you want it. I'll look after you.' The concern in her voice was genuine and her grandfather was moved.

'No, no, Jenny, nothing like that. I'm a tough old fraud and I'll last a long time yet.' He squeezed her hand. 'But you know I appreciate the offer.' Then he sat forward until their heads were almost touching. 'I'm going to tell you a story. It's an exciting one, it's very sad, and it concerns you.'

When he had finished, they sat in silence, Jennifer still holding one of his hands between the two of hers.

It was only on the way home, passing the high curved woods near Hampden House, that she remembered the prophetic rainbow she had seen on her outward journey.

* * * * *

And so the Christmas term ended. The boys departed, leaving the echoing silence of empty rooms and corridors. And if one took Thomas Hardy's view of an immanent Fate, one might say that the key pieces were in place for the eventual consummation of tragedy.

Candlemas

Chapter 6

It was the Candlemas term, the traditional name for the spring term at Merchet. But there was nothing springlike about the second day of February. It was cold, flint-cold; low clouds held back the dawn and sleet gusted against the windows.

Charles Moncrieff, housemaster of Ryders, was woken by Wood, his butler-cum-housekeeper, the last old-fashioned servant left at Merchet. There had been a time before the war, and for some years after it, when every house had its butler and a battalion of servants to minister to the needs of the housemaster and his boys; but Wood was the last, a social relic preserved by loyalty to Moncrieff and the simple fact that having no family and no money, he had nowhere else to go. A stunted little man, mild when sober, aggressive when drunk, he was, like most servants, intensely conservative, vying with his master in his attempts to hold back an alien modern world.

'Good morning, sir,' he said, putting down a cup of tea and drawing the curtain. 'Dark today. Trying to snow.'

Moncrieff heaved his bulk into a sitting position, blinking short-sightedly; he smoothed back his white hair and stretched for his glasses on the table at the side of the bed.

'The boiler's playing up again,' said Wood. 'The radiators on the top landing are as cold as charity. They're not getting no 'eat at all.'

Moncrieff grunted and inclined his head in a gesture of acknowledgement and dismissal.

'It could be furred pipes,' went on Wood. 'Or it could be young Mr Darcy in Room 22. Probably got 'old of one of them keys that turns the valves. Turns up the radiator in 'is room till it's so 'ot you could fry an egg on it. Then everyone else freezes. Anyway, there ain't no 'eat on top landing, that's for sure.'

Moncrieff adjusted his spectacles, made a characteristic puffing noise, then spoke for the first time. 'All right. See Darcy and find out if he's been messing about. Now let me get dressed.' He was used to Wood starting the day with a catalogue of gloom and was adept at brushing it away.

Moncrieff was outdated and totally unaware of it. In a curious way he had much in common with Wood: for both men Ryders and the boys were the centre of existence; and neither had made firm plans for the retirement both faced at the end of the summer term, though it was assumed that wherever Moncrieff went Wood would go too.

He was a snob and a misogynist – other traits he shared with Wood. He had resigned from his London club when it admitted women and it was he who had coined the nickname Mad Millie for Pamela Baskerville. With some reluctance he was prepared to invite women to his dinner parties, but he preferred them to have a title, to own racehorses, or inhabit country houses to which he could be subsequently invited. Female cleaners at Ryders had strict instructions to finish their work and be off the premises before he got back from teaching at lunchtime. The only resident female in Ryders was the house matron, the unfortunately named Miss Broad, an amazon of forbidding appearance with a luxuriant moustache.

Moncrieff got out of bed and put on his dressing-gown; as a cord he used a frayed regimental tie. He went to the window and reviewed the day before him. Not a bad one on the whole. Only two periods up to school, both with Sixth Forms, whom he found more congenial than younger boys. A parent had asked to see him before lunch. He didn't know what that was about, but Sir Roger Treece was a father of whom he approved, even if his son – brilliant at both work and games – could be unpredictable. In the afternoon there was a house match against Drydens with an easy win guaranteed against the most intellectual and least athletic house at Merchet;and in the evening the Candlemas Feast, the occasion of the grandest dinner in the Merchet calendar, shared by governors, masters and boys – but not wives: it promised to be a good day.

Dawn was breaking over the Downs. The sleet had stopped, but he could still hear the wind. Beyond the grey pile of the abbey the winter fields stretched geometrically beneath the curve of Gallow Down with its clump of trees. Like Paul Nash, he mused, and his mind flicked to his recent Nash acquisition, a purchase dictated by investment potential rather than aesthetic appreciation: a good buy. He wondered what Sylvester Ford would say when he told him.

And then he saw Jennifer Wentworth walking her dog. He pulled the curtain and crossed to the wash basin to shave.

* * * * * *

James Wentworth lay in bed, looked at the empty whisky bottle on the bedside table, and faced the fact that he was a failure. Theobalds was not the sort of house he wanted it to be; however hard he worked it seemed he could not make a jot of difference to its casual, philistine character. 'Housemasters make houses' was the rune inscribed on the psyche of Merchet, but he appeared to have achieved nothing. He wanted a cultured, helpful community with boys who would put their hearts into everything and eventually lead useful adult lives. And what had he got? An idle, unreliable crew of layabouts whose guiding principle was love of self. No, that was too strong, a reflection of his prevailing mood, but it was what it often felt like. Of course, there were times when he knew he had agreeable boys, boys of stature and character of whom he could be proud; but somehow the gilded butterflies of Chelsea and their jet-set cousins with penthouses in New York or Buenos Aires always seemed to make the running, setting the tone, influencing gullible new boys , and giving Theobalds a reputation for self-indulgent irresponsibility. He regarded the other houses with envy.

The early morning was a bad time for Wentworth. A depressive who set himself exacting standards he was never able to meet, he constantly took stock of his shortcomings. The house was bad enough, and it had come to dominate his life in a way he was still objective enough to see was unhealthy, but he knew he was a failure as a husband too. Why else should he be sleeping in a single bed staring at the pink brocade of the spare-room curtains?

Of course, this personal failure was at the bottom of everything; just occasionally he admitted it was the real reason he threw himself so wholeheartedly into the house. He had realised the mistake within a month of the wedding and, as an honest man who faced facts, he blamed himself as much as Jennifer. The truth was that they were incompatible. He was staid, conscientious, and, he admitted it, pedantic; Jennifer was vivacious, full of inconsequential chatter, always living in the present rather than the future, and exuding a sexuality that attracted men from miles away. Friends said they were the most ill-matched couple they knew and wondered how they had come together in the first place. Actually it was simple. Jennifer had made the running because she was attracted by academics and, bluntly, found the prospect of life at

Merchet socially desirable; to her credit she had rarely said other-wise. Brought up by a dominating mother, James had toppled the moment Jennifer showed an interest in him; indeed, once his emotions were modestly engaged, reason drove him on to disaster by urging him to take the first opportunity of marriage because it might be his last.

Their relationship had come to grief before his appointment to Theobalds; the housemastership merely confirmed the situation. Wentworth now committed himself to every facet of the boys' lives, compensating for the vacuum in his own. His wife maintained a façade and went through the motions required by Merchet convention. Dinner parties for colleagues, teas for new boys, sherry for unexpected parents, standing in at surgery on matron's day off – she did them all, but never with enthusiasm. She often wished she was back in the Bond Street art gallery where she had worked before her marriage. Beyond the shell of that marriage Jennifer lived a life of her own. She was attracted by men and although she never completely laid the ghost of her guilt at betraying James, she had soon betrayed him so often that custom dulled conscience. They had stopped sleeping together several years ago and he no longer questioned her about unexplained absences.

So Wentworth did not contemplate the day with relish. He had already heard Jennifer moving about and assumed she had gone out with Sabre. Funny, they didn't even share Sabre; he was *her* dog. And where had she been last night? He hadn't heard her come in. The question he always tried to avoid raised itself again. Who was she sleeping with now? He understood her needs well enough to know there must be somebody. Acceptance of the situation did not mean he was immune to hurt. His private pride had long been shredded; he just hoped there was some rag of public respectability left to him, that his colleagues weren't laughing behind his back. Perhaps they assumed it was all sweetness and light? Perhaps they envied him his pretty wife.

He laughed, a harsh sound. Only one answer to that sort of nonsense: start the day. He got out of bed and even as he did so the house took over. He ran through the boys he wanted to see before the morning service; he had to ring a parent about a blatant piece of cheating, a parent who would find it hard to believe

41

anything critical of his son; and then, according to Matron, who reported unmade beds and untidy rooms, it was high time he carried out an unheralded inspection to support her authority.

He looked at himself in the shaving mirror. The pall of depression was not lifting. He saw only the receding hairline and the fleshiness in his neck suggestive of too much alcohol. He looked down at his premature paunch. Once, in the days when he cared what Jennifer thought of him, he would have been concerned; now he did not care. He wondered if his wife positively disliked him. He remembered that she had been almost as upset by her first affair as he was. Or that was the impression she had given. He laughed again, brushing shaving soap round his chin. Now it was all very different.

And what were his own feelings now? He sensed his tolerance, his indifference, were changing. Was that bitterness he detected the beginning of hatred?

* * * * * *

Tristan St. Leger heard the alarm clock shuddering near his ear. He turned it off without opening his eyes and pulled the blankets back over his shoulders. 'Your turn to make the tea,' he said.

There was no response from the pile of blonde hair on his left.

'Your turn,' he repeated, louder.

'I did it yesterday.'

'Your memory's failing. Yesterday was Monday. I got the tea, I fed the cat and I went to the abbey. Today is Tuesday. You get the tea, you feed the cat, I do not go to the abbey and I'm not in school until period three. You will recall that I reserve my strength to deal with the noxious Remove containing Skirmish and Beaver. Now, my darling, get the tea.'

Melanie stirred marginally. 'I'll bet Jennifer doesn't get the tea.'

'She probably gets something else. Now come on, Woman, get going. Or even I might be tempted.'

* * * * * *

Mark Calverley sat at his solitary breakfast table in Drydens and viewed the coming day with unalloyed optimism. A mixture of

42

emotions coursed through him, but one overrode all others. He was in love. Irrationally, hopelessly, gloriously, irrevocably in love – and for the first time in his life. It had come upon him suddenly and as a fifty-year-old married man he knew he should have known better. But reason did not come into it: the fact could not be denied: he adored Jennifer Wentworth. And all the signs were that she loved him.

The trouble was that he had a wife and she had a husband. He was sufficiently old-fashioned to see this was a problem. Not that it had hampered them unduly so far, of course. He smiled involuntarily, recalling the eroticism of the two previous nights. But it was only chance that had taken Mary to Wales to look after an infirm mother, and he had no idea how long he could count on Wentworth's seemingly blind acquiescence. His wife's absence was only temporary and although her mother enjoyed notoriously bad health Mary would see it as her duty to be back with him as soon as possible. Once back in Drydens she would be far too shrewd to miss the transformation he felt he had undergone. Poor Mary –he viewed her with almost brotherly affection – poor, kind-hearted Mary had tried so hard. But their relationship was totally prosaic and mundane; there had never been a real spark. As he looked back at twenty years of childless marriage he saw care and respect, rational compromise and intellectual dialogue, but no passion, none of the irrational feelings overwhelming him now.

They were irrational, he knew that. Was it really possible he had fallen like the others? He was not a gossip, but he was aware Jennifer had a past, and even if only part of what he had heard was true he was taking dangerous steps. As a highly intelligent man he could see how his heart was ruling his head. But that was irrelevant. The emotions unleashed, quiescent for so long, were all that mattered.

So for the moment life was good. For the first time he was living as if each second was his last; the years of respectability peeled away to leave him bewildered at his own behaviour. He was deliriously happy, even if a still small voice told him it could not last.

With this perspective the problems, major and minor, littering a housemaster's desk dwindled into insignificance. There was the loss of a watch, an expensive one which an idiot parent should never have given to a boy at school, and investigation into that would take time; a boy whose family background was so complex he always had to look at his file to see which of his ex-wives his father was likely to bring to

43

Speech Day was causing trouble in form – a characteristic of sons with much-married fathers – and needed a sympathetic dressing-down; and beer cans suggestive of illicit drinking had been found in the dustbins. The most tedious was a note from the local Social Services department giving notice of an imminent inspection. The woman who usually came, an earnest female with preconceived ideas about boarding schools, had the darkest suspicions of everything she did not understand – for example, the communal bathing arrangements after rugger – and wrote unreadable reports in execrable, jargon-ridden English. But all this, the day to day grind of the house-master's life, became mere triviality before the fact of his love. He lived again the softness of Jennifer's eyes and the erotic feasting of the previous night.

There was a knock at his door and Paul Sandbach, his head of house, came in. He was a dark-haired boy who looked older than his eighteen years.

'Sorry to bother you, sir. I've taken call-over, but you asked me to remind you about seeing the House before they go down to breakfast. We're ready when you are. All except for Keighley, that is. He was still in bed, but I've got someone dragging him out. He'll be there by the time you are.'

'Of course, I'd forgotten. Hang on to them. Paul. I'll be right down. Thanks for reminding me.'

Calverley stretched for a piece of paper and looked at it blankly. He knew he wanted to talk to the house about something important, but he couldn't for the life of him think what it was. He really would have to pull himself together.

* * * * * *

Alastair Munro looked out of his kitchen window at the wind-blown sleet. Dressed in his cassock, he waited for his egg to boil; he timed it methodically, watching the second hand on his watch jerk its progress through the essential three and a half minutes. A bachelor of forty, neat, well-organised, with a tendency to hypochondria, he had a meticulous routine which ordained boiled eggs on Tuesdays and Fridays. It was the time of day for thought; the solitary breakfast before telephone, colleagues or boys intruded, when he faced himself as he really was, warts and all; a ritual self-examination before conducting the morning service in the abbey.

Recently one thought had come before all others. Why was he still a bachelor? Why had he never made a satisfactory relationship with a woman that might have blossomed into something more lasting? It wasn't that he didn't find women attractive. Quite the contrary. And it wasn't his vocation decreeing celibacy for a higher cause, though there had been a period of self-denying idealism in his twenties when the idea had been tempting. No. It was – and he was beginning to face this more honestly than he had once – it was that women were not attracted to him. They didn't exactly avoid him, he could not say that, but they didn't seek him out, they didn't give him the attention he saw them lavishing on other men. They were civil and friendly, yes, but not warm, not close...Was there something about him that was off-putting? Could it be the fact that he was a priest? Did they think the cloth somehow emasculated his manhood? Looking round at his colleagues, their wives, their girl friends, he saw an easy familiarity he had never known. He was envious.

Through the window he saw Jennifer Wentworth walking back to Theobalds. Even beneath her thick tweed coat her innate sexuality was clear to the world; her alsation walked obediently behind her. Munro felt the stirrings that always disturbed him when he saw her: unsatisfied physical desire struggling with a Calvinistic sense of guilt. At the same time, inevitably, he recalled the knowledge revealed to him under the cloak of his priesthood the previous summer. She must have been to blame; no objective observer could decide other-wise. But she had paid a high price. And what about young Treece? How was he now? The responsibility of his confessional position in the school weighed heavily upon him when unbidden secrets were revealed.

'Why not me?' he suddenly said aloud. He remembered his parents and the suffocatingly puritanical upbringing he had endured. 'The last of the Victorians,' he said. He cut viciously into the egg. 'I'm the last of the bloody Victorians.'

* * * * * *

And so the day of the Candlemas Feast began. By a quarter to nine the boys had answered call-over in their houses, breakfasted, and attended the short daily service in the abbey. There was then a quarter of an hour of relative calm before the tolling of the bell in the abbey tower sent the boys, grey-suited, and masters, miscellaneously-suited and gowned, scattering in all directions to the first period of the day.

It was light now, as light as it would get. The wind whipped the gowns of the masters and threw birds about the sky like pieces of charred paper. By half-way through the first period it was starting to snow.

Chapter 7

Sylvester Ford started the day with a free period and for once he was going to spend it on his own painting, a luxury he rarely allowed himself during the term.

The light was poor this morning, barely adequate. Although his studio had high eastern-facing windows and a fanlight, the winter gloom was pervasive and Ford peered at the two watercolours he had on easels side by side. Not bad, he thought, but still not good enough. He looked at his watch to see when the period ended. Ten minutes to go. Just time for a touch here and there. Somehow the stonework on the castle wall was not quite right. The sunlight still suggested a hot summer afternoon and he needed the soft quality of evening sun. The February gloom did not help, but it really was time he finished this one. The bank manager's last letter had been quite explicit.

Not for the first time he blessed the moment he had got to know Jennifer Wentworth. Her connection with the Cellini Gallery in Bond Street had proved a boon in so many ways. The daily chore of teaching was now much more acceptable.

Once more he peered at the paintings, his brush poised. 'Nearly there,' he breathed.

He sniffed, then pulled out his handkerchief and blew his nose noisily. He had a headache again.

* * * * * *

For Mark Calverley the euphoria of the early morning did not fade. He taught the bottom Fifth with such high good humour that even the egregious Simkinson escaped the detention his prep merited. Simkinson, a boy whose name appeared on punishment lists at all points of the school compass, was aghast. Returning to his desk, he said to his neighbour: 'Something's up. That's the first time Calverley's accepted my prep this term. We've got to watch him.' As a ubiquitous wrongdoer he treated the slightest sign of generosity from

47

authority with suspicion. Apart from anything else his reputation was at stake.

At break in the masters' room Calverley detached himself from the gowned figures drinking coffee, nibbling biscuits and holding desultory conversations about the trivia of the day. He sat apart, metaphorically clutching his secret to himself, wallowing in the self-glorification of the man who has satisfied a woman. Across the room he saw James Wentworth talking to the headmaster. He watched him curiously.

In the last period before lunch he was able to let himself go. He was doing Romanticism with a Sixth Form and the subject was so sympathetic to his mood that he enthused even more intensely than usual. 'We are dealing,' he said, pushing back his hair and giving his gown a characteristic twitch, 'we are dealing with the world of feeling, with the winding stair of the imagination. The stately artificialities of the eighteenth century, nurtured and sustained by the cool light of reason and logic, are under threat. Enthusiasm and emotion sweep all before them The more direct and spontaneous Man's experiences are, the more authentic and valuable they seem to the Romantics. Skate with Wordsworth on the midnight ice, wander through the Appenines with Byron and Berlioz; feel the despair of Schumann, the savagery of Goya and' – his voice dropped, as if to impart a confidence – 'revel in the eroticism of Wagner.'

He turned to the compact-disc player at one side of his desk and the opening bars of the Prelude to *Tristan and Isolde* permeated the room. 'Listen to this and the *Liebestod* that follows. You'll see what I mean when I say we're in a new world...'

Calverley sat down and threw his head back as though contemplating the ceiling. Before him fourteen attentive faces faded into a limbo of their own; he closed his eyes and let the sensuous waves of the *Liebestod* sweep over him. The sheer physical impact of the music took him back to Jennifer. To himself he said: 'We're in a new world...'

Through the window he saw that the roof of the great hall was white with a dusting of snow.

* * * * * *

It would be neat to say that parents at Merchet fell into three basic groups: landed, monied and professional. Neat but untrue. For, as sociologists have discovered through extensive research and lesser mortals by simple observation, English society is not given to easy categorisation. Certainly the man sitting in Moncrieff's drawing-room at the end of the morning sipping a delicate Fino did not fall into any neat pigeon-hole.

Sir Roger Treece, Baronet, came of an old family, or at least one that became armigerous in the gentry boom of the seventeenth century; his substantial wealth, however, came not from the shires, where it is true he had broad acres and a notable seat, but from the old North American colonies, where a Victorian Treece had shown initiative and other entrepreneurial qualities the less sympathetic might call ruthlessness to carve a personal empire out of the old frontier. Succeeding generations had shown similar qualities and the transatlantic Treece fortune was now firmly based on extensive 'real estate', together with a flourishing firm making plastic wrapping for take-away meals.

The present incumbent of the title was short, almost squat, with a head set forward on his shoulders as though he had no neck; he was a man used to speaking his mind and getting his own way, though there was a kindliness about his eyes that did something to modify the aggressive impression of his body. He was the sort of parent Moncrieff considered important and the two were on Christian name terms.

'Well, Roger,' Moncrieff opened. 'What's it all about?' He knew Treece was not given to sentimentality. He did not visit his son or his housemaster without good reason; his old-fashioned view was that having chosen a school to educate the boy it should be left to get on with it.

'Something's up, Charles. I thought I smelt something wrong last summer, but I'm damned sure of it now. Haven't you noticed?'

Moncrieff was wary. To agree would be to invite the question of what he had done about it, to disagree would suggest a lack of proper observation. He took refuge in a platitude. 'All boys are odd at one time or another. That's adolescence. And he's got a lot on his plate. He's got to get straight 'A',s in the summer if he's going to confirm his place at Merton and he's keeping his games going full blast. A lot of boys begin to take life seriously round about now. What have you noticed?'

'He's stopped ringing up. He never writes, of course, but ever since his prep school days he's rung up like clockwork. When he was little he

49

was full of enthusiasm for this and that – mostly his success at sport. As he got older it was often school gossip or a request for money, but he always rang, he always maintained the contact. I'm often abroad on business, of course, but Margaret has come to expect it. Then last term he just stopped. Just like that. We wrote a couple of times, but got no reply. He's got his own mobile. So something's up. It's as simple as that.'

'Nothing go wrong in the holidays?'

'No. Though he wasn't his usual self either last summer holiday or at Christmas.'

'In what way?'

'He just didn't communicate. He wouldn't say why he hadn't rung. Spent a lot of time alone in his room with his computer or walking on his own with the dogs. He claimed to be working.'

'Did you doubt it?'

'Not at first. He's always been truthful. Besides, we *want* him to work. His reports last year suggested too much concentration on games, so a bit of work seemed a good idea. He's got to get his priorities right if he's going to get this Oxford place.'

'Did he see any friends in the holidays?'

'No. That's another odd thing. We were down at Cannes in the summer and he usually has a friend or two to stay. But he didn't want anybody last time, in fact he actually put off one chap who was coming. When we said anything, he told us bluntly he wanted to be on his own. Almost told us to mind our own business. It was the same at Christmas. No – something's up. In my day, Charles, there was only one thing at the bottom of a change like this. Sex.'

'No sign of another boy. I would have seen it.'

'Glad to hear it. What about a girl?'

'Difficult. We're much freer than we were in your day, so I suppose he might have met someone. You didn't ask him?'

Treece was momentarily embarrassed. 'Not really. He's been away at school since he was seven, so there's a bit of a gulf. Difficult to ask, you know.'

'Could he have met someone at home?' Moncrieff hoped he could shift the problem away from the school.

'It's possible. But my impression – and it's only an impression – is that the change took place at Merchet. He was perfectly normal when he went back at the start of last summer term. Anyway, I'm leaving for

50

the States at the end of this week and I promised Margaret I'd clear it up before I go. For some reason I get on better with Oliver these days than she does. That's why she didn't come.'

Moncrieff could well believe that. His own reading of Lady Treece was that she was a selfish woman interested primarily in clothes and her own social life; she was certainly not greatly given to maternal sensibilities. It was more likely that Treece's visit was prompted by his concern rather than hers.

'There was one odd thing,' went on Treece. 'I wouldn't have noticed normally because I'm so often away, but last summer I was at home for most of the holiday and I noticed that Oliver always wanted to get to the post first when it arrived in the morning. When he comes home he's usually so tired he sleeps in until about eleven, but right through the last two holidays he's been up first thing waiting for the post to drop onto the mat. I asked him if he was waiting for something and I felt he was evasive and furtive. Said he was expecting post from a compact disc club or something like that. Quite unlike him. He's an open boy normally. We've never had to worry about lies. And he spends hours on his mobile. I've been horrified by his bills.'

'I've had a lot of complaints about that. But if parents buy sons mobiles they must take responsibility for the bills.'

'I accept that, Charles. I'm more interested in whoever he's talking to. I'd put money on a girl down here.'

'It's possible, Roger, I can't deny that. Now I know there's a problem I'll look into it. But you see what you can do today. Take him out to lunch – as long as you get him back in time for the house match this afternoon. And don't give him too much to drink.' Moncrieff laughed. 'I don't want him dropping every pass at fly-half in this damned snow. If we can handle properly we'll win easily. If you go now, you'll just catch him coming out of the last period.'

'Right, I'll go and get him.' Treece did not respond to Moncrieff's lighter tone. 'I can't stay for the match, but I'll telephone this evening. We're going to get to the bottom of this, Charles. There's not going to be any nonsense like the Mackenzie boy's drug business three years ago.'

'He was in Theobalds. Too many social butterflies there. In any case, I don't think Merchet has a drug problem now.'

'I think Oliver's too sensible for that, but I'm not ruling anything out. We'll speak this again this evening.'

The two men shook hands and Treece retired to find his son. Moncrieff sat down to finish his sherry. Through the window he watched boys walking down to the great hall for lunch; casual, hands in pockets, they seemed in no hurry. He frowned. He did not want anything to go wrong with Treece's final year. If he captured the Oxford place, he would stand an excellent chance of a Blue for rugger or cricket. He thought back with self-congratulation to the way he had wined and dined the boy's prep school headmaster to make sure Oliver had transferred to his house. He had always been good – many would have said ruthless – at getting the boys he wanted.

He went over to the fire and stirred one of the logs with his foot. The boy's father worried him. There had been an intensity about him he'd never seen before. It would be wise not to cross him – and Oliver was an only son. He kicked the log again and as he did so his eyes, worldly and shrewd, narrowed. He had not noticed anything much wrong with Oliver this term or last, but what about the end of the summer term? What about what Sherlock Holmes might have called 'The Curious Case of the Undrunk Beer'? Yes, that had been unusual.

After winning the house match final, a match in which young Treece had scored a fifty and taken five wickets, he had sent Wood round with a crate of beer for the team. He always did that when a cup was won, a housemasterly gesture the boys appreciated. Normally it vanished within minutes, downed in the excitement of the moment. But later that evening, going round the house in his normal way, he had dropped in on Treece to congratulate him. Treece was not in his room and his beer was on his desk unopened. Yes, that *had* been odd.

* * * * * *

By the afternoon the rugger fields were under a light dusting of snow, though not enough to stop the house matches. The fields lay on both sides of the lane linking the village with the main road, edged on one side by the Downs, on the other by woodland. From the school, on higher ground, the players were small coloured figures moving on a green and white chess-board.

House matches are important at Merchet. Although the school

has a corporate sense and there is a curious quality the *cognoscenti* may identify as the hallmark of Merchet – a desire not to be thought overtly enthusiastic about anything, yet notably reliable when the chips are down – the real loyalties at the school are to the house. This is best seen in the average boy's relationship with the headmaster. For most he is a remote figure, a dispenser of justice, a fount of honour whose presence lends weight and dignity to abbey services and other school functions. An ordinary boy needing no magisterial reprimand, acquiring no monitorial status, may pass through Merchet without meeting him more than twice: at the beginning and end of his career when the great man formally shakes his hand in welcome and farewell.

Compare this with the boy's relationship with his housemaster, the man who sees the best and worst, who guides him through the hazards of adolescence, deals with the daily minutiae of his life, and from whom little can be hidden. The focal point of a boy's existence is his house. He lives and sleeps there, his whole being is bound up with its own tight little community with all its sins and virtues. So houses have a powerful corporate loyalty and house matches are blood and thunder affairs in which even boys whose main interest is in books rather than boots are prepared to die in the breach. Thus, although popular opinion had it that the blue-blooded hearties of Ryders would thrash the pallid aesthetes of Drydens, no-one could be certain of the result until the final whistle.

Moncrieff arrived in time for the kick-off. Wearing a voluminous coat redolent of a past age, together with a shapeless tweed hat with trout flies stuck in it, he propped himself up on a shooting-stick on the half-way line. To his right and left he looked along the straggling line of boys who had turned up to support their respective houses. It was compulsory in Ryders and he would have noticed immediately if anyone was absent.

Calverley was not enthusiastic about house matches in normal circumstances, but today was not normal. Still glowing internally, he strode down to the fields and arrived on Big Side only a few minutes after Moncrieff.

He said: 'Looking for a cricket score, Charles?'

'Twenty points will do.'

'Come on, Charles, don't be so modest. My best player's a 2nd XV Scarf. You've got three 1st XV Colours and God knows how many

Scarves. You'll murder us.'

'Our strength is outside, but it's too cold for handling. The forwards will get the ball but the backs will drop it.'

'I've got Figgis on the wing and he doesn't play at all except in house matches.'

'Scholar, isn't he?'

'Yes, he's writing a novel. Precocious.'

'Pretentious in my book. I don't like scholars. Don't have 'em if I can help it. Go for blood every time. Ah, Clode's reffing. He's all right in open play, but doesn't see what's going on up front. Better than Charteris, anyway. He thinks he's the cat's whiskers and doesn't see anything at all.'

Clode blew his whistle and the match started, to the accompaniment of frenzied cheering from the groups of spectators huddling against the wind in overcoats.

'The pageant's making progress,' said Calverley. 'Tristan's finished the script and Pilgrim's started casting. First rehearsals next week. You don't approve, do you?'

'No.'

'We've got to put on some sort of show. Tristan and John will do it well.'

'There's more than enough going on in the summer term without all this self-congratulation. The parents pay to get their sons through examinations and into cricket teams, not to put on fancy dress and satisfy Pilgrim's egotism. Besides, the summer term's so short now cricket gets hit every time. Look at the fixtures we've lost this year.'

'It was Tristan's idea.'

'He always has ideas, but he can't organise anything. What about those historians he took to Jervaulx last year? They all got on the wrong train and ended up in Newcastle. And he lost Penberthy-Brocket on the way back. The little beast was drinking at King's Cross and got picked up by the police. Just the sort of publicity we can do without.'

'Tristan thought his parents had picked him up.'

'Tristan thinks too much. No, Merchet doesn't need an orgy of celebration. It's lasted five hundred years and that's good enough for me. We operate best when we're out of the public eye. Run, you wretched boy, run!'

This last was bellowed at the Ryders' left wing, who had been put away after a classic fly-half break by Treece. As he neared the line the winger cut inside and was tackled by the full-back.

Moncrieff grumbled aloud: 'Always go outside, Burns. How often do you have to be told? Good tackle by your boy, Mark, but he ought not to have stood a chance. No, I'm not letting many of my boys take part in the pageant. Just the ones who aren't doing anything else. You know Pilgim's productions when they get going. Late night rehearsals and goodness knows what. All wrong in the summer term.'

Calverley, who considered the pageant a good idea but did not want to get involved in an argument, looked for an opportunity to disengage himself. The chance came a few minutes later when one of his few competent players picked up a loose ball, broke through the Ryders' line and scored an unexpected try entirely against the run of play. He thought Moncrieff was about to suffer a seizure and as he went stumping up the line brandishing his shooting-stick at the unfortunate centre who had missed his tackle Calverley retreated in the opposite direction to join a parent who had materialised near the corner flag.

'See you at the feast, Charles,' he called. To himself he laughed: 'And watch your blood pressure or you won't reach retirement at the end of the year.'

The parent Calverley greeted was one of the fathers for whom he had notable respect, an academic whose struggle to pay the fees meant that he had no car but who nevertheless turned up to support his son more frequently than those more fortunately endowed. They chatted in desultory fashion for a while – long enough for Ryders to equalise and shortly afterwards go into the lead – and then Calverley saw Jennifer walking her dog at the far end of the field.

He excused himself hastily and went to meet her.

Chapter 8

The origins of the Candlemas Feast were obscure. Some said it dated from the installation of a Cambridge Whig headmaster in the eighteenth century, appointed by Walpole to destroy the influence of a string of Oxford Tories with Jacobite sympathies; another theory linked it with a visit by the Prince Regent to celebrate the battle of Trafalgar; more prosaically, and probably more accurately, it was seen as a continuation of the feast held by the original monks to mark the collection of the Candlemas rents. Whatever its origins, the feast had become a notable event in the Merchet calendar, an occasion of formality and splendour, attended by masters, senior boys and those governors still capable of locomotion.

The great hall at Merchet was the refectory of the original abbey and had never lost its original use. Oak tables and benches, dark with the patina of age, stretched its length at right angles to high table. The walls were oak-panelled, providing a sombre background to the portraits of headmasters encircling the hall. Of the latter, some were works of quality, others lacked artistic merit; all were set in heavy gilt frames. Above high table hung the one painting of distinction, a view of the busy pageantry of the Grand Canal by Guardi. Overhead was the fourteenth-century hammer-beam roof that formed the climax of the guided tour laid on for tourists. This evening the hall was candlelit and silver gleamed on the long tables. On both sides of the hall, half-way down, log fires burned in two enormous medieval fireplaces. For masters, governors and monitors it was a dinner jacket occasion, for the boys formal dark suits. The whole was a muted canvas of brown and black with flickering candles and shadows. The smell of woodsmoke hung in the air.

In the past the governors had sat on high table with the headmaster, but in these democratic times they were on the lower tables mingling with the boys. 'That way we hear the gossip and find out what's really going on,' observed one of their number, an Old Merchet with a reputation for shark-like dealings on the Stock Exchange. As a result the headmaster was freed from the necessity

56

to make small talk with governors who enjoyed nothing so much as reminiscing about their own schooldays and could make up high table according to his own wishes. On this occasion he had invited, among others, St. Leger and Pilgrim, to bring him up to date with progress in the pageant.

Irving turned to St. Leger on his right: 'So you've got the overall plan more or less straight, Tristan?'

St. Leger put down his soup spoon, dabbed his lips with his napkin and moved to one side to allow his plate to be taken by one of the waitresses specially hired for the evening. He said: 'The main scenes are drafted, Headmaster, and we've done some preliminary casting. Some of the script still needs polishing – and we can always add things if anyone has a really bright idea. John's produced a timetable for the first rehearsals.'

Pilgrim, sitting opposite, said: 'Tristan's script is excellent.' His voice reflected respect, yet at the same time sounded mildly patronising.'Of course, we've discussed the main scenes and tried to work in as many people as possible.'

'We thought about including the burning,' said St. Leger,'but eventually decided against it.'

'Burning?' Irving looked puzzled.

'Mary Weaver. Haven't you heard about her?'

'No.'

'She was a local woman burned at the stake in the sixteenth century for murdering her husband. It happened down at the crossroads in the village.'

'We thought we might burn one of the matrons,' joked St. Leger.

'Why did you decide against it?'

'Well, we've got to have Abbot Greenfield's execution earlier and we don't want to overdo the morbidity. Besides, there are strong sexual overtones. There was a live lover as well as a dead husband. And there's an unhealthy interest in female executions. Look at Ruth Ellis – or the way the hanging of Martha Browne affected Thomas Hardy.'

'Some of the women might object.' He coughed. 'I'm not sure Pamela Baskerville would approve.'

'I hope you're going to get the women in somewhere,' said Irving, whose limited imagination foresaw more complaints arising from their omission than possible issues of taste.

'We've persuaded Jane Osgood to be Jane Shore in the opening scene, Headmaster. And we can get plenty of wives and matrons into the suffragette riot. They'll enjoy dressing up for that. Several have already volunteered to help with make-up and costumes.'

'I hope you'll find a slot for Pamela,' said Irving.

'I'm sure we can find something for her,' replied St. Leger. 'Assuming she wants to take part.'

At the end of the table an unidentifiable voice, only just *sotto voce*, said: 'How about going back to the burning?'

Smiles went round the table; here and there eyes met; Irving appeared not to have heard.

'The costumes will cost a good deal,' said Pilgrim. We need so many different periods and we can't cut corners on this one. And there'll be heavy expenses setting up stands, lighting and so on. We shall need some sophisticated equipment once it gets dark.'

'Anything you need, John – just ask,' said Irving. 'We really shall be on show and I'm sure the governors will wear it. Within reason, of course,' he added hastily, suddenly recalling the expenditure on Pilgrim's last production. Just to make sure, he repeated it: 'Within reason.'

'How do you see the timing of it?' asked Paul Rathbone, who was sitting next to St. Leger.

'We haven't worked out the details yet,' replied St. Leger. 'But the basic plan is to do the early centuries in daylight. We want it completely dark by the time your Corps chaps perform in the Great War. That will give you the chance to have flares, lots of explosions and so on. And the CDT department has promised us a model Bristol Fighter. That will need darkness at the beginning and end of its flight.'

'Ambitious,' said Irving. 'How do we get that in?'

'A man called Fawcett, Headmaster. An old Ryders' boy who won a VC in 1918. Brought his plane back and saved his gunner's life though he'd been so badly shot up he died the same night.'

'And it needs to be dark for the fireworks at the end. We're finishing off with a display of the Merchet coat of arms.' Pilgrim took a studied sip of his claret. 'I hope that doesn't sound too hackneyed. We've thought about it and I don't think it can be bettered as grand finale. It'll bring the Merchet story full circle – and most people are suckers for fireworks. It'll be expensive, of course.'

Irving was nodding. 'Don't worry. I like the idea. It'll go down well with the press. If I get in touch with the right people we'll probably get a front page picture in one of the nationals. He always had an eye for publicity possibilities. 'As long as it's safe,' he added. The cautionary note was equally characteristic.

'It's quite safe, Headmaster,' said St. Leger. 'We've got a special firework firm to lay it on. They're doing it all the time – a really professional job. They plan to set it up well beyond the acting area and the stands. And the boys won't have anything to do with it.'

'Thank heavens for small mercies,' said Rathbone.

Irving was frowning. 'All the same we shall have to make sure someone like Skirmish doesn't sabotage it. He's been sent up to me more than any other boy in my time at Merchet.'

'Can't you sack him before the summer term, Headmaster?' asked St. Leger, jocularly.

Irving took the question seriously. 'You may be near the truth, Tristan. He's already had a last warning and I know James suspects he's at the bottom of the drink circle in Theobalds. He's got a record as long as your arm. His parents' fault, as usual.'

'What's wrong this time?'

'Poor little rich boy syndrome. Father ran off with a French film starlet when he was at prep school and mother consoled herself with drink and an Arabian sheikh. Neither wants to take responsibility for him, so they get rid of their guilt by giving him money. The wretched boy doesn't stand much chance. But he's our problem now and I should like to think Merchet can do something for him. He's no fool and he's got guts. He tackled like a lion in the Colts match against Tonbridge on Saturday. He's got character. Thinking back to the pageant, Tristan, he's the sort of chap I might go over the top with. I wonder if Fawcett had problems at Merchet?' Irving turned to Tawney, who had been silent so far. Irving had invited him onto high table as a mark of respect to the favourable impression he had created. 'Have you come across the egregious Skirmish, Matthew?'

'No, Headmaster. It sounds like a pleasure in store.' Tawney, unsure of himself when surrounded by so many senior masters, was at his most reserved.

'You're bound to have him next year in the Lower Sixth,' said Pilgrim. 'He's opted for a French A Level, so he'll be in your division. If he lasts, that is.'

'He won't last,' chimed in Rathbone, as the circle of conversation widened. 'We monitor everything he does in the chemistry labs. One false move, Headmaster, and he'll be up to you so fast his feet won't touch the ground. We can do without boys like him.' Rathbone had a reputation for blunt, unimaginative opinions and could rarely see both sides of an argument.

'I've a soft spot for him,' said St. Leger. 'There's a basic honesty about him. Whatever you think of him in the chemistry labs, he wouldn't do anyone else down. In fact, I suspect he takes the rap for other people sometimes just for the hell of it. There are one or two others I wouldn't trust an inch.'

Irving retreated from the conversation as the discussion of boys' personalities widened. As the ultimate authority it was not for him to reveal his opinion to other masters. He noticed that Tawney, who had only spoken briefly, had withdrawn likewise. He was quietly observant, he missed nothing, but plainly saw no need to take part in what was becoming common-room gossip. An impressive young man, Irving decided. The thread of steel he detected under the youthful exterior would be a rarity in any walk of life. He congratulated himself on an excellent appointment.

* * * * * *

Merchet is a male institution from top to bottom. When similar public schools recruited girls into their Sixth Forms – 'To keep the beds full,' as one governor accurately but indelicately put it – Merchet's reputation ensured that there were always plenty of male bodies available and it continued to turn away almost as many as it admitted. Until recently, with the exception of a few part-time music teachers, the staff had also been entirely male. However, a combination of the Equal Opportunities Act and a shortage of well-qualified scientists had led to the appointment of Jane Osgood and Pamela Baskerville.

Jane, a bright chemist, proved a great success. She accepted both masters and boys as they were and fitted into the male prejudices and idiosyncracies of Merchet without any real problems. Crucially, she was a natural disciplinarian – always more important than academic qualifications in a teacher – and she made it her business to fit in. She was not a games player, but turned out to watch the lst XV, and had even gone on a Field Day exercise with the Corps. In short, though she put up with occasional puerile jokes about being a mistress, she was a successful schoolmaster and the boys called her 'Sir'. With her trim blonde hair and slim build she was also attractive, a circumstance approved by both masters and boys.

The problems had started with Pamela's appointment. Her arrival was unexpected. She was originally the token woman on the short list and the post had been offered to an Oxford man with a good cricket pedigree. Unfortunately he was hi-jacked by the B.B.C. at the eleventh hour and when Irving returned to his list he found all other candidates had been snapped up except for Miss Baskerville. Although Irving liked to see himself as progressive, he had not really wanted another woman because he was aware of the cricket lobby, whose interests he had only modestly supported in recent appointments. However, the academic claims of the Physics department had to come first and in the event he had little choice.

Pamela's feminism had caused problems from the first. A tall woman with unkempt hair and a seemingly permanent sardonic expression on her lean, high-cheekboned face, she challenged Merchet traditions head-on. The office staff had been startled when she announced her wish to be MS rather than MISS in all official school publications and she had followed this by publicly querying the title 'masters' meeting' for the first formal meeting of the term; likewise, she wrote to the headmaster suggesting the 'masters' room' should be renamed the 'staff room' to recognise the presence of Jane and herself. By the end of her first term her political correctness at an institution that must be one of the most politically incorrect in the country had roused mirth and resentment in equal quantities. Even Jane, who might have been expected to share a certain fellow feeling, was embarrassed by her uncompromising stance. The soubriquet Mad Millie was adopted by all.

Previously Jane had declined the invitation to the Candlemas Feast on the grounds that it was a male occasion and she did not want to be the only woman. Pamela, however, insisted on attending and persuaded Jane that her duty to womankind was to do likewise. Accordingly, they were now sitting either side of a governor, a retired bishop who believed, wrongly, that he would have made Canterbury or York had it not been for his wife's reputation for gossip and interference. Irving's wife, who was responsible for the seating plan and who was not, of course, attending the feast, relished her mischievous juxtoposition. She found both the bishop and Pamela tiresome. Around them were several younger masters, and Andrew Korn, who had been put on Pamela's right on the grounds that he might have some sympathy with her iconoclasm.

Initially Pamela listened to the ramblings of the bishop with a measure of courtesy, but once she realised it did not matter whether she responded to the monologue or not and that he was in any case more interested in the nubile attractions of Jane's low neckline on his left, she turned to Korn and launched into one of her diatribes.

'This place needs a bomb under it, Andrew. Look around you. Can you believe this is happening in the last years of the twentieth century? Just two women here! And all these penguin suits and gowns. Outsiders wouldn't believe it.'

Korn was cautious. While his own views were anything but traditional, he realised how isolated Pamela had become. He said: 'It's been here a long time. I've sniped away for the last fifteen years, but not much has changed. The real power lies with the housemasters, you know. Moncrieff's retirement may make a difference.'

'What are you doing for this bloody pageant?'

'Nothing much. I've volunteered to keep an eye on the car parking and picnics in the park. The ground staff will do most of the work, but there'll have to be a master to take overall responsibility. Are you keeping out of it?'

'Certainly not. I'm going to be in the suffragette scene. Some rampant feminism won't come amiss.' Her taciturn face lit up at the prospect. 'I think it might become the most memorable episode of the whole evening.'

She did not know how prophetic her words were to be.

* * * * * *

The feast progressed through four courses. The noise level rose, for the boys had been drinking cider while the adults had wine.

Irving, who invariably mixed business with pleasure, turned to his left where the moon-faced Sylvester Ford had been talking to

Geoffrey Killigrew and Richard Pomeroy, the head of school, whose privilege it was to dine on high table on any formal occasion. The headmaster felt he had a finger on the pulse of the pageant and was now considering other areas where Merchet would be on display in the summer.

'What about the art, Sylvester?' he asked. 'Special exhibition?'

Ford was a methodical man. He adjusted a small piece of brie on a biscuit before replying. 'I'll do my best, Headmaster. We've accumulated some good work this year and the current crop of Sixth Formers are better than usual.'

'The place will be crawling with visitors next term, so we must put on a show.'

'Exams must come first if you want my department grades to keep us up the league table.' He spoke without looking at Irving and was apparently concentrating on another piece of brie.

It was Irving's stated policy to ignore academic league tables on the grounds that they took no account of entry standards or other elements of a Merchet education, but he was aware parents often saw things in simpler terms. An unexpected rise in position was useful for public occasions; a sudden drop could be damaging. A school with Merchet's high profile had to be careful.

'No, you needn't risk your grades, Sylvester. But you've already produced some outstanding pictures this year. Those portraits by Fairclough you've put up in the cloisters remind me of Francis Bacon. Frighteningly good. He's safe for an 'A', isn't he?'

'Oh yes, he'll walk it. I'll let you into a secret. Headmaster. Do you know who the portraits are?'

'No. They're so cruel I thought they were imaginative.'

'Sadly not. They're all members of the masters' room, though they don't know it. Fairclough's a bit of a rebel, but no harm in that.'

'More cruel than I thought. Has anyone complained?'

'Spooner recognised himself and had a moan. But – saving your presence, Headmaster – he wouldn't be happy if hadn't a complaint somewhere. There are some other interesting pictures you haven't seen yet. Mark Calverley's general studies division is doing Romanticism and has been working with me as well. He covers literature and music and I do a turn on art. They've been putting ideas inspired by Keats's poems on canvas. Pomeroy here – he indicated the head of school across the table – has produced a splendid nocturnal forest

63

based on the *Ode to a Nightingale*. Very evocative.'

Pomeroy, whose maturity had marked him out as a future leader from his earliest days at Merchet, smiled with pleasure. 'It's a marvellous course, Headmaster. General Studies aren't popular, as I suspect you know. Most boys think it's all pretty irrelevant and want to concentrate on their A Levels. But Mr Calverley's enthusiasm gets everybody going. He had us listening to Wagner this morning – it seemed to mean so much to him. Boys respect that. And then doing the painting with Mr Ford helps bring it all together.'

'A nice vote of confidence, Hugh.' Irving was avuncular. 'But to go back to next term' – he turned back to Ford – 'we shall obviously have to put the Manners collection on display in the Dorter gallery. It's high time it had another airing. I know you prefer to show the boys' work, but the Manners hasn't been up for several years now.'

Ford's eyes narrowed. 'Several frames need attention. And it does involve a lot of work to set it up, not to mention the extra insurance. Perhaps we could just display a sample.'

'The Manners family will expect it, Sylvester. It's some time since any of them came back, but the old man is bound to come for the quincentenary. The collection was given to us in memory of his brother who was killed piloting a Lancaster on that disastrous Nuremburg raid in 1944. Enormous losses that night. I think we must have the whole lot up. He'll expect it for a celebration year.'

'Very well, Headmaster. I'll see to it in the Easter holiday.'

'Good. What we really need, Sylvester, is a new gallery; then it could be up all the time. I'll try to get it into the next appeal on the strength of your excellent results.' Irving never missed an opportunity to praise a head of department and just at present art was one of the jewels in the Merchet crown.

At the same time he registered Ford's clear reluctance to put the Manners collection on display. Strange.

* * * * * *

Geoffrey Killigrew, sitting on the far side of Ford, leaned forward. He was in his way as serious-minded as the headmaster.

'The French *assistante* is finally fixed up, Headmaster.'

Irving, who was still thinking about the Manners collection, in particular the outstanding nineteenth-century watercolours, did some hasty mental adjustment. 'Yes?'

'A certain Monique Ducatillon. She was over earlier today and I confirmed what you and I had agreed. A term's appointment this summer and the possibility of a further year. If she's a success, she'll improve the French conversation enormously. The boys just need to get over their self-consciousness and I suspect they'll do it more readily with her than with one of us.'

'Was that the lady I saw you showing round this afternoon, sir?' asked Pomeroy, emboldened by the wine which he and the other monitors were sharing with the masters.

'Yes, she came over for the day on Eurostar.'

'Very pretty, if I may say so, sir.' As head of school, Pomeroy felt this a permissible comment about someone not yet on the staff. 'It'll help her with the boys.'

'Yes,' replied Killigrew vaguely. An academic noted for absent-mindedness, he had obviously not considered the matter. 'Yes, I suppose it will.'

'How old is she?' asked Irving.

'Twenty-two.'

'I suppose we shall have to fit her into the pageant as well,' said Pilgrim, picking up the conversation.

'Another suffragette,' said St. Leger. 'We can cope with all the women in that scene. One more or less won't make any difference.'

* * * * * *

It was something of a tradition for masters' wives to hold and informal party on the evening of the Candlemas Feast. This evening it was Sarah Charteris's turn to act as hostess and she had arranged a fork supper. She was a big blonde woman, cheerfully untidy, the sort who takes anything in her stride and expects others to do likewise. Her house, the old Merchet Farthing rectory, was Georgian and one of the more desirable residences provided by the school for its masters. A lock of unruly hair fell across one eye as she opened the door to early arrivals.

'Come in, come in,' she said to Rachel Pilgrim, taking her coat. 'Red or white? Help yourself. It's on the table by the piano.'

'Thanks, Sarah. It's freezing out there. Have we got many coming?'

'A good turn-out. Several here already.'

'Is Joyce coming?' The presence of the headmaster's wife gave an imprimatur to a party that had originally had a seditious tinge, being born of resentment at the exclusion of wives from the feast.

'You wouldn't keep her away. She and the headmaster have got old Bones staying the night and she's looking forward to telling him how she spent the evening. Hullo, Jane' – this to Jane Hillyard, a pale girl who had recently married the head of music – 'Come in, my dear, and get warmed up. Red or white? Take a glass and help yourself. We're independent tonight.'

'Who's Bones?' asked Jane.

'Sir Ralph Harcourt-Jones, one of the governors. A nice old buffer really, no malice in him. But pretty geriatric and thinks the school is still as it was when he was here. We had him last Founder's Day. Do you know he actually left a tip in his bedroom when he left. He thought we had a maid. It never occurred to him it was his hostess running round after him.'

'I hope you pocketed it.'

'You bet I did. But it's the sort of thing that does the governors no good. Fortunately they've appointed some younger ones recently. One or two quite dishy.'

Other wives arrived, among them Joyce Irving. She was conscious of her ambivalent position and determined to make her attitude plain. She said: 'We ought to do this more often. We don't have to wait until the men push us out. Can I give you a hand, Sarah?'

'Thanks, Joyce, but everything's under control, I think. Just come in and get yourself a glass of wine. Grub will be up shortly.'

The drawing-room and dining-room were soon full. Sarah had provided a lavish spread, as she always did, though the house had not been tidied and children's toys and clothes were scattered around.

Melanie St. Leger and Lucy Killigrew had their heads together in a corner. They were roughly the same age and shared a common interest in that both owned holiday cottages in Norfolk.

'What's this about wives in the pageant?' asked Lucy. She was usually the first to pick up items of news and was mildly irked to have to ask about it.

'Tristan wants suffragettes. Going to volunteer?'

'Edwardian costume is rather fetching. I might.'

'At one time they wanted an unfaithful wife to burn, but they've dropped the idea.'

'I can think of a candidate for that one.' Lucy dropped her voice. 'Or is Jenny lined up for Jane Shore?'

Melanie lowered her voice to the same conspiratorial level and giggled. 'I doubt if she'd have time for rehearsals.'

'She doesn't need rehearsals.'

'We're being bitchy. Jenny's all right really. James is a bit of a stick and she should never have married him.'

'As long as she isn't after your husband. I don't suppose she'll be here this evening. No men.'

'You're wrong. She's over there.'

Indeed she was. Jenny Wentworth, looking younger than her thirty-odd years, wearing high heels and a navy and white dress with a trim waist and full skirt, was talking to Kathy Tichbourne. Her face was animated, as usual; her sexual attraction was apparent, even to another woman.

'She's enjoying herself.'

'She always enjoys herself.'

Lucy Killigrew would have been mortified if anyone had called her a gossip, but that is what she was. She lowered her voice again. 'Look at Mary Calverley over there. Do you think she knows about Jenny and Mark?'

Melanie was cautious. 'Careful, Lucy. There may be nothing to know.'

'Don't you believe it.' She eyed the back of Mary's square shape through her unfashionable dress. 'Mark's still got plenty of life in him and Mary looks as though she's given way to comfortable middle age. Just look at her. All the danger signs are there. And you never see her in a pair of high heels. You know what men like. And Mark's a very attractive man – just the sort of intellectual Jenny goes for. If she wants him, she'll get him.'

Melanie looked down at her own flat shoes. She made a little sideways nod of her head which those who knew her interpreted as determination. 'If she goes for Tristan, I'll kill her.'

Chapter 9

The feast drew to its conclusion. The boys fell silent as the headmaster stood up. He toasted the memory of Abbot Greenfield and a scholar said a Latin grace. The boys remained quiet as governors and masters processed from the hall.

In the cloisters Alastair Munro saw Matthew Tawney walking on his own. Munro had detected his isolation in the masters' room and at the same time felt mildly guilty he had not been more sociable himself. He went over and tugged the sleeve of his gown.

'Come back and have a drink, Matthew.'

Tawney looked surprised, then smiled engagingly. 'Thanks, I'd like to. Anything to put off marking my Remove essays. I gave them an imaginative title, 'A great gulf fixed', and told them to get on with it. It didn't work. Most of them walked to the edge and fell in. I shan't be daft enough to do that again.'

'I didn't know you taught any English.'

'Just this Remove and one of the bottom Shells. The head man asked if I was prepared to take a bit of English when he appointed me. I enjoy it.'

Munro warmed to the younger man; he suspected he was less reserved than some of his colleagues had made out. He suspected they had reacted defensively to a clever northerner. He said: 'Curious occasion.'

'Very. But none the worse for that. I like tradition. Not much of it at my school.'

They threaded the cloister, left the straggling line of gowned figures and turned across the quadrangle towards the Old Infirmary. It was already freezing and their feet crunched in the light covering of snow; their breath steamed before them.

' *Pious incense* ,' said Tawney.

'Keats.' Munro frowned. 'Where? I can't place it.'

' *The Eve of St.Agnes*. My favourite poem – though it's not very fashionable at the moment. I know most of it by heart.'

'No-one learns poetry these days.'

'I make mine learn something regularly. They enjoy it. Easy to do and a sense of achievement at the end.'

'I couldn't agree more. I've never regretted anything I had to learn,' said Munro. 'I prefer Keats to Shelley. Shelley was a selfish swine. Treated his women appallingly.'

Tawney looked at his companion. With his gown wrapped around him and his gaunt, bearded face outlined against the lighted windows of the great hall, Munro seemed the last person to have opinions on romantic poetry or Shelley's love life. Perhaps he had misjudged the austere Scotsman. Perhaps he longed for a woman as much as he did himself. He smiled at the idea. Then it occurred to him that he might seem just as austere, a young intellectual with sublimated instincts. The exchange was over, both men shying away from their emotions.

The Old Infirmary had survived the Dissolution unscathed and, like the Almonry and the Abbot's House, had been adapted to provide accommodation for masters. As chaplain, Munro had one of the best sets of rooms, his sitting-room having linenfold panelling and leaded windows looking out across farmland towards the South Downs.

'A bit dark in winter,' said Munro, 'but it has style. I don't suppose the central heating is doing the panelling any good, but I'm going to turn it up. It's damned cold. Now, Matthew, what can I offer you? Port? Whisky? Or we could pick up where we left off at dinner. I've got a bottle of the same Pomerol. I bought a case when the bursar was stocking up the hall.'

The world of wine was relatively new to Tawney. With teetotal Methodist parents he had barely known the taste of alcohol before Oxford. Since then he had indulged, occasionally over-indulged, and he now enjoyed a drink; he was also anxious not to appear gauche.

'The claret was good. Are you sure you don't mind opening it specially?'

'Of course not. Just as long as we finish it. It won't be the same tomorrow.' Munro laughed throatily. He worked hard to show his dog-collar did not preclude worldly enjoyment.

Tawney relaxed into an armchair. Munro busied himself with glasses and a corkscrew.

Munro said: 'Well, what do you make of Merchet?'

'I like it. I've made some gaffes — and it's hard work. But it didn't take too long to see why the independent sector usually scores over the state. There's no nine to five mentality here. One of my first mistakes was to ask Jim Clode if he'd had a good week-end. He looked at me as if I was mad. 'What on earth do you mean?' he asked. 'I took the Junior Colts to Marlborough on Saturday and didn't get back till ten in the evening. I got up early on Sunday to mark some Upper Sixth essays and spent the afternoon going through them with the boys. What week-end are you talking about?' I felt I had to apologise for being stupid.'

'Try this.' Munro handed him a glass.

'My parents both taught in state schools. Advised me against it. They couldn't stand the interference of the local authority – and they didn't think much of the NUT. They said it had done more harm than good to the teaching profession. No- Merchet's fine. And it's got something I didn't expect.'

'What's that?'

'Variety, individuality. I used to think public schools were battery farms turning out clones with Oxford accents. I'm struck by the way we encourage the boys to do their own thing.'

'It depends on the house. You can be an individual in most houses -say Drydens or Muchelney. But you'd better not try it in Ryders. Moncrieff expects you to toe the line. Woe betide you if you don't throw yourself into games or support the house. Did you see all his boys down on the touchline this afternoon? It's a three-line whip and they'd be gated if they didn't turn up.'

Tawney thrust out his legs before him in a confident and unchar-acteristic way; the evening's alcohol had done its work. 'I don't disap-prove of him as much as some do. He's a snob, but he cares about his boys and you can't deny that Ryders is one of the most successful houses. There's a lot to be said for team spirit. Remember, I never had it. This wine's good. By the time we've finished the bottle I'll think my Remove essays are touched with genius. Probably find I've got a Hazlitt or De Quincey.'

'You're an optimist. I thought I was one of the last.'

'You have to be, don't you? Part of a priest's professional posture. Or is that rude? It's not meant to be. I considered holy orders myself during my last year at Oxford.'

Munro looked with new interest at the young man relaxing before him. Intelligence radiated from him, but there was none of the off-putting arrogance so often found in the able academic. When he had first arrived at the beginning of the Christmas term, he sensed suspicion, the suspicion of the outsider who withdraws in self-defence; now, he saw an inner warmth available for those prepared to break through the reserve.

'What stopped you?'

'No real vocation. But only after a lot of soul-searching. Did you decide easily?'

'No, I don't think anyone does. I'd considered it in a vague sort of way, but eventually realised what I had to do after a religious camp in Devon. Then I fought against it. We're complicated creatures. You'd be amazed if you'd seen one or two of the boys here who have gone into the church. If you'd told them when they were here they would end up as vicars, they'd have said you were mad.'

'You get to know the boys well?'

'Some of them. The dog-collar's a barrier in public, but they come when they've got problems. Some become genuine friends. And when they open up you'd be surprised at the things I discover about the school.'

'The confessional angle?'

'Something like that. We only know part of what goes on at Merchet. There's a sort of underground life we only touch on. Housemasters glimpse it from time to time, but only the boys know the whole truth. It's the same at all boarding schools. Do you know, at my place we had a chap who built himself a private study way up in the roof. He was an electrical boffin and set up a bugging system that included the headmaster's study. It wasn't discovered until three years after he'd left. I thought he was rather sinister, but he had his admirers and he's now a top man in the Ministry of Defence.'

'How long have you been here?' The question was simple, courteous, obvious; but the perception of the questioner gave it untoward weight. Munro felt Tawney's shrewd eyes carried supplementaries: 'Why have you stayed? Should not a priest with a vocation be caring for those with fewer advantages than Merchet boys?'

'Twelve years. I suppose you think I ought to get back to a parish to battle with the real problems of life. It's a point of view. But, in a curious way, there are some boys here who are as under-privileged as any in Brixton. Their money doesn't compensate for the emotional needs many of them have. Take a boy like Brand in Muchelney. He's been looked after by nannies and au pairs for the whole of his life.

He told me once he looks on the school as his real home. All the money in the world doesn't compensate for that. Besides, there's missionary work to be done. We've got some marvellous parents here, crippling themselves to pay fees they can't really afford for the sake of their children. But one or two homes are as pagan as any in the country – veritable temples to the great god Materialism. No, there's certainly a job to do.'

Munro refilled their glasses, then he too lay back and stretched his legs out. 'Or am I just justifying my position? Perhaps the truth is that it's a comfortable life for a bachelor. Nice rooms, stylish dining facilities, congenial company. A boarding school community has a lot going for it.'

'It's all new to me.'

'You feel settled?' Munro felt himself moving towards the pastoral angle. 'You get on with everybody?'

'I don't know everyone yet, but people have been very hospitable. Besides, the place is big enough to pick and choose. I haven't much in common with the Duke of Cambridge lot – but their all affable enough.'

'My dear boy' – Munro felt the patronising tone justified – 'My dear boy, nor have I. It's all beer, birds and leg-breaks – and jokes at Pamela Baskerville's expense. But don't underestimate them. Jim Clode's a First, you know. In any case the school's reputation rests partly on its games. If we can't keep a good XI and XV we shall stop getting boys from the prep schools. The academics bleat about intellectual standards, league tables and all that, but it's all meaningless if we don't keep the beds full. There are still plenty of parents who want a rounded education and expect good games results as well as A Levels. Irving's always understood that. The whole independent school thing depends on numbers. That's why Moncrieff has survived. He may be a dinosaur, but Ryders is always full to bursting. In a crazy way he's one of the most successful housemasters in the business. Of course, he doesn't always know everything about his boys. In fact, I could tell you...'

Tawney felt Munro near the edge of a confidence that might be unjustified on their short acquaintance. His reticence shied away. He said quickly: 'Is the Duke of Cambridge circle difficult to break into?'

'Not if you're prepared to pay for a big round. Just go down there one day. You'll probably get lumbered with some reffing or umpiring:

72

that's the other price to pay. Either that or Rathbone will have you crawling over Barton Heath with the Corps. I went down in my first term and found myself on the next night exercise. It poured with rain and Rathbone's dog ate my supper.'

Munro poured more wine and for another hour the two men discussed the strengths and weaknesses of the school. But although they broke initial barriers, they did not progress beyond certain formal limits. At no point did the conversation descend to personal gossip. And neither of them mentioned Jennifer Wentworth.

Eventually Tawney, who had long ago decided his Remove would have to wait for their essays, took his leave. He was up to school for the first period next day, so there was no chance of a lie-in.

When he had gone, Munro tidied up the glasses and got himself ready for bed. He found Tawney stimulating and he went back over their conversation. He thought about Tawney's comment on his confessional role. He realised with a shock what he had nearly revealed. But the facts were there and he still did not know if he had handled them correctly.

It was all very disturbing. He could not believe that nothing would ever come out. Why had Sir Roger Treece been at Merchet earlier in the day?

* * * * * *

Sylvester Ford walked straight back to his cottage in the village after the feast. He kicked the snow off his shoes as he opened the door, but he kept his overcoat and scarf on and went straight to the telephone. He put on his spectacles to look up a London number and then rang it.

'Hullo? Fanshawe? Ah – good. I'm sorry to call you so late. I hope it's not too late.'

A puzzled voice replied: 'No, I'm still up.'

'It's Ford, Sylvester Ford. I just want to check something. Have you still got that Copley Fielding – *Brighton Beach* ? It was in the front gallery the last time I was up with you.'

'Yes, things have been quiet recently. The market's been dead over the winter. There'll be no interest until the spring. It'll go when the Americans start arriving.'

'Good. Hang on to it, please. I'll speak to you later – in fact, I'll come up to explain in a day or two. But don't let it go whatever you do.'

'Very well, Mr Ford. I'll take it down and put it in the stock-room tomorrow.' The disembodied voice was accommodating and friendly. 'How's the term going?'

'We haven't reached half-term yet, but it's the shortest term of the year and that's something. Now I really mustn't keep you up. I'll try to see you within the next week. I'll telephone you before I come.'

Having achieved his aim, Ford cut the conversation short. The eyes behind the steel-rimmed spectacles, narrow, shrewd, even cunning, reflected relieved satisfaction.

Chapter 10

And so the day of the Candlemas feast drew to a close. Senior boys, anxious to contain the high spirits of their cider-lubricated juniors, turned out lights and retired to their own rooms either to work on overdue essays or continue their own partying with illicit supplies of beer or gin. While the headmaster worried about drugs – and from time to time there had been drugs at Merchet – alcohol was a more serious problem and many boys had access to it. Nervous housemasters, like Wentworth, went on tours of inspection, finding excuses to visit boys in their rooms at unexpected times; old hands, like Moncrieff, relaxed over a nightcap, knowing that if senior boys wanted to drink no amount of pussyfooting inspection would beat them.

Moncrieff poured himself a small whisky and sat down in his drawing-room. He was not one of the world's great thinkers, but he usually gave himself five minutes for reflection at the end of the day. By eleven o'clock the house was quiet, Wood would never disturb him after ten unless he was called for, and it was a Merchet convention that no phone calls were made after ten-thirty.

Not a bad day on the whole. The match against Drydens had started badly, but class had told in the end and Ryders had cruised home. The feast had been a success, too. He'd sat next to old Stannard and engineered a week-end's shooting in September. This was a coup in itself because the moor had a notable reputation. But Stannard's house parties invariably attracted distinguished City names; with shrewd management – and his track record was good – he would get enough inside information to guarantee an improved portfolio performance the following year. Thus the twin pillars of his life, social snobbery and financial greed, had been serviced. He took a sip of the single malt whisky he always kept for himself and savoured it.

Unexpectedly and irritatingly, the telephone rang.

'Moncrieff.'

It was Sir Roger Treece. He made no apology for calling late, but launched straight in: ' I've got an inkling of what's wrong with the boy. It's sex. I told you it was.'

'Go on.'

'I haven't got it all, but he's got a crush on someone. That's what we used to call it. He was led on and now it's all gone wrong. You know what it's like when you're seventeen. It happened last year. He says his whole world fell apart and that's why his work was so bad last term. He's even lost interest in sport. When that happens it's serious.'

'He played well enough today. Scored the final try.'

'I'm glad to hear it. Sorry I couldn't stay to watch. I did get the feeling the worst is over, but he admitted he felt suicidal more than once last year. Not the sort of thing sons say to fathers, is it?'

Moncrieff took off his spectacles with his free hand. 'So who is this crush on?'

'He wouldn't say. Said it was his business and he was going to put it straight. He's never spoken so directly to me. There was a determination I've never detected before. Somehow he seemed more mature. But it's definitely a girl and not a boy, that's something.'

'Girl in the village? Or Brighton?'

'No, he wouldn't say any more about that. He just laughed when I suggested it might be a boy. He actually said he wished it was a boy. Said it would be easier to cope with. The one thing I did glean is that he feels badly let down. Apparently she made all the running and to begin with he didn't want to get involved. Then he obviously fell for her and she just dropped him. She sounds a first-class bitch and I would guess he's well out of it. That's not the way he sees it, of course. But there's something odd about it, something he's not letting on.'

'What do you want me to do? There are limits, you understand, Roger.' As an old-style bachelor housemaster, he already felt himself withdrawing from a matter that threatened to be emotional; besides, he believed there were certain areas of a boy's life where interference might do more harm than good.

'Say you've talked to me. See if he'll open up any more. He respects you, Charles, and he just might come across with a name. He's very bitter. And there's something important I haven't got. I just hope to God there isn't a pregnant girl somewhere. See what you can do.'

'I'll do my best. But remember, Roger, if Oliver has done anything foolish he's virtually adult now. We're not dealing with a child. He must take a measure of responsibility himself.' The unspoken comment, the message Moncrieff always conveyed to parents when it looked as if they might shift the burden of their offspring too uncompromisingly towards the school was: 'And don't forget he's your responsibility too.'

Treece sensed the rebuff and softened his tone. 'Just do your best, Charles. I want Oliver to get to Merton and he won't do it if this girl messes up his A Levels.'

Moncrieff made reassuring noises and put down the 'phone. Though he might appear a superannuated old buffer to some of his younger colleagues, he had a sharp mind and years of experience. He was already considering possible contenders for Treece's infatuation. There were several nubile girls who served in hall and one or two masters' families had au pairs. The Pilgrims, for example, had a delectable Norwegian who trailed clouds of admirers. And what about wives? Moncrieff's bachelor misogyny ruled no-one out. Rumour had it that twenty years ago an errant master's wife had initiated a whole generation of boys before finally being caught *in flagrante* in the squash courts with the bursar. And there was always the village or Brighton. The days when the boys hardly ever left the abbey grounds had long gone; senior boys were always asking for leave to go somewhere or other. But it would be easier to deal with if the relationship – whatever it proved to be – was right off home territory.

He sat down again and picked up his Glenmorangie. Yes, it had been a good day. The Treece affair was of minor importance; much more significant were the boy's competent handling and tackling in the afternoon. Moncrieff's mood of complacency remained unshaken.

* * * * * *

Mark Calverley and Jennifer Wentworth sat in the back of Calverley's Ford Mondeo parked on the fringe of Parker's Wood. The car was in the shadow of the outlying trees; out in the open the snow-covered fields glistened in the light of the moon. Half a mile away the blunt outline of the abbey tower was dimly visible and here and there the pin-prick of a lighted window.

Mark pulled Jennifer close and pushed his face down into the tangle of her hair. 'You smell good.'

'I've just washed it.' She laughed. 'I thought I'd finished with the backseats of cars when I left my teens. I'm too old for this sort of thing.'

'So am I. But beggars can't be choosers. We'll do better in the holidays. We can go to my brother's cottage in Wiltshire. He's got a four-poster you could lose an army in.'

'Mary will know something's up. She's no fool, Mark.'

'Just at the moment her mother means more to her than I do. She's not at all well, so Mary will be up in Wales for a good part of the Easter holiday. I'll have to go with her for a few days just to put in an appearance, but I can get free for at least a week.'

'How did you escape tonight?'

'I've gone over to the St. Legers to discuss this damned pageant. Tristan's getting too enthusiastic about it.'

'She won't ring you there?'

'No. She'll do her usual tidying of the house and then go to bed.'

'Tidying the house? At this time of night?'

'She can't leave domestic things alone. She's desperately house-proud. We have a daily cleaning woman, but Mary's done everything before she arrives in the morning. Ridiculous, really. I don't know what we pay her for.' He pulled Jennifer closer. 'I have priorities that come before the washing-up. Come here, woman.'

They kissed. The car windows were already beginning to steam up.

'Will you be able to get away from James to come down to Wiltshire?'

'I can manage anything you can. James doesn't mind where I go or who I go with, just as long as he's spared the details. We have an unspoken arrangement.'

'It's strange to have reached one's fifties before realising what love really is. Doesn't that sound trite! I feel like a schoolboy.'

'You won't leave Mary.'

'How do you know?'

'Men don't leave their wives.'

'A bitter remark?'

'Realistic.'

'Experience?'

'Perhaps.'

Her tone, hard-edged and flat, made him feel insecure. He felt for another schoolboy line: 'You do love me?'

'I've wanted you a long time, Mark. But I'm no blushing virgin. I've been here before and I know more about men than you do about women. I also know myself. I've a track record and I'm hard. It won't do for you to jump in too deep. Love? No, let's keep it simple. We can enjoy each other's company – we can enjoy each other. You're good in bed, even if Mary's never told you so. But don't look for complications. Don't look for permanency.'

He was silent. Then: 'God, it's cold out here! Don't worry, Jenny, I'll have you on any terms. Has anyone else told you that? You see, I'm jealous already.'

'Plenty of men have said they loved me, but none of them meant it.'

'Don't underestimate me, Jenny, that's all I ask. It would be a mistake.'

'I never underestimate men, believe me. Now come on, darling, warm me up.'

* * * * * *

Later Jennifer crept into Theobalds by the back door, went quietly upstairs, threw off her clothes and was in bed within minutes. As she slid down between the chill cotton sheets, she wondered for the first time whether her affair with Mark was a good idea. She was certainly enjoying it, but was it possible that it might be less under her control than she thought? Normally her flippant, light-hearted style dictated the terms; her lovers were kept at arm's length and forced to play the game by her rules. Mark was different and there were signs he might be difficult.

Why was she so promiscuous? 'Give your favourite nymphomaniac a kiss,' she had once said to a spectacularly temporary lover. At the time she was joking, but her blatant enjoyment of her libido did sometimes disturb her. Never more so than when a man threatened to take her seriously. She liked Mark, she had wanted him for a long time and she relished their lovemaking, but she knew it wouldn't last. It never did. And there had been disasters. She thought back to the previous summer. How on earth had she got involved in that? And why had she been so careless? It had all been her fault. She couldn't blame anyone else.

She pulled the bedclothes tightly round her. 'That's the last time in the back of a car,' she reflected. And there was something else: she sensed that Mark had found it vulgar. She didn't mind a little vulgarity herself, indeed she enjoyed it, but she shied away from inflicting it on intellectual men.

In the room next door James lay awake. A shaft of moonlight cut through a crack in the curtains, illuminating a nineteenth-century print of his Oxford college. Where had she been this time? Who was it? More material for a sniggering masters' room? He felt his innermost being had been reduced to a dried, empty husk. Life was pointless.

Suddenly the telephone rang. Wentworth picked it up and found that his wife, who had an extension in her room, had also done so.

A female voice said: 'Mrs Wentworth?'

'Yes.?

'I'm sorry to disturb you so late. My name is Sister Reynolds and I'm speaking from the A and E department of Stoke Mandeville hospital. We've got your grandfather here and he's asking for you. I believe you're his only relative.'

'Yes. What's wrong with him?'

'Heart attack, I'm afraid, Mrs Wentworth. I must tell you, sadly, that the prognosis is not good. Can you come straight away?"

'Straight away?'

'Yes, I think so. If you want to see him.'

There was a pause as Jennifer assimilated the news. 'Of course, I'll come immediately. It'll take a moment or two to get organised, but I'll be with you as soon as I can. I'll just tell my husband.'

'It's all right, he's heard.' Wentworth spoke on the shared line. 'You go ahead, Jennifer. You'd better take an overnight bag in case you have to stay.' In his bitter mood he thought, but did not say: 'You won't be missed here.'

Jennifer quickly got dressed again, packed a suitcase, said goodbye to James and was on the road to Buckinghamshire before midnight. 'God, I'm tired. Just the last thing I wanted tonight,' she said aloud as she accelerated out of Merchet Farthing. 'But I always was a selfish bitch.'

As she drove north towards London and the warmth of the car's heater began to make her relax, a more generous mood took over. 'Poor old man. I hope I'm not too late. He'll have no-one there.'

At the back of her mind was another thought altogether, one of which she was not proud. She congratulated herself for remembering to put a spade in the back of the car.

Trinity

Chapter 11

The Trinity term opened in the way that had become something of a tradition. Two days before the boys returned for the summer Irving gave an evening drinks party for all the teaching staff and matrons.

'We've still got ten minutes. Do you want a drink before we go down?' Joyce Irving, trim and businesslike in a simple grey dress, knew her husband did not enjoy the occasion.

'Please – a gin and tonic.' Irving straightened his tie in the mirror and smoothed back the greying hair at his temples. 'I never like this term. The summer always produces more problems than the other two terms put together. Discipline falls apart once the exams start – and they start earlier every year. This time we've got the pageant on top of everything else. It'll be just our luck to have a drugs scandal in the middle of the quincentenary.'

'Nonsense. The school's probably having its best period since the war. It's got plenty to celebrate – and your nine years have a great deal to do with it. Even the masters' room isn't critical any more. How many headmasters can say that?'

'Don't you believe it, Joyce. Three years on probation, three struggling to make a change or two, and three trying to prove I'm not over the hill. You can't free-wheel here. It's difficult to win at Merchet. If you don't alter anything, the young staff think you're fossilized; if you change too fast, you've got the governors and Old Merchets breathing down your neck saying you're a revolutionary. Remember the fuss when I altered the time of evening school by a quarter of an hour? You'd have thought I wanted to demolish the abbey.'

'Here, drink this.' His wife brushed a piece of dust off his shoulder. 'You don't look too bad on it.'

'I couldn't do it without you.'

'Rubbish.' She was brusque. 'You do it all yourself.'

Irving was momentarily taken aback by the way his affectionate remark had been swept aside. 'Come on. Share this.' They drank alternately out of the glass. 'I hope James Wentworth's more cheerful than he was last term.'

'He's one of your most dedicated housemasters. Look at the time he spends with his boys. He's down at every match from start to finish. Rugger, cricket, fives, squash, fencing – he throws himself into everything. Of course, Jennifer's not very interested.'

'He works hard, but he's not a good housemaster. He takes a personal interest in his boys, no-one can deny that, but Theobalds is the scruffiest house in the school. He's no idea how to get the sort of discipline we need here. Do you think he and Jennifer have got a problem?'

'Could be. I've picked up rumours, but no-one would tell me. Now finish your drink. It's time we were down there.'

Irving drained the glass and together they left the house and crossed the lawn to the Old Library, the Jacobean room they used for all large scale entertaining. Haskins, the major-domo of the masters' dining room, and three black-dressed women from the village had prepared the room and were putting drinks on trays ready for the first guests.

'At least no-one's here before us this time,' said Irving. 'Remember that wretched man Clift last year? He'd downed a couple of glasses before we got here. He had to go. I could just about put up with his boorish manners, but he couldn't keep order and that's the one test you can't fail at Merchet. Thank God he couldn't keep order.'

Joyce smiled, then realised her husband had missed the humour of his own remark. She did not comment. She had lived with him long enough to know it would be useless to try to explain. She said: 'There was a lot to be said for Evelyn Waugh's Captain Grimes. I always had a soft spot for him.'

Irving was not listening. 'The pageant's only nine weeks away, you know, but there's an enormous amount to be done if that rehearsal at the end of last term was anything to go by. Tristan was doing the battle of Flodden and the casualty rate was nearly as bad as the real thing. Ferguson was kicked by a horse and a new boy nearly had his eye put out by that fool Skirmish. It was a shambles.'

'What in heaven's name has Flodden got to do with Merchet?'

'Not much. Thomas Howard, the Earl of Surrey, gave us the Howard Acre after he'd won the battle in 1513. A sort of thanksgiving to the church.'

'It's a bit thin.'

'Pilgrim's keen on it. It gives him a chance to employ all those sons of Scottish lairds who can't be relied on to do much but fight. They like wearing kilts too. It'll be very colourful. Pilgrim says the only problem is making sure the right side wins.'

'Are you going to be involved?'

'Tristan has asked me to do a small walk-on part at the end – as myself, just to tie it all up. But that's all. The main headache will be coping with competing interests once Pilgrim turns the rehearsal heat on. You know how demanding he is. He does it brilliantly, but he upsets everyone. Ah, here they come...'

They moved forward as Haskins opened the double doors at the end of the room to admit the first guests.

* * * * * *

Within twenty minutes the library was crowded and noisy. Irving and his wife circulated dutifully; Haskins and his minions dispensed claret and Chablis.

The party pattern developed in the usual Merchet way. House-masters drifted together, mulling over the likely problems of the new term; the cultural divide emerged as intellectuals fled from sportsmen and vice versa; wives who enjoyed talking to men flirted, those who didn't congregated together to gossip about those who did.

Analysts of the party scene would have found interesting material. This was no Hampstead or Islington party centred on the vogue attitudes of the media and the arts, laced with the cynicism of politics; nor yet the golf and gin brigade of Sonning and Sunningdale, consumed with profit and loss and the conversational banalities of fast cars. Here was a party within a closed institution whose participants shared a similar educational background, one or two boasting pedigrees linked with the world of the great nineteenth-century educators – the Arnolds, the Butlers, the Huxleys. An outsider would have found much of the conversation parochial, and parochial it often was, yet at the same time it managed to combine the ironical detachment of an Oxford high table with the material preoccupations of the boardroom.

A party at Merchet was a self-confident affair bearing the hallmarks of the mandarin society it reflected. Schoolmasters are not given to uncertainty – they cannot afford to be, performing daily as they do before an astute and critical audience; they are talkers rather than listeners, prepared to pontificate on subjects they may or may not know anything about.

Thus, as Irving cast his eye over the bent heads and clinking glasses, he might have seen a classicist noted for a monograph on Minoan Crete laying down the law on the qualities needed by an England cricket captain; a chemist discoursing with confidence on the Mafia; and the head of IT, who taught no history, explaining the mistakes made by Napoleon at Waterloo.

Irving, at ease now the party was under way, viewed the scene with a measure of detachment. Then duty called. He saw Geoffrey Killigrew pinned to the wall like a butterfly specimen by the voluble Miss Broad. He plunged to the rescue.

* * * * * *

Moncrieff stood on the edge of the throng at an open window giving onto the trim lawns between the library and the Old Buttery. He sipped his claret. He was about to utter when St. Leger, standing at his elbow, spoke first. He indicated the claret. 'Better than last time, Charles?'

'It could hardly be worse. I don't know where Irving gets it. You'd think the head man of Merchet would know a decent wine merchant.'

'You're impossible, Charles.'

'Not at all. I'm an élitist and proud of it. Elitism has become a dirty word so that we can all be dragged down to the common denominator. If you're spending money on wine, you might as well get something worthwhile.'

As second master, St. Leger could be blunt with Moncrieff in a way younger colleagues could not. 'If you can afford it,' he said. 'Now what's this I hear about you taking boys out of my pageant?'

'It's true. You can't have Crawford-Morrison and Wharncliffe. They're both doing A Levels and they can't possibly do the pageant as well as their cricket.'

'Come on, Charles. They haven't much to do. I want them for the Somme scene. Two of your blonde aristocrats leading their men to disaster.'

Moncrieff smiled complacently. His hide was proof against St.

Leger's mocking tone. 'No, they're both likely to be in the XI and that still means something at Merchet. Wharncliffe's father would never forgive me if the boy lost his place because he was poncing around in your pageant. Besides, I value the Wharncliffe shoot.'

'And his title.'

'Of course.' Moncrieff was twinkling now, his circle of white hair bobbing up and down. 'Poor Wentworth would like a title or two in Theobalds. He thought he was going to get young Staggers, but I snapped him up. The Yorkshire Staggers, of course.'

'They bought the baronetcy from James I,' observed St. Leger, who as head of history knew some pedigrees better than Moncrieff. 'Part of the Duke of Buckingham's money-making racket. Not much to be proud of.'

'Hallowed by time, dear boy, hallowed by time.'

'Young Staggers doesn't look any great shakes to me. I've given him a pike to hold in the Elizabethan scene, but I think it's too heavy for him. He's dropped it at every rehearsal so far.'

'Too much inbreeding. The Staggers were a close-knit lot in the eighteenth century. Still I'm glad he's appearing. Prop him up if you have to. His mother would like to see him do *something*.'

Moncrieff was looking over St. Leger's shoulder. 'You must excuse me, Tristan. The head man wants a word. I gather he's dining with the Maceys at Downe. Probably wants to know if it's black tie.' He looked over his half-moon spectacles quizzically. 'He's as much of a snob as I am, you know. And you can't have Crawford-Morrison or Wharncliffe. That's final.'

* * * * * *

Calverley was enjoying himself. He ran his fingers through his hair and looked affectionately at Jennifer Wentworth, whom he had manoeuvred into a corner of the room. After their successful holiday in Wiltshire he felt proprietorial.

'You're going to be a suffragette?'

'Don't sound so disbelieving. The wives usually get roped in to do the make-up or sew up cod-pieces. I wasn't getting involved in any of that nonsense. But Tristan was persuasive about the suffragette scene.'

'I think I'll fancy you in Edwardian dress.'

'Careful, Mark. Mary's only just behind you.' Jennifer looked over his shoulder, then turned in such a way that she could speak without being overheard. 'I've got to talk to you, Mark. Something serious. Can we get out of here for a few minutes?'

'Difficult.'

'It's important. It's about my grandfather.'

'You miss him a lot, don't you?'

'Yes. I didn't see him very often, but he was always there. He seemed indestructible somehow. He was a link with the past and I haven't got many of them. His death has made me aware of my own mortality in a way I never was before.' Jennifer looked down at her feet, avoiding Mark's eye. 'There's something I didn't tell you in Wiltshire.'

Calverley looked at her. 'I was flattered that you told me anything. It was quite a confidence.' He thought back to the evening in the cottage when she had told him of her final visits to her grandfather. Briefly he had felt that this independent spirit had needed him in a way she hadn't before.

'I didn't tell you everything. I suppose I was protecting him in a funny sort of way.'

'Tell me now.'

She shook her head. 'Outside.'

'Difficult,' he said again.

Jennifer moved closer and bent forward until their heads were nearly touching. 'It's about a gun.'

Calverley felt he had not heard properly. He looked puzzled.

'A gun,' she repeated.

He responded immediately. 'Slip out of here in a couple of minutes. I'll meet you in the Dorter gallery. I've got a key.'

* * * * * *

Jasper Hillyard – 'Fingers' Hillyard to the boys – was talking shop with Patrick Dangerfield, his second in command in the music department. A small man with wild hair, wild eyes and a large aquiline nose, he held a glass in one hand and a sausage on a stick in the other. The prospect of organising the music for the pageant filled him with gloom.

'It's all very well for you, Patrick,' he said. 'You're not ultimately responsible. Just look at the problems.'

Dangerfield was a tall, thin man, with a stoop that made him seem shorter than he really was. He was an enthusiast who radiated optimism at all times. 'Nothing that can't be overcome.'

'Take rehearsals,' went on Hillyard as though Dangerfield had not spoken. 'It's bad enough trying to get anything done in the summer term at the best of times. Cricket will come first, second and third, pageant or no pageant, so we'll never get the full orchestra for the Elgar – unless it pours with rain and cricket is cancelled. Then look at the Byrd, the *Mass for Five Voices*. We can't hope to do that without Rutherford and he's Captain of the XI. We'll never see him.'

'The Byrd's ambitious. Where does it fit in?'

'We're only doing a small extract, but it's got to be good. Tristan wants it for the Gunpowder Plot scene. There was an Old Merchet working in Cecil's spy network. I suspect Tristan wants to have a dig at the Catholics. You know his family's got an estate in Ulster and they've had trouble with the IRA?' Hillyard speared a sausage from a passing tray and shrugged his shoulders. 'As for the first world war songs, I give up. I only managed to get the boys together once last term. The Corps get in first every time. Rathbone says his bangs are more important.'

'Tipperary doesn't need to be very musical.'

'It certainly won't be with louts like Carpenter and Hosegood singing. God knows how those two got into Merchet.'

'Got to keep the numbers up. Quantity before quality these days. Merchet's not immune to modern diseases.'

Sylvester Ford, who had been lurking on the edge of the conversation, chose this moment to join in. 'You're not the only one with problems, Jasper. I've got to get the school plastered with boys' paintings, I'm still hanging the Manners collection, and now Pilgrim wants innumerable bits of scenery. It's a nightmare. As far as I'm concerned, the whole thing's a waste of time.'

Distracted from his own grievances, Hillyard changed the subject. 'Look over there. Jennifer's found a new toy.'

Dangerfield and Ford glanced towards the corner of the room where Jennifer Wentworth, making her way to the door, had stopped and was laughing with Matthew Tawney.

'He's too green for her,' said Ford.

'Nonsense, she's omniverous. She could do a Leporello catalogue in reverse.'

'I thought Mark was still the lucky man,' said Dangerfield.

'Jennifer's a butterfly,' said Hillyard. 'She doesn't settle for long.' He looked across the room to where Jennifer and Tawney were still laughing. 'She won't do Tawney any good.'

'Tawney's old enough to take care of himself.'

'Only just.'

At that point Jennifer edged away from Tawney and slipped out of the door. Joyce Irving chose the same moment to join the Hillyard group.

'Come on, gentlemen,' she said. 'You're either talking shop or gossiping. They're forbidden at my parties.'

'Guilty,' said Hillyard, 'of both.'

'If I weren't the headmaster's wife, I'd love to hear the gossip. As it is I have to be diplomatic and nobody tells me anything. Isn't it a shame?'

Joyce Irving's arrival gave Ford the opportunity to move away from the group. He did so pensively, thinking back to his first meeting with Jennifer and all that had happened since. She had opened up so many possibilities. He smiled inwardly with egotistical complacency.

Haskins circulated with the claret. Snatches of conversation drifted across the room, a disjointed verbal collage.

* * * * * *

'Of course Karajan was a Nazi. He joined the party as early as 1933.'

'No, no. He didn't join until he was appointed to Aachen in 1935. He didn't have much choice. In any case Hitler couldn't stand him.'

'Does it really matter? Have you heard his Mahler Ninth? Anyone who could conduct a performance like that transcends politics.'

'And Mahler was a Jew.'

'Did you know that when Alma Mahler was in labour with her second child Mahler read Kant aloud to her to take her mind off it. She didn't understand a word, poor girl.'

* * * * * *

'Do you remember a boy called Sutherland? He was sacked some time in the 1980s. He's just been imprisoned for misappropriation of funds in the City. Apparently he wore his O.M. tie in the dock, hoping the judge might be sympathetic to a public school man.'

'No good?'

'No, Sutherland got it wrong again. The judge's wife had just run off with another O.M. He was sent down for four years.'

* * * * * *

'Did you see Mark and Jennifer go out? They both went within minutes of each other.'

'Not very clever to be so open. Jennifer's usually more discreet.'

'I hear they saw a lot of each other in the holiday. Mary will find out soon if she doesn't already.'

'I'd have thought Mark had more sense.'

* * * * * *

'We live in an age of moral relativism. You won't find a vicar anywhere who will condemn anything. When did you last hear a sermon threatening divine punishment?'

'Universal dumbing down. Vicars want to be popular like everyone else. Populism rules O.K. The government rules by focus groups, the media play to the groundlings to compete for an audience. No one knows better than anyone else. Beethoven has no more value than...Give me a pop group beginning with B.'

'The Bastards.'

'Exactly. Beethoven is no better than the Bastards.'

* * * * * *

'There's something wrong with Sylvester this term. I was talking to him just now and his hands were shaking. He doesn't drink, does he?'

'No more than most of us. Funny, I thought he looked ill too. Very pale.'

'He was moaning about the pageant.'

'He always moans. Hope he's not sickening for something. We don't want to start the term by providing cover for him.'

* * * * * *

'The trouble is that no-one knows the difference between 'few' and 'less' any more. Just listen to the BBC.'

'At least Marks and Spencer got it right at the check-out.'

'Only because someone complained.'

* * * * * *

'Have you spoken to Mad Millie?'

'She's on the warpath again. The head man said she couldn't wear trousers for teaching. She's determined to make him change his mind.'

'She makes life so uncomfortable for herself – and everyone else. She doesn't understand the word compromise. Terrible mistake to have appointed her here. This is one of the last male chauvinist bastions. She'll go too far one day and someone will hit her. She takes advantage of our good manners. Do you know what she said to Jim Clode the other day when he held the door open for her and let her go through first?'

'No.'

'*I'm more than capable of opening a door myself, Jim. I'd take it kindly if you'd start treating me as an equal.*' Jim was flabbergasted. You know how courteous he is. He couldn't see what she was getting at.'

'I hope she doesn't turn the new French *assistante* into a disciple. Have you seen her?'

'No. Where is she?'

'Over there with Killigrew and all the linguists. She's a real looker. Plenty of admirers already. We certainly don't want Millie's talons into her.'

* * * * * *

'Fifteen thousand a year is a hell of a lot out of taxed income.'

'Parents will still pay it if we get it right. At bottom they want two things: academic standards and social credibility.'

'Social credibility? You mean accent?'

'Speech, not accent. It's all to do with lavatories.'

'Lavatories?'

'The public school teaches you what to call them. The bog, the rears, lavatories, even the loo, are acceptable. Toilet is not. If you come out of Merchet talking about toilets you've missed the point of the whole exercise. Fifteen thousand a year down the bog, so to speak.'

* * * * * *

Conversation around the room reflected the prejudices and values of a conservative, male-dominated society. The universal approbation of the French *assistante* meant that Killigrew had to force his way through an admiring crowd of young bachelors to introduce her to the Irvings. She was dark and pretty, and spoke English with an accent that came close to a cliché; furthermore, she was vivacious and dressed in a style normally associated with a mature Parisienne.

'Where exactly do you live in France?' asked Irving.

'Montsauche. In the Morvan.'

'I'm afraid we've never been there,' said Joyce Irving. 'We come to France quite often, but it's usually Normandy or Brittany. I missed your name, my dear. There's so much noise.'

'Monique – Monique Ducatillon. We don't get many visitors to the Morvan. And there's a French saying *No good comes out of the Morvan.*' She laughed delightedly and her eyes darted round her audience. 'The only things it's noted for are the wood from its forests and its – I'm not sure of the English here – its milk-nurses. No, I think you call them wet-nurses. Rich families used to hire them. Morvan nurses were best.'

The Irvings were impressed by the bubbly young woman. As they moved on, Irving said: 'She looks good value.'

'So did her suit. I wouldn't mind one like that.'

'You'd need a longer skirt, I think,' said her husband.

Just for a moment Joyce thought he was making a joke, but when she looked at his face she saw he was completely serious. She should have known better.

* * * * * *

In spite of Moncrieff's criticism of the wine, Irving's parties were popular. The previous headmaster had been something of a puritan and parties had always ended at a prearranged time, regardless of how well they were going. Irving had decided early on that relations with the masters were the essence of success and, whatever he felt about parties himself, his hospitality was generous and highly regarded. On this occasion the drinks had been advertised for 6 to 8 pm, but

Haskins was still refilling glasses at 9.30 when the last guests were leaving.

Jennifer and Mark had returned from their rendezvous in the Dorter gallery and had now split up. Jennifer had gravitated once again to Matthew Tawney.

'Why don't you come back to Theobalds for a bite to eat? James and I are only having a salad, but you're very welcome. And James could show you round Theobalds before the boys get back. Have you been round any of the houses?'

'No. I should like that. Most housemasters guard their empires jealously.' Tawney looked closely at the attractive woman beside him. She had the knack of standing provocatively and he wondered if any of the whispers he had heard could possibly be true. He was also aware of his own response. He said: 'Thank you, Mrs Wentworth. I'd love to come.'

'Jenny, please. You mustn't make me feel too old.'

* * * * * *

The party drew to a close. As at all parties one or two individuals were left like driftwood on the beach when the tide has receded.

St. Leger had gone to discuss the pageant with Pilgrim, but Melanie, in a bright red dress, was still there talking to the elegant and affected Stephen Higham. They were discussing politics and both had been drinking steadily.

'I've had a basinful of Moncrieff's prejudices,' said Melanie. 'He's about as near a fascist as we get round here. When I listen to him I wish Old Labour were still around. After all, they did at least talk about getting rid of public schools. No chance with New Labour. Can *you* justify our existence?' She had an intense side which did not always endear her to Merchet.

Higham had a cigarette in one hand and a glass in the other. He waved the cigarette ineffectually and it was easy to see why the boys called him 'Stephanie'. 'Of course, Melanie dear. But I'm much too drunk to make a speech about it now. Besides, I'm also drunk enough to say I find your trendiness tiresome. How does Tristan put up with it?'

'Oh easily. He's marvellously tolerant, haven't you noticed? He's the sort of self-confident conservative who tolerates everything because he can't really believe anyone thinks differently. Just let people think and say what they like and they'll come round to his right-headed view in the end. Infuriating.'

'But you love him?'

'What an indiscreet question, Stephen! You really are drunk. Yes, I love him. Of course I do. But that doesn't mean I couldn't have an affair with someone else. Fancy me, Stephen?' She laughed.

'Good God, Melanie! Now you're being *outrageous*. Stop teasing me, there's a dear. It's time we both went home. Come on. Me to my virtuous bachelor couch, you to the joys of the marital bed. Melanie, don't you *dare* say anything like that again. Just think of my reputation!'

They laughed loudly, thanked the Irvings, and, still laughing, left the library.

Stephen Higham, too, albeit wholly unwittingly, was to be a minor player in the unfolding tragedy.

Chapter 12

The Dacre Club at Merchet was created for the Upper Sixth in the 1920s. Worried when he discovered a group of boys coming back from a nightclub in London and suspicious that others were escaping regularly to pubs in Brighton, the headmaster of the time founded a prestigious club where senior boys could drink under a degree of supervision. Such legal sanction did not eliminate bootleg liquor elsewhere, nor did it end illicit visits to local hostelries, but membership of the club had a certain cachet and provided a place where boys of different houses could meet.

Three weeks after the beginning of the Trinity term a few members of the 1st XI were having a drink after nets. They were still wearing whites and cricket sweaters.

Clive Raybould, a robust boy with prominent cheekbones and deeply-set eyes, sank into an armchair, clutching a glass of lager. 'God, I'm exhausted! And St. Leger's expecting an essay from me in the morning.'

'Get an extension. He's not unreasonable,' said a dark-jowled boy wearing a blue blazer with its collar turned up in an old-fashioned way.

'Not a hope. It's already three days overdue. Even St. Leger isn't that generous. Besides, he's ratty this term. This bloody pageant thing's getting on his nerves. Do you know, he wanted me to dress up as some sort of herald?'

'He ought to get Stephanie to do it. He'd love waving his hat and pouffing it up.'

'Are any masters in it?'

'Not as far as I know. Halstead's doing the lighting – you can't keep him away from anything electrical. He's the original anorak. St. Leger said something about the head man bringing the whole thing to a triumphant conclusion before the fireworks. I expect rain will save the day and it will all be cancelled at the last moment.'

'La belle Wentworth's in it.'

'I didn't think she'd be kept out of it. A born exhibitionist.'

'She shares it out, you know,' said a boy with insensitive eyes.

'Does Wentworth know?'

'I doubt it. Half his house goes to Brighton at the week-end and he still doesn't twig.'

'Touching faith in the public schoolboy.'

'He's all right,' said a boy in Wentworth's house who had been in the club before the cricketers arrived. 'We like him.'

'So would I if he were my housemaster. Bryant's bloody awful. He snoops around the rooms and that's not the Merchet style. I wouldn't be too keen on Tichbourne either.'

'I wouldn't mind a touch of Jennifer Wentworth,' said one of the cricketers who had not yet spoken.

'You're not old enough, Freddie. She likes the mature types – like me.'

'I wonder if she's tried Stephanie.'

They laughed the loud laughter of the sexually inexperienced.

'I fancy this French girl. What's her name? She doesn't teach me – no such luck. But I see quite a lot of her because she's often in Killigrew's room. Her legs are quite something – and she doesn't mind showing them. Almost enough to make me take up French again.'

'What do you think of her, Woody?' Raybould turned to Gatewood Foster, an American spending a year at Merchet.

'I'm too worried about this pageant to have time for women.' He was a tall, serious young man with a soft, unaggressive accent. 'Mr St. Leger's written this Virginia scene especially for me and I don't want to foul it up.'

'Got to keep the colonials happy. What have you got to do?'

'It seems this Old Merchet helped Raleigh get the Virginia charter from Queen Elizabeth. Then he was scalped by the Indians.'

'Sounds depressing. I should want something more heroic.'

'I told Mr St. Leger we don't call them Red Indians any more. He said he knew that, but there wasn't going to be any politically correct nonsense in *his* pageant.'

'Pilgrim's got Stephanie training the bottom Shell as Indians. That's all they're capable of.'

'They're giving Stephanie hell.'

'He hasn't a clue how to control the younger boys. He's fine with Sixth Formers, but they shouldn't give him the juniors. They run rings round him.'

'Do you find it very different over here, Woody?'

The American was about to give his considered opinion when the club steward, an ex-guardsman and old school retainer, came across and broke them up. 'Time please, gentlemen. You must be back in your houses in five minutes.'

'All right, Joe, we're off.'

They drained their glasses quickly – for all his old-world courtesy Joe Thorburn was not a man to be trifled with – and left the club.

Outside, Oliver Treece, one of the cricketers who had not taken part in the badinage, took Raybould to one side. 'You're not serious about Mrs Wentworth, are you? She's not really like that?'

Raybould gave him a dig in the ribs. 'You're a dark horse, Oliver. Burning a bit of a candle, are you?'

Treece turned away, glowering. 'You glib fool. Go and write your bloody essay.'

* * * * * *

That same evening Calverley took his wife to the local railway station. She was spending a night in London with a friend and then going on to Wales to see her mother for a few days. He found her a seat and put her suitcase on the rack.

'Take care of yourself,' he said.

'I'll be back on Saturday if she's all right. I've got three Shell boys coming to tea on Sunday and I've already put them off once.' Calverley knew his wife well and he detected a tone he hadn't heard before. He looked at her sharply as she spoke again: 'I know about Jenny, of course.'

Thinking about it later, he realised he had been waiting for her to say something like this for some time. Mary was an intelligent woman and his behaviour had been anything but cautious. 'Do you want to discuss it now?'

'Don't be foolish, Mark. The train's about to go. It'll keep. I don't suppose it will make any difference anyway.'

'I knew you'd find out.'

'I never thought you could be such a fool.'

He got out of the train. As it started to move he watched his wife's face. It was hard and taut and she did not look at him.

Calverley drove slowly back to Merchet. Although he had been expecting his wife to find out, it had still come as a shock. At the same time it was a relief that the secrecy was finished. He was not at bottom a deceitful man and recent weeks had been a strain. At least he could now be honest. Curiously concern about Mary's discovery was not uppermost in his mind. What was really worrying him? He thought back to his meeting with Jennifer in the gallery during the headmaster's party. That had been reassuring because he had felt trusted and needed, just as he had when she had first confided in him at the cottage. But afterwards he realised talk of love and commitment had all been on his side. Once she had unburdened herself of her secret and asked his advice she seemed to have taken a step backwards. Nor had he seen as much of her this term. He had been busy, of course, but somehow when he had been free she had not been. In the previous term she had always been available, or so it seemed; indeed, she had usually taken the initiative. Committed to a passion he had never felt before and did not understand, he found the idea that Jennifer's ardour might be cooling more worrying than his wife's discovery. However, she was coming over this evening now Mary had gone.

He arrived back at Drydens and went up to his study. Waiting for him were Paul Sandbach and Clive Raybould, his second-in-command, still in cricket whites.

'It's late, Paul. Can't it wait until the morning?'

'I believe I ought to tell you now, sir. You decide if it can wait. We – Clive and I – think it's important.'

'Very well. Sit down, both of you. What's the problem?'

As head of house Sandbach was the main spokesman. 'One of this year's new boys – Desai, down in the bottom corridor. You can probably guess what I'm going to say.'

'Homesick?' Calverley was not optimistic.

'No, sir. That's not a problem.' He was a shrewd boy and guessed his housemaster had evaded the issue. 'Prejudice, sir – colour prejudice.'

'I was afraid you might say that.'

Sandbach broke out in anger: 'Look, sir, I've been at Merchet for five years and we've had all shapes and sizes in Drydens. A couple of Nigerians, several Arabs and Jews – even old Mitsu from Japan. Pink, black brown or yellow – it's the Drydens tradition it makes no difference.'

98

'We're hotter on it than any other house,' broke in Raybould.

Sandbach went on as though no-one had spoken. 'With respect, sir, I think we see the tolerance and equality on our side of the door better than you do over here. I even got Gold and Farouk to share rooms last year. Their parents couldn't believe it. Now this Desai chap's arrived – he's bright by all accounts – and his life is being made hell by a nasty little group in the Removes. Clive and I will do something at our end, but we thought you ought to know so that we can make it a joint effort. In any case, we know what you feel about this sort of thing.'

Calverley looked at him with respect. He had always known he was a boy of mettle – his own contemporaries had marked him out as a future head of house from his first term – but now he saw a passionate idealist.

'Who's at the centre of it?'

'Smedley. An unpleasant boy. I can say that, sir, though I know you can't as his housemaster. He's the ringleader, with lesser lights like Garside and Moulton as followers. There'll be other weak characters joining in if we don't make a stand now.'

'Has Desai complained to you?'

'No' – Sandbach smiled – 'I think he's more frightened of me than he is of them. I gave my pep talk to the new boys at the beginning of the year and I always try to create a tough impression. I remembered your advice when you first made me a monitor. "Be strong from the start and show you mean business. You can always ease up later. One thing's certain: you can't do it the other way round." The best bit of advice I've ever had. Some of the new boys need taking down a peg when they first arrive. They've usually been little kings at prep school. Some of them behave like spoilt brats.'

'That's Smedley's problem.'

'Spoilt?'

'Totally. He's got feeble parents who give him everything he wants. Most of our parents are outstandingly good, but the imbecilities of one or two of the others make you gasp. The Smedleys come high in the league table of ineptitude. That's confidential.'

'He's a real horror, sir,' said Raybould. 'If you don't clip his wings now, he'll be big trouble in the senior part of the house.'

Calverley looked at the two concerned faces before him. His personal problems faded and the priority of the house took over. He said: 'How about a glass of beer?'

Sandbach accepted the invitation. Raybould pulled a face. 'Thanks, sir, but I had one at the club and I've got to work on an essay for Mr St. Leger that's already overdue. I'd better have something soft.'

Calverley poured the drinks, then sat down behind his desk. 'Right, now we'll deal with it like this. I'll talk to the house tomorrow about bullying – because that's what it is – and I want you to have a word with all the monitors, particularly those with rooms in Desai's part of the house. Make it clear that the slightest sign of anything untoward is to be reported to me. I shall see Smedley and throw the book at him. Anything else I ought to know before I see him?'

'He's a smoker.'

'Heavy?'

Sandbach looked at Raybould doubtfully. 'Difficult to say, sir. I've smelt it on him, but he's a cunning little so-and -so and keeps out of my way. He's probably like most Remove boys. Does it for kicks and to impress his peers.'

'Useful ammunition. If he goes on like this, I'll get his parents out here and give them a dressing down, too. I should never be surprised if they let him smoke at home.'

Calverley and the two boys sat talking for another ten minutes and it was nearly eleven before he suggested they went to bed.

'One thing, sir,' said Raybould as he was leaving. 'Could you possibly have a word with Mr St. Leger, just in case my essay doesn't make it. This has all taken up time and I didn't finish nets until six-thirty.'

Calverley smiled. 'I'll see what I can do, Clive. When was it due?'

'Three days ago, sir. There just isn't enough time in the Trinity term if you're a cricketer.'

'Do your best, but don't stay up all night. Thank you both for coming to see me. We'll crack it between us. Goodnight.'

It was only as the door closed that Calverley realised Jennifer had not turned up. It was the first night she had failed to come to see him when Mary was away. For one idiotic moment he thought he was going to burst into tears.

* * * * * *

Matthew Tawney found it hard to believe Jennifer had accepted his

100

invitation. They had met down at the swimming pool. Merchet had the sort of luxurious indoor pool a school with its reputation has to have these days and certain times were sacrosanct for masters and their wives. Matthew swam regularly as part of his keep-fit regime; Jennifer only went occasionally, but this evening they had met by chance and had the enormous pool to themselves. They went their separate ways for supper, but Jennifer had agreed to go round for a drink with Matthew afterwards.

Tawney's hand shook as he poured them both a whisky. Out of the corner of an eye he saw she had tucked her legs under her on the settee.

'I ought not to be here,' she said.

'No, I'm sure you shouldn't,' replied Tawney, hoping he sounded sophisticated.

'I don't mean that. I ought to be somewhere else. I've cut a previous engagement.'

'Very flattering. Where was that?'

'Don't be naive, Matt.'

'I don't know.'

'Really?'

'Really.'

'Well, I never know who knows what, but my impression is that my affair with Mark Calverley has been common knowledge for some time.'

'I didn't know.'

'You haven't been here long. Most of the oldies know I'm tainted goods. I've never pretended otherwise.'

He handed her a glass and sat down beside her. 'Are you very unhappy?'

She laughed, then stopped when she saw the expression on his face. 'You've been listening to too many psychiatrists. I'm hard, Matt. And not worth much. The kindest thing I can do for you is drink this and then go.'

'But you don't want to.'

'I don't want to.'

'You'd like to stay?'

'For a little while. Come here and give me a kiss. I know you want to. I won't bite.'

'Of course I want to kiss you. You're a very attractive woman. But

I'm not just going to be one of a line.'

'You can't avoid that. I've got a past, Matt – and a present.'

Tentatively Tawney leaned forward and brushed her cheek with his lips. 'You say you're hard, but you're not really. I believe you've got a very soft centre.'

She took his hand and held it gently. 'You must take me on my terms, Matt. There can't be any romantic nonsense. I went through that phase a long time ago. There was a lot of pain – mostly for other people. I made a mistake in marrying James and it was my fault as much as his. He's not a bad man – quite the opposite – but it's a bad marriage and we're lumbered with it. I don't think I'm a wicked woman either. But I like men and, let's be frank, I enjoy sex. Does that shock you?'

'Did I look shocked? I didn't mean to. Don't be too honest. We none of us really know ourselves. Don't write yourself off.'

She moved towards him and kissed him, gently at first but with increasing strength. 'I want you, Matt. And it may be that I shall have you. But not tonight. You must get to know me better – to see the dark side of the moon. I'm not just the trollop the gossips imagine. There may be a soft centre, as you say. But I'm bad news for most men and I don't want to wreck your career when it's only just begun.'

She stood up. 'I'm going now. I'll still be around when you've had time to think – and when you don't stick me on a pedestal. Now give me another kiss. You kiss nicely – has anyone ever told you that?'

They kissed again, he more confidently; she moulded her body to his and pulled him close. Then she pushed him away.

'Goodnight, Matt. Wait a little while, then we'll see...' She raised an eyebrow in the provocative way he had come to recognise. He saw her to the door of his flat, letting his fingers run over her hair as she went out.

When the door had closed Tawney stood for fully a minute just looking at it. Aloud he said: 'You tried to be honest with me. I give you credit for that.'

He went back to his sitting-room and picked out a CD he kept for moments of contemplation. The haunting melody of Finzi's *Eclogue* permeated the room. He lay back in his chair; his body still tingled from Jennifer's proximity. Reason dictated caution; emotion gave him no choice.

* * * * * *

102

Jennifer went back to Theobalds. It did not worry her that she had stood Mark up; she had done it before and he had never borne malice. Besides, as an unromantic realist she recognised the pattern. She liked Mark, she had wanted him, and she appreciated his warmth; but whatever she might say in moments of passion, she did not love him and she already recognised the signs of an affair drifting to a close.

James had gone to bed and she was alone in the large Edwardian drawing-room of Theobalds. She poured herself another whisky and sat down by the bay window overlooking the park. It was a starlit night and the trees fringing the park were black against the lighter sky. She felt a dark mood settling, a mood more frequent since her grandfather's death. Self-disgust was a large part of it. Why did she drift from man to man? Why did she give herself so easily in a physical sense yet keep her innermost self apart? As she saw a new relationship about to start, she already wondered how long it would last. Why did she *need* a man so badly? Not for the first time her self-appraisal made her wonder if she was abnormal.

She did have a conscience. Outsiders would have said – did say – that she trifled with emotions and thought nothing of the consequences. But the men she went for were usually those looking for what she had to give. She had never broken up a marriage and her affairs with married men – like Mark – had only taken place because there was a flaw in the marriage. If Mary had been as interested in sex as Mark, he would never have strayed.

The boy Treece was different. She was worried about that. He was handsome, naive, though not the virgin many might have thought, and she had taken the initiative when she saw his interest. But it had been a bad mistake and she had closed it down with relief and guilt. The complications of the previous summer had been horrific. What a fool she'd been! Never again would she go near a boy.

What about Tawney? She wanted him, she knew that; all the signs were there. But she sensed danger. Somehow it was different. It was not just his obvious inexperience: that had not stopped her before. It was more subtle, more disturbing. He obviously wanted her: that was normal, expected. There was something else. She had seen it in his eyes, a remote look coming close to adoration: that was frightening. The simple man who wanted a woman, the notional notch on the cane, she could cope with; in a way even young Treece's puppy love had fallen into this category. But this was deeper, unexplored territory. Almost for the first time in her life she felt unclean, stained. For heavens sake! How had she managed to get involved with a first-class rat like Sylvester Ford, for example. He had used her, of course, and she supposed she had used him. They always avoided each other now. It was as though it had never happened.

Matthew Tawney was not her only problem. There was also her secret. She got up and went over to her writing desk. She opened the bottom drawer and felt under the three files. Yes, they were still there, the two heavy bags and the box. She was relieved she had told Mark. She knew she could trust him even if their sexual relationship ended.

Her fingers ran over the rough surface of the wooden box. Again she questioned her own behaviour.

Why hadn't she taken his advice?

* * * * * *

The same evening Sylvester Ford finally finished hanging the Manners collection in the Dorter gallery. He stood back and looked at the last picture, a David Cox watercolour of haymaking. A bit pallid, he thought, compared with the clear, no-nonsense lines and sharp colours of Francis Danby's *The Avon near Bristol* hanging next to it. It was a relief to have finished. He looked down the length of the gallery with its subtly lit cases and matching cream and brown carpet. It was a big job, but always worth the effort once it was done.

He only wished he felt better. He'd seen the doctor earlier in the week, but he hadn't seemed worried. 'Just ease up, Ford,' he'd said. 'You're not the first who's been to see me this term, you know. There's too much going on.'

Of course, he had his own suspicion of what was the matter. But that was not something he was going to discuss with Dr Armstrong and fortunately the doctor's examination was no more than perfunctory. If he had looked at him properly, he couldn't have missed the tell-tale signs. Ford was an arrogant artist of the worst type. Confident of his own intellectual superiority, it did not occur to him to linger over consideration of his most obvious weakness.

Chapter 13

The day chosen for the pageant was late in June during the last week of term. Virtually all public examinations were over; it provided a focus for the energy of those who had been taking them and, being at a loose end, might have made a nuisance of themselves; and, with a bit of luck, it was hoped the weather might be reasonable for an open air production. In the event the day dawned blue and hazy with the Downs barely visible towards the sea; by noon it was a hot summer's day and with a favourable forecast those responsible for possible wet-weather crisis arrangements relaxed.

The pageant was due to start at eight o'clock in the evening. Most parents arrived early and had alfresco supper parties in the park. Here and there brightly-coloured gazebos had been erected; others brought the full paraphernalia of a sophisticated picnic and sought out congenial sites on the edge of the woods or by the lake. The school had erected a marquee for those who wanted to dine 'inside'. It had also been suggested that as it was a unique occasion black tie would be suitable and the majority of men were wearing dinner jackets.

Andrew Korn, who was supervising the car parking with several groundsmen, winced at the sound of popping champagne corks and braying voices. Not for the first time he wondered why he taught at Merchet when all his socialist instincts reacted against his surroundings and the clientele he had to deal with.

'Bloody hypocrite, I suppose,' he muttered to himself as he waved a large Mercedes towards a group of trees near the old carp ponds. 'It's too comfortable here and I earn more than a poor sod at a comprehensive. I'm just another liberal intellectual who parades his conscience from time to time to keep it quiet.'

By the time parents started to wend their way up to the school wine had produced garrulity.

'It's like the second half at Glyndebourne,' said a red-faced, white-haired man who had dined well and looked a strong contender for a cardiac arrest, 'except that there aren't any sheep.'

'And that you managed to get here on time,' replied his wife with acerbity. 'We missed the first act of *Don Giovanni*, you will remember, because you couldn't get away from the office. I'm glad you got your priorities right when your own son is performing.'

'He's a soldier on the Somme.'

'He gets shot.'

'Most of them did.'

'Did you lock the car?'

'No-one's going to pinch anything here at Merchet.'

'Don't you believe it,' responded his wife, a sharp-looking woman in a dress with too many spots. 'Look at all these cars. What a haul for some local lad with light fingers. The school can't possibly police this lot and I don't imagine they're trying. Give me the keys. I'm going back.'

Similar conversations, some punctuated by vacuous laughter, marked the desultory drift of parents and guests across the fields.

The pageant was to be performed in Old Quad, a wide grass area between the abbey cloisters and the Abbot's House. A high terrace of wooden seating had been built around two-thirds of the quad, leaving several small exits and entrances at strategic points and one open end for the main acting area. Ten minutes before the scheduled start most of the audience of over a thousand had taken their seats, shepherded by Hugo Charteris and a team of senior boys. Now they sat expectantly, with the growing sound of conversation rising within the curve of the auditorium.

John Pilgrim, who was to be the narrator, listened to the noise and hoped his actors would judge the acoustics correctly. Rehearsals had been watched by small groups of boys, but the seats had not been completely filled before. As an experienced producer, he had warned them it would be different on the night. From his specially constructed box, sound-proofed and raised high at one end of the terracing, he could see both the grass acting area and the cast assembling off-stage. In an adjacent box to his left, surrounded by banks of switches and coloured lights, sat Roger Halstead, together with three senior boys fascinated by all things electrical, who were to control sound effects and lighting. Above the curve of the terracing towered metal pillars with the lights they were to operate.

Pilgrim checked his watch, gave the last latecomers climbing to their seats time to settle down, then spoke to St. Leger, who was backstage, on the telephone system rigged up by the signals section of the Corps.

'Ready, Tristan?'

'As ready as we ever shall be,' was the response. Tristan had long ago regretted his brainchild and now only wanted it to be over with as little pain as possible. 'I've just caught Henry VIII having a quick drag in the Infirmary garden. Let's hope that's the worst. It probably isn't. Millie's on the warpath. She's been unspeakably rude to the head of school. She just doesn't understand this place. All right, John. Ready.'

'Right, let's get the show on the road.'

He pressed a button to his right that communicated with the actors and gave a thumbs up sign to Halstead in the box next door.

Three boys dressed as heralds in yellow tabards marched to the edge of the arena, raised silver trumpets and signalled the opening of the performance with a medieval fanfare. When they had finished, bowed with artistic flourish and retired, the audience fell silent.

Pilgrim looked down at his script and made a minute adjustment to the microphone in front of him.

'The story of Merchet begins,' he said, 'in the reign of King Edward IV.' His confident, well-modulated voice dominated the quadrangle, shrewdly placed loudspeakers producing a sound that enveloped the audience without reverberating from the sur rounding buildings. 'The sun of York who turned the winter of discontent into glorious summer was an able man with many of the attributes of a successful medieval king. From an early age he showed his skill as a general, as well as his ruthlessness; yet he was more than a brutal survivor in the period we designate the Wars of the Roses. He was also a capable ruler who did much to restore the reputation of a tarnished monarchy; and in this age which saw strange mixtures of cruelty and culture he captured something of the spirit of a Renaissance prince, revelling in magnificent clothes of the latest fashion, collecting a fine library and becoming a patron of the printer Willam Caxton.

'While contemporaries agree about Edward's capacity as a king, they also agree about his passion for women. Philippe de Commynes, viewing him from the rival court across the Channel, said that "Edward thought upon nothing but women" and although this may be seen as characteristic Gallic optimism, there can be little doubt that Edward pursued the ladies. At the point where our story begins his mistress was one Jane Shore, a woman whose attraction for men was self-evident from the number who wanted her. The other consuming passion of Edward's life – as with all medieval kings – was hunting. He and his courtiers spent hours in the chase and the chroniclers marvel at the number of horses he could exhaust in a day. It is to these twin passions, women and hunting, that Merchet owes its foundation.'

Pilgrim paused and pressed the cue button to his right. Off stage came the sound of hunting horns, the barking of dogs and excited shouts. Into the arena cantered a richly-attired Edward IV on a sorrel horse; behind him on a white pony came a pretty girl, recognisable as Jane Osgood, and various hunters, some armed with bows and arrows, others restraining dogs.

Pilgrim resumed: 'One late autumn day Edward and his mistress were hunting in the forest near Merchet Abbey, the Benedictine house standing here at Merchet since Saint Dunstan founded it as a daughter house of his own great abbey at Glastonbury. At the end of a strenuous day it started to rain and the king and his party decided to seek shelter at the abbey. The abbot and his monks came out to welcome them.'

From one of the small side entrances in the terracing a group of cowled monks moved to greet the king. Special effects contrived a rumble of thunder.

'Foul weather, Father Abbot,' said Edward IV. 'I fear we must impose upon you...'

Pilgrim switched off the microphone and turned a page of his script as the action and dialogue opened on stage. He looked to his right and saw another party of courtiers, out of sight of the audience, ready to enter with the charter. He could see Tristan talking to the actors, and one of the matrons, already dressed as a suffragette for her own part later, moving among the courtiers making final adjustments to dress.

So far, so good.

* * * * * *

Seated in a central position surrounded by governors and their wives, Bruce Irving began to relax. As he had predicted, the pageant had created a rare crop of problems, but with a bit of luck most of them were now over. He had fielded complaints from the bursar about the cost, from housemasters irritated by the way Pilgrim was pressurising the boys, keeping them rehearsing until the small hours, and there had even been complaints from the village about late-night noise and lights disturbing sleeping babies. In most cases he had supported Pilgrim; it was, after all, a unique occasion and Merchet would be on display in an unprecedented way. Looking round at the audience he knew he had been right. Quite apart from parents and influential old boys it contained a cabinet minister, an ambassador, and three heads of Oxford and Cambridge colleges; moreover, the press was there in force and he had already given two interviews to national dailies. As the opening scene unfolded he was relieved to see his support had been justified.

'Pretty girl, that,' said Lord Padstowe, the Chairman of the Governors, indicating Jane Shore.

'Young Jane Osgood,' said Irving. 'She teaches chemistry.'

'I like the look of Edward IV,' whispered Lady Padstowe, sitting on Irving's left, who had heard her husband's remark. 'I've always fancied a toy boy.'

Irving stirred uneasily. He had heard rumours of Padstowe disharmony and did not want to be involved; his fastidious nature, which frequently distanced him from the masters' room, now reacted against possible embarrassment. Blandly he whispered: 'Young Hugh Pomeroy. I must say he's got a good seat on a horse. I didn't even know he could ride. His father's a general, of course.'

Irving viewed the scene with satisfaction. This was, after all, *his* school. It was a great school, it was showing off and it had something to be proud of. At the same time his meticulous administrative mind noticed where people were sitting.

The most distinguished guests – the cabinet minister, the ambassador, the heads of colleges, together with a Prussian aristocrat with an inordinately lengthy title and a tincture of Queen Victoria's blood – sat just in front of him. The masters were scattered around the arena. In the front, to the right of the stage, was Sylvester Ford. The high dome of his head and his round, bearded face were unmistakable even at a distance; beside him was a girl friend with artistic aspirations who had turned up in a patchwork skirt and sandals to defy the evening's dress code. Nearby sat one or two younger masters, members of the Ford clique, with their wives. Irving could guess the type of cynical comments they would be making. Irving disapproved of Ford, but recognised the strength of his department.

Most housemasters had hosted dinner parties in their houses. The Calverleys had invited the Sandbachs again, together with the parents of other monitors; the Wentworths had also asked parents and had included Alastair Munro in their party; Jennifer had already gone backstage, but the two groups were close together in the front row.

As a retiring housemaster, Moncrieff had central seats not far from the headmaster. His guests were predictable: two Scottish peers and their wives, a City banker, and a millionaire socialist whose wife had insisted their sons should be entered for Ryders. Moncrieff had also invited Spooner as the two were retiring together. Neither fitted the image Irving wanted to create for a modern Merchet; he would be glad to see both of them go.

Until the dress rehearsal Stephen Higham, who always helped with dramatic productions, had been the prompter. However, the rehearsal had produced a number of minor hiccups and Pilgrim, a perfectionist, had decided Higham's experience would be more valuable behind the scenes to deal with unexpected crises on the night. To take his place as prompter Pilgrim had approached Tawney, who had readily agreed to take over at the eleventh hour. He was sitting, Irving noticed, in the front row at the very end of the terracing.

* * * * * *

Tawney agreed to act as prompter because he had not been asked to do anything else and was feeling left out. The late invitation had mollified him and he set about the task with his usual conscientiousness. He sat with the script on his knee following every word.

Nevertheless, his mind was not fully in gear and his concentration wavered as King Edward, lovingly supported by Jane Shore, presented the foundation charter. He found his own feelings overriding those artificially created before him on stage. His emotions had been in turmoil for weeks now and simply to see the representation of a passionate relationship brought his own problems

110

into focus. Briefly he was able to stand back and look at himself in a detached way.

He loved Jennifer, he knew that, and he loved her in a way that frightened him. As an intellectual he always tried to rationalise his feelings, but he was aware of a dark tide he could not begin to understand. He thought back to that May evening when she had telephoned him unexpectedly.

'I've been hoping to hear from you. I normally expect the man to do the chasing.' He could hear the humour in her voice.

'I wanted to ring you.'

'Why didn't you?'

'Nervousness, I expect. And something else.'

'What?'

'Difficult to explain. A mixture of jealousy and dislike of myself.'

'You're too complicated, Matt. I'm very simple.'

'Come round for a drink tonight. Simple enough for you?' In a couple of seconds he had destroyed the rational caution he had cultivated since her first open sexual invitation.

'All right.'

'After supper, say eight-thirty?'

'I'll be there at nine.'

And she had been. They had had a drink and he had been seduced swiftly and efficiently. His senses still reeled from the experience. The fulfilment of physical desire opened a well of emotion his instincts wanted to disown. He wanted her and his jealousy of Calverley drove him to loathe a man he had previously admired. Did she still see him? She said it had all finished, but could he believe her? Love and hate were close cousins. He loved her, but why did he hate her too? Each day he lurched between hope and despair: hope that they would be together, if only for a short time; despair at the thought of those who had had her in the past and the suspicion he would not be able to keep her. And just beneath the surface he sensed the powerful streak of puritanism bred into him, the puritanism that led to self-disgust.

He felt the anger rising within him, an anger he had not felt before. The words of the script blurred before him as his eyes filled with tears.

On stage the pageant was advancing: Thomas Howard, Earl of Surrey, won the battle of Flodden. Large numbers of pikemen milled about before being surrounded and summarily massacred. Once

111

more the abbot and his monks paraded, promising prayers and masses in perpetuity to a blood-stained benefactor.

Pilgrim concluded the scene: 'Thus Merchet acquired the Howard Acre. For the last hundred and fifty years it has been the site of the lst XI cricket pitch, that hallowed patch of ground which has for generations of Merchets provided a goal for ambition, a field for personal glory and tragedy.'

Tawney relaxed during the fighting. No-one had any lines to forget, so a prompter was superfluous. The next scene was different. The Reformation, with the dissolution of the abbey and execution of Abbot Greenfield, meant substantial on-stage dialogue.

He looked round the audience, seeking out the men Jennifer had favoured. In a moment of abandonment she had told him all of them. Then he hunched over the script, wishing he could deaden the pain.

Chapter 14

It was going well. In his eyrie on the terracing Pilgrim smiled the self-confident smile that irritated so many of his colleagues. He quietly turned a page of the script. Backstage even St. Leger, who had been sunk in gloom after the final rehearsal, sensed the growing success of the evening. The production had pace, the boys – as they usually did – were doing their stuff with style and panache now they knew it was the real thing, while the audience, delighted to see its progeny perform and conscious of a sense of occasion, responded with spontaneous applause. St. Leger thought it was all too good to be true. He looked at his watch, then anxiously up at the sky to see how near to dusk it was. As the only begetter of the whole enterprise he knew how important it was for the later scenes to be done in darkness, particularly the battle of the Somme. He need not have worried. The timing so far was impeccable.

So the years passed. The abbey was dissolved by Henry VIII, the monks were driven out, and Abbot Greenfield, defiant to the last, went nobly to execution. The school survived and after several years of touch and go under Edward VI and Mary Tudor achieved stability under Elizabeth I. In spite of Jasper Hillyard's earlier qualms, a boy performed creditably on the lute to mark a visit from the Virgin Queen, while the ethereal sounds of Byrd's *Mass for five voices* echoing round the quad signified the continuing catholic tradition and prepared the way for the Gunpowder Plot, in which an Old Merchet had so unwisely got involved.

The American Gatewood Foster's appearance in the Virginia scene evoked loud cheers. His lanky physique and obvious good nature had endeared him to all levels of the school in the short time he had been there. His determination to try everything had included games he had never played before like rugger and cricket, and he had even signed on in the Corps so that he could go out on Field Day. Now he performed with his usual seriousness before being carried off by hordes of small befeathered Indians to a gory scalping off-stage.

Some scenes were short – an obscure Caroline poet wearing ill-fitting hose read a poem and a young man who claimed to have been a lover of Lady Castlemaine carried out a swift and demure seduction – and some were long. The Civil War skirmish on the Downs took at least a quarter of an hour by the time troops and horses had been assembled for carefully choreographed fighting and subsequent drunken revelry, the latter notably realistic.

The eighteenth century included a bibulous cleric who had achieved episcopal status as a result of insider dealing during the South Sea Bubble and what might be described as an under-the-cassock relationship with Sir Robert Walpole, who wanted to strengthen his control of the bench of bishops in the House of Lords. As a decayed borough Merchet Magna had for years returned two members of Parliament, both usually Old Merchets, until the Great Reform Act and this gave the opportunity to portray the hustings as well as to celebrate a significant reform. Old Merchets had fought on the Heights of Abraham with Wolfe and sailed the seas with Captain Cook, while one aristocratic member of Lord Lansdowne's so-called 'Bowood Circle', a group of radically inclined political philosophers, got himself guillotined in Paris while taking too close a look at the practical application of some of his ideas.

The nineteenth century paid tribute to the flagellant headmaster who had done so much to increase the reputation of the school with the upper classes, as well as the holder of that office sacked by the governors for taking an unhealthy interest in the boys' bathing arrangements. Discipline, as with so many schools of the time, was clearly a problem. A group of boys, including a future archbishop, were expelled for trying to blow up one of the side-chapels after reading Shelley's *The Necessity of Atheism* ; a boy destined to be the first Merchet Prime Minister was publicly flogged for leading a rebellion against the headmaster; and a brawl between the scholars of Merchet and the local boys of Merchet Farthing was only ended when a posse of the newly-formed police force ejected the 'gentlemen' from The Duke of Cambridge, which they had captured as a bridgehead in the village.

Darkness was falling by the time they reached the Boer War and the first Merchet Victoria Cross. Halstead and his minions in the box next to Pilgrim, hitherto concentrating on sound effects, now extended their operations to the technicalities of floodlighting and spots. The visit to Merchet by Queen Victoria near the end of her life brought the century to a close with the stage bathed in purple.

* * * * * *

Moncrieff's disapproval of the pageant did not stop him appreciating its success or enjoying the compliments of his guests. He also took pleasure in pointing out boys coming from county families, particularly those in Ryders.

He growled in an undertone to Spooner: 'Better than I thought. Pilgrim usually pulls it off. But it's not worth the trouble it's caused. Anyway, acting just gives the show-offs a chance to ponce about. Not my idea of education, but I expect I'm old-fashioned. Too much damned touchy-feely self-expression these days. I'd like to go back to a few early morning cold baths and a bit more self-control.'

As a man who always knew exactly what was going on in the school, Moncrieff's eyes were as much on the audience as the performance. He kept up a grumbling commentary *sotto voce* : 'I see Tichbourne's not in a dinner jacket. Typical. The only housemaster to let the side down. Even Ford's properly dressed – though there's a frightful woman with him who looks like a gypsy. Ah, Calverley's had enough.'

'What do you mean?'

'He's just gone out. Probably to check on his house. Easy for a boy to slip back and get up to something nefarious while all this is going on. Good smoking opportunity – or worse. That's the problem with evenings like this when all the normal discipline is upset. I've told my head of house to do an inspection.'

Spooner peered round him The acting area was bathed in flood-light, but the audience was in darkness. 'You've got good eyesight, Charles. Do you check up on all of us?'

Moncrieff chuckled. 'Of course. Come back for a dram and a gossip when this pantomime's over. My guests aren't staying, so we'll be on our own. Merchet won't be the same when we've gone.'

* * * * * *

Pilgrim continued his narration: 'The death of the old queen and the turn of the century marked the end of an era. For Britain it had been an age of empire, of wealth in high places and poverty in low, of style and splendour, of squalor and exploitation. But democracy had advanced, albeit slowly, and Parliament stood as a symbol of freedom in a world still dominated by regimes in which democracy played little or no part.

'Democracy, however, was not complete. The first working-class MPs had only recently been elected and as yet women had no direct say in the running of the country. The opening of the new century saw the start of a campaign for the female vote and Merchet, for once in the van of progress, played its small part in support of the movement for women's suffrage.

'The women who mounted this campaign drew attention to their cause by militant action in public places. Cabinet ministers were hounded, government buildings attacked, and in 1913 Emily Davison ensured her place in history by throwing herself in front of the king's horse in the Derby and being killed. The Merchet connection came as a result of a demonstration in front of Buckingham Palace in the same year.'

The acting area, dark after the last scene, was flooded with light. Diagonally across one corner stood the railings outside the palace. From the opposite corner entered a gaggle of women in Edwardian costume carrying banners and shouting. At the front, gaudily prominent and raucous, were Pamela Baskerville and Melanie St. Leger; just behind, clutching a banner demanding 'Votes for Women' were Jennifer Wentworth and a house matron; behind them marched a miscellany of wives and matrons, with the delectable Monique Ducatillon and the Herculean Miss Broad bringing up the rear.

After much shouting and waving of parasols, a posse of police appeared and began to make arrests. Struggling violently the majority of the women, together with their banner, were removed. Two remained, Pamela Baskerville and Jennifer Wentworth, who had chained themselves to the railings. Both wore cream-coloured dresses emphasizing their femininity and vulnerability.

Pilgrim continued the story and explained how one Robert Staniforth Q.C., a defender of liberal causes, had taken up the cases of the women who were charged and obtained an unexpected acquittal. The case had enhanced his reputation and suggested, said Pilgrim, that even in those days Merchet had nurtured diversity of view and independence of mind. He omitted to mention that a case which had initially pushed forward Staniforth's career had ultimately wrecked it when it was discovered he was enjoying a lubricious affair with one of the defendants, an affair only ended by a random shell at Ypres.

The moment Pilgrim stopped speaking all floodlights and stage lights were extinguished; the whole acting area plunged into darkness and the women attached to the railings vanished. Off stage an enormous explosion announced the arrival of the Great War.

* * * * * *

Backstage the advent of the war brought more confusion than at any other time in the evening. For the first time every light was out and there was total darkness.

Rathbone was bringing up troops and equipment from the changing rooms and make-up areas in the buildings behind the abbey. The actors were in two columns and heavily laden with tin hats, packs, rifles and other military impedimenta. Just as they rounded the buttresses at the end of the nave and came within range of the blacked out arena they met the suffragettes hastening off stage in the opposite direction. In spite of strict injunctions against noise of any kind, there was a restrained mélange of oaths and giggling as the two columns met. Fortunately it was at this point that a not very musical choir stationed in the cloisters started to sing 'Tipperary', at the same time stamping their boots up and down on the flagstones.

Stephen Higham, posted for just such an emergency, did his best to unravel the confusion, holding a torch in one hand and a mobile phone in the other. Rathbone materialised beyond the abbey when he realised his troops had halted. For no apparent reason, since he did not appear on stage, he too was wearing a tin hat. He seized one of Higham's windmilling arms and hissed: 'What the hell's going on?'

'Slight cock-up.'

'What's stopping them?'

'Suffragettes. They were meant to be further over.'

'Get them out of the way. My troops must have priority.' There was a note of hysteria in his voice.

Behind them another explosion took place. 'Tipperary' increased in volume and the marching on the spot stepped up a gear.

Rathbone went past Higham in the dark. To no-one in particular he said: 'My men must get on stage. What's happening now? Get these bloody women out of the way.'

'Who are you telling to get out of the way?' Pamela Baskerville's voice was unmistakable. 'Get your boys out of our way. They're in the wrong place. How dare you blame us? Who do you think you are, you silly little man?'

Higham caught Rathbone up. 'Please, ladies, move to your right. *Please*.' He waved his torch ineffectually and, aware of a figure in front of him, illuminated Miss Broad.

'We were told to come this way.'

Beyond the confusion a boy's voice, anonymous in the dark, said: 'Stephanie's pouffing it up as usual.'

'If you don't get out of the way...'

Rathbone's threat never materialised. Just as Higham's torch momentarily revealed his face suffused with fury and his tin hat absurdly tilted over one eye, the mobile phone crackled into life. It was Halstead. 'Third explosion coming up. Stand by.'

Another explosion rent the air.

The troops were moving again now. The worst was over. Higham shone his torch at the retreating women as they rounded the abbey.

Coming in the opposite direction was the dinner-jacketed Mark Calverley.

* * * * * *

The third explosion was the cue for continued narration from Pilgrim. 'Tipperary' and the marching feet faded.

'The First World War was one of the great watersheds of history. When the lights went out over Europe, a world of birth and privilege received a blow from which it never recovered. And everywhere the young men of birth and privilege, like those at Merchet, contributed to their own demise. Read the Merchet war memorial in the cloisters and you will see the names of some of the most distinguished families in Britain, families whose remote country house existence might linger on for a few years but in reality was finished. But they went with bravery and style. Merchet men won five VCs, their deeds scattered from the Somme to Gallipoli, one even being awarded to that new arm of battle, The Royal Flying Corps. As examples of the bravery of a generation at Merchet and other more humble homes throughout the kingdom, we will follow the two young men who gave

118

their lives and achieved the ultimate accolade during the battle of the Somme.

'It is night on the Somme in July, 1916. Along the battered trenches the guns have fallen silent for a brief respite. A raiding party is about to go out into no-man's land...'

To one side a small group of soldiers were spotlighted putting on their equipment and checking their weapons. A young officer inspected their darkened faces and gave a final pep talk. Then they climbed silently out of their trench through sandbags and barbed wire.

And so the pageant marked the Great War. For ten minutes tense silence alternated with seemingly uncontrolled noise and violence, not only in the main acting area but right across the parkland beyond the abbey. Explosions loud and small formed a counter-point to the rattle of small-arms fire; coloured flares rose and fell in the distance; soldiers ran or crawled, cried out in triumph or pain. It was a pyrotechnical display of some indulgence. Rathbone and the Corps were enjoying themselves.

It came to an end at last. A model Bristol Fighter swooped low over the battlefield, glinting in the spotlight briefly before vanishing into the darkness of the night. And that was that.

Pilgrim turned on his microphone. 'And so heroism had its day. All over the country those left at home mourned the dead, those whom poets like Wilfred Owen believed to have died in a pointless cause. He did not, of course devalue the courage of those who died, or those who came home with shattered bodies and minds never to be the same again.'

A spotlight picked out a solitary white cross in a field of poppies. Off-stage a trumpeter sounded the Last Post, followed more distantly by a piper playing the lament, 'The Flowers of the Forest'.

The audience, cynical and worldly though much of it was, was moved. There was silence as the light on the cross faded and the final notes of the piper died away.

For a full fifteen seconds there was total darkness to accommodate the emotional transition from the horrors of war to the next scene, a light-hearted farrago about the 1920s. Pilgrim turned a page of the script. In the box next door Halstead checked his stop-watch, looked across at Pilgrim for approval, then pulled a switch.

The whole arena was bathed in light. All round the terracing eyes blinked in the unexpected brightness, not immediately taking in what they saw.

Eventually it dawned on those watching that something was wrong. The stage should have been empty. But it was not. On the extreme right hand side, slumped against the railing at the edge of the acting area which had been used to represent the palace railings in the suffragette scene, was a crumpled form in a cream Edwardian dress. The head had fallen sideways with its hair hanging downwards over the face; one arm was outstretched and a leg appeared twisted, with a shoe protruding unnaturally: the whole posture was grotesque. The figure was completely still.

Pilgrim, who had turned on his microphone, found it hard to take in what he saw. Briefly, irrationally, he was aware of a flash of anger as he assumed St. Leger had changed something without telling him. He looked into the box next door and saw Halstead's startled face staring at him. He just had the presence of mind to turn off the microphone before he blurted out: 'Jennifer? What in heaven's name...?'

Then the momentary anger was overtaken by the realisation that something terrible had happened.

Chapter 15

Pilgrim was good in a crisis. As master of the microphone he saw he was the only one who could take immediate control. He did so. He called for a doctor and asked the audience to remain seated until advised to do otherwise. On the backstage telephone he told St. Leger what had happened and asked him to take charge of the actors.

If the problem had occurred in a theatre, the obvious thing would have been to pull the curtain. Here there was no such solution. The next few minutes were played out in full public view with the hushed audience taking in every move.

Strangely, considering he was a man of some bulk and not noted for athleticism, the first person to react was Sylvester Ford. Even before Pilgrim had finished speaking over the public address system he had sprung from his seat and run to the crumpled figure on stage. With the help of one of the younger masters who was just behind him he cradled the top half of Jennifer Wentworth and eased her gently to the ground. He was feeling for her pulse when James Wentworth arrived and knelt beside his wife. Wentworth was accompanied by one of his parental guests, a distinguished surgeon called Cuthbertson. The latter bent low over Jennifer and announced in a matter of seconds what many had known from the moment they saw the twisted body. Jennifer Wentworth was dead.

Wentworth was holding his wife's hand. 'How?' he asked.

'Difficult to say.' Cuthbertson put a compassionate hand on Wentworth's arm. 'Obviously some sort of heart attack is a possibility.'

Wentworth, pale-faced, was suddenly aware he was kneeling in front of an audience. He stood up and looked helplessly round the massed faces. He spoke quietly, but such was the silence that his voice carried to the back row of the terracing. 'She's dead,' he said. 'She's dead.'

Within seconds the small tableau, seemingly frozen by shock, was joined by other figures. Pilgrim came down from his eyrie, St. Leger appeared from backstage, Irving left his party in the audience and Alastair Munro did likewise. Another doctor had materialised and he and Cuthbertson, incongruous in dinner jackets, put Jennifer's body on one of the stretchers used during the Somme scene and carried it to the nearby Abbot's House. Meanwhile Irving, after a swift consultation with Pilgrim and St. Leger, turned to address the audience.

This was Irving at his best. He was brief and to the point and, whatever he felt inside, master of the situation. Speaking clearly and slowly he confirmed the death, said everyone would share his shock, and asked all guests to leave quickly and quietly. Boys should go back to their houses immediately. He then collected all ten housemasters, asked them to see the boys to bed and to be ready for an emergency meeting as soon as he had clarified the situation. He would telephone.

The auditorium emptied slowly, but it was more or less clear in under ten minutes. A handful of randomly selected boys, whispering to each other, dealt with the lighting or shifted props and bits of scenery. A scattering of masters and wives lingered in a limbo of inactivity, speculating in low voices. In the distance car engines revved down in the park as their owners began to drive away into the night.

Irving, St. Leger and Pilgrim stood together on stage. 'Poor Jennifer,' said Irving.

'Poor James.'

'It was going so well,' said Pilgrim, still trying to change mental gear and not thinking what he was saying. 'Sorry.'

'They'd been married sometime,' said St. Leger. 'Whatever the problems they must have shared something.' He searched their faces to see if he had spoken out of turn.

'She was so young and seemed so fit.'

'And such fun and so lively. Things were never dull when she was around.'

'*Memento mori.*'

'Muriel Spark.'

'Have you read it?'

'Yes. One of her best.'

'If it doesn't sound patronising, Headmaster, I thought you handled that very well,' said St. Leger.

'Thanks. One of the more difficult ones. We clearly had to get rid of them all.'

The conversation was desultory and disconnected. They were still talking when Cuthbertson and the other doctor came back.

Cuthbertson spoke with quiet authority: 'It wasn't a heart attack, Headmaster. Mrs Wentworth was shot.'

* * * * * *

Looking back at it afterwards, those who stood in that small group on the stage realised that Cuthbertson's simple statement came as much of a shock as the fact of Jennifer's death itself. As an experienced public school headmaster, Irving had inevitably dealt with death before. He recalled having to tell a boy his mother had been killed in a car crash; coping with the problem of a master who died of a heart attack refereeing a rugger match; and, the most difficult, within a month of taking over his first headmastership, having to tell parents their son had hanged himself in a lavatory. They had all been horrific in their way, but however deep the emotions, they had all been private tragedies. This one had been played out, literally, on the public stage in the full glare of the quincentenary publicity.

Besides, this was different. Jennifer had been shot. Obviously it could have been an accident. He thought of the rounds fired so liberally by the Corps during the last scene and wondered whether by some dreadful chance a live round had conceivably been mixed with the blanks. But Irving knew better than that. Whatever explanation he might dream up, he really had no doubt. This was murder.

He looked round the deserted seats, listened to the departing cars and, turning to the darkness beyond the main stage, saw the scaffolding supporting the huge firework coat-of-arms intended to be the grand finale of the evening. The whole year's celebrations were turning to ashes. Instead of a climax to years of headmastering he saw nothing but the wreckage of a career.

Then he saw the indulgence of such self-pity and was horrified to find he had almost forgotten the problem that had caused it.

'I'll telephone the police,' he said.

* * * * * *

After the dramatic events of the evening the arrival of the police was something of an anti-climax. They came in the form of two young uniformed constables from Merchet Magna, one a woman. Both were young and inexperienced and neither had dealt with violent death before.

They were taken into the Abbot's House by Pilgrim. Jennifer's body still lay on the army stretcher in the hall, covered by a rug. Cuthbertson and the other doctor had been joined by the school doctor. Cuthbertson raised the rug for the constables and pointed to the blood which had now seeped through the canvas stretcher onto the floor.

'She's been shot in the back,' said Cuthbertson. 'Very little bleeding to start with. We didn't notice the blood until we got her in here.'

The two constables, pale, earnest, and anxious to do the right thing when faced with the first real problem of their careers, took refuge in police jargon.

'Suspicious death,' said the girl.

'Suspicious death,' agreed her colleague. 'I'll tell the station.'

Chapter 16

The two young officers, their nervousness not initially diminished by finding themselves entirely surrounded by men in dinner jackets, proved capable and energetic. They took statements from Cuthbertson and the doctors, inspected the railing where Jennifer had been found, and asked Pilgrim, St. Leger, Ford and Wentworth to give preliminary accounts of events as they saw them. They made sure no-one went near the acting area again before CID arrived and drew up lists of names of those who might be expected to know something because they were near the scene of the action.

They were already cross-checking certain aspects of what had happened.

'And you say you managed to get to her first?' said the young male constable, eyeing Ford's girth doubtfully.

'Yes. I suppose I realised something was wrong before most people. And I was one of the nearest. I was in the front row.'

'And you started to move her before anyone else arrived?'

'One of the new young masters helped me. Yes, we moved her immediately. She was so crumpled and hanging so awkwardly we had to move her. Anyone else would have done the same. She looked grotesque. I suspected she was dead simply because of the position she was in.' Ford ran a hand down one side of his face to his greying beard, then back over the dome of his head. 'We had no alternative.'

'You put your arm round her?'

'Yes.'

'So that's probably when you got that blood on your sleeve.' The constable pointed at the smears of blood on Ford's dinner jacket and white shirt cuff.

Ford looked down at his arm like a prospector examining an interesting sample for the first time. 'My sleeve? Ah, yes – I expect so. I imagine several of us have got bloodstains. That's the first time I've noticed it.'

While this was going on Irving collected together St. Leger, Pilgrim and all the housemasters except Wentworth. They met in Irving's study, a high-ceilinged room with a painting of the abbey hanging over the fireplace.

With the clock approaching midnight there was no time for the discursive discussion characteristic of housemasters' meetings. Decisions were taken swiftly. They decided there should be a meeting of all masters at 8.45 am the next morning, followed by a short service in the abbey for the whole school at 9.15. Thereafter it was agreed there was little alternative but to continue with normal routine as though nothing had happened. Internal end of term examinations would continue; those who had finished A Levels or GCSEs would be allowed to carry on with whatever arrangements they had made. All this, of course, would depend on police approval.

'What about leavers' parties?' asked a housemaster called Scott. 'I've got mine tomorrow evening – and there are dinners or parties every night this week. We put everything off until after the pageant, so they've piled up.'

The others looked at him gratefully. It sounded insensitive, but he was only putting into words a question they all wanted answered.

'We must stick to normality,' reiterated Irving firmly. 'The Trinity term falls apart anyway. If we let this business – this sad business – upset everything, we shall have no idea where anyone is or what anyone is doing. Besides, it's obviously best to keep everyone occupied.'

'And the Harrow match?'

'It goes ahead. It's all planned for and we've no idea how this is all going to work out. We may find by tomorrow the whole thing's a ghastly accident. And some of the parents who came down for the pageant are staying on for the cricket as well. The police must get on with their job and we'll get on with ours.'

'Stiff upper lips all round,' said Tichbourne sardonically.

'We shall hit the headlines tomorrow, Headmaster,' said St. Leger. 'Who's going to deal with the press?'

'I'll look after them myself. And I shall record every word I say. If it's possible to twist something they will. The anti-public school spin is inevitable, but we can try to limit the damage. Who knows what angle they'll go for? They'll dig up some dirt if they can, we all know that. We've got to make sure they don't talk to the boys. We've no more to hide than any other institution, but we're always vulnerable and this gives them an entry point. Remind me to say that to the masters in the morning. One or two of them can be just as indiscreet as the boys.'

Moncrieff cleared his throat. The desk light caught his spectacles, masking the eyes behind them. 'We've nothing to be ashamed of, Headmaster. It should soon be clear who killed Mrs Wentworth. Most murderers are known to their victims. That's an accepted fact.'

The housemasters, sitting in a rough circle round Irving's desk, looked at their feet.

'Yes, Charles,' said Calverley, who spoke for the first time during the meeting. In the artificial light his face looked more lined than usual. 'There are going to be some awkward questions for a lot of people.'

Calverley resented Moncrieff's detached, complacent tone. His own emotions were in turmoil. He had been into the Abbot's House to see Jennifer's body and he realised he had probably seen her disturbing beauty for the last time. If only she had known the depth of feelings she stirred up in men. As yet he had not been able to weep.

* * * * * *

At about the same time Irving's meeting was breaking up, the first members of the CID were arriving, together with a forensic team. They had been hastily assembled and were for the time being headed by one Sergeant Taylor, a red-haired man with battered features who tended to take a pessimistic view of new cases.

When the constables had given him a quick summary of events, he inspected the body and then went on to look at the acting arena. The floodlights were still on; the whole area was strangely silent.

'Everything's been moved and mucked about,' complained Taylor to one of the white-overalled forensic men. 'A pity no-one realised she'd been shot before she was shifted. Now, exactly where was the body?'

'Up here,' said Pilgrim, who was guiding him. 'The railing hasn't been moved.'

'And she was here right through the Somme scene?'

'She must have been. No-one seems to have seen Jennifer after the suffragette scene, so we're all assuming she didn't get off the stage. But you'll have to check that. Yes – she was against this railing. We piled these sandbags on one side and it became part of the German front line, but there was no action just here. The whole scene was played out in darkness and it was the British side of no-man's land over there that got any light going. This bit was completely dark. I certainly didn't see Mrs Wentworth until the lights went up at the end. Halstead said the same.'

'And no-one else saw her?'

'I've only spoken to one or two people. Halstead was probably in the best position because he was controlling the lights. Members of the audience I've spoken to said they saw nothing until the floodlights came on at the end. Then it's surprising how many thought she was dead. It was the position of the body.'

'And the actors?'

'I haven't spoken to any of them. We got the boys back to their houses just as soon as we could when we realised we had a tragedy on our hands. You'll have to ask them. I can give you a list of those on stage for the Somme scene.'

'And you didn't hear a shot?'

Pilgrim laughed. 'The whole scene was punctuated with shots and explosions, Sergeant. Flares went up in the park, we had an artillery bombardment on tape, Rathbone was throwing thunderflashes around like a child with toys, and most of the boys fired their rifles. It was meant to be military mayhem – and it was. No-one would have noticed an individual shot. Was it just one shot?'

'We'll have to wait and see. There won't be a post-mortem report until tomorrow.'

'It wouldn't matter how many shots there were. It could have happened at any point in the scene and none of us would have been aware of it. Whoever killed Mrs Wentworth chose the time well.'

'No chance of an accident?'

'Hardly. The boys were firing blanks. We never have live ammunition at the school. They only fire live on the ranges. But you should speak to Rathbone about all that. He commands the Corps and this was very much his scene.'

'Thank you, Mr Pilgrim. That's a start, anyway. It looks as though there may be more to this than I thought. Most shootings are clear-cut. Detective Chief Inspector Barnaby's coming in the morning, but

I must have a few facts clear before then. Just one thing. If I've got the picture right, anyone could have got to that side of the stage during the Somme scene. They could have got there from backstage – or from the audience.'

'I suppose so.'

Pilgrim agreed reluctantly. The truth was that he had not thought about it. So far all he could register was that a successful dramatic production had been ruined.

Around them blue and white police tapes were already in place.

* * * * * *

To say that Merchet was shocked by the violent death of one of its housemaster's wives would, of course, be an understatement. However, an institution with five hundred years of history has an integral sense of balance not easily disturbed. Even a murder – for realists saw there was no other explanation – may to some extent be taken in its stride.

The next morning Alastair Munro led prayers for Jennifer in a short service in the abbey; the headmaster spoke briefly, expressing the sadness of the community but also stressing the need for normality; by ten o'clock the school was back to its usual routine. This did not, of course, stop strenuous speculation at both boy and master level, but the ship of state was steady. Only one or two foolish masters trying to curry favour with boys allowed any sort of gossip to develop over the master-boy divide.

The house most obviously affected was Theobalds. Irving had visited Wentworth the night before to express his sympathy and at the same time deal with practical issues. He suggested that Jim Clode, who had once been a house tutor in Theobalds, should move in temporarily to help with the day to day running of the house while Wentworth coped with his personal tragedy. Wentworth, still struggling with shock, was ready to agree to anything.

'But I must have something to occupy my mind,' he said. 'I can't just sit and do nothing.' Random thoughts pursued each other in his head. His worried eyes looked straight at Irving. 'I can't hand over next year's Lower Sixth options. I'm half way through. No-one else can be responsible for them. The boys have been discussing them with me for the past year.'

'None of us is indispensable, James,' said Irving gently.

'Who did it? Who could possibly *want* to do it?'

Irving's own mind had been so occupied dealing with governors, police, parents, housemasters and press that he had not yet confronted this issue.

'God knows,' he said. 'You realise I don't know what to say. I'm so sorry, James. Are you going to be all right?' He extended a hand and almost put it on Wentworth's arm.

'I'm on automatic pilot. I'm sure you don't need me to tell you our marriage was not perfect. From my point of view the problem was that Jennifer had too many friends, not enemies. She was gregarious by nature and I'm not. Why should anyone kill her?'

'Impossible question for me.' The brief moment of warmth for Wentworth had gone. Irving the administrator was already pondering the problems to be faced if one of his masters turned out to be a murderer.

* * * * * *

The arrival of Detective Chief Inspector John Barnaby immediately after break came as a relief to Irving. His conversations with Sergeant Taylor and the forensic men had not been reassuring. He was conscious of their suspicion of, almost hostility to, a milieu they found confusing and alien. He wanted to talk to someone who would appreciate his problems in keeping the school running and also tell him what was going on. So far he felt he had been told nothing.

The choice of Barnaby to head the investigation was not chance. One of his earliest successes had been a murder at a Somerset prep school and more recently his reputation had been enhanced by his handling of the Beaufort College affair at Oxford. The chairman of the governors had contacted the Chief Constable immediately it was discovered Jennifer had been shot and he had promised someone who would not be entirely at sea in academic surroundings.

Barnaby himself would not have claimed any particular knowledge of, or sympathy with, the groves of academe. He was not a university man, nor had he attended a boarding school, but experience had taught him one basic lesson: closed institutions are organic structures having *mores* of their own, as well as a network of subtle relationships the outsider ignores at his peril. Likewise he never thought of

130

himself as imaginative, but he knew the value of tact and saw the need to gain the confidence of those involved. Certainly it would be a cardinal error to alienate them.

On first acquaintance the most notable aspect of Barnaby was not his mind but his physical structure. He was a tall man with deep-set eyes that gave him a haggard appearance and made him seem older than he was. He usually wore a faded but well-cut tweed suit with a waistcoat, even in the warmest weather. When he walked, his motion was disjointed and ungainly; when he walked quickly, as he usually did, a casual observer might have seen him as a figure of fun, a match-stick man pulled by strings. But the casual observer would have been wrong. Barnaby might look odd, but he was a man of energy and intellect who had earned an enviable reputation over a long career and who, with retirement round the corner, maintained the respect of both contemporaries and juniors.

By the time he arrived it was another hot day. He stood at the window of Irving's study looking out over the cricket fields. Nothing seemed to move except the groundsman rolling the wicket on the Howard Acre.

'How do you want to play this?' asked Irving, standing beside him with his hands in his pockets.

'I've already spoken to Sergeant Taylor, so I've got the basic picture. I gather he set up camp in the bursar's office last night. We've got a mobile incident room coming up this morning – we can discuss the best place to put that later – but I should like a room to myself, somewhere central.'

Irving eyed the gaunt policeman about to invade the school. He was aware they were weighing each other up.

'You can have the registrar's drawing-room in the Old Almonry. He sees prospective parents there, but we can easily find him an alternative for the time being..'

'Taylor tells me you're sticking to normal routine.'

'It's the only way. Boys are creatures of habit. As long as they're fed and watered and kept occupied I don't anticipate any problems. A few members of the Upper Sixth who have finished A Levels have been allowed out of school and one or two not involved in the pageant have gone home. But most of them are here because we have leavers' parties all this week.'

'I understand Taylor's got hold of last night's seating plan. I may need to get some parents back.'

'Hugo Charteris – one of my masters – dealt with all that. Tickets were issued for individual seats. You'll keep me informed about progress, Chief Inspector, won't you?

Barnaby detected Irving's sense of unease at the invasion of his fiefdom.

'Yes, Headmaster, of course. One question for you, sir. You have an overall view of the school and you must have a detailed knowledge of your staff. I'm starting absolutely from scratch. Can you think of any reason at all why anyone should kill Mrs Wentworth?'

Irving looked hard at Barnaby, bringing into play the steely-eyed technique he used when faced with a refractory boy. His chin was tilted upwards, his nose became more dominant.

'No, Chief Inspector. I can think of no reason at all. I don't know what goes on between individuals and their families. I can only say that we are a large community and there must be likes and dislikes everywhere. Any group of people thrown together as we are must produce petty feuds of one sort or another.'

'Hardly a petty feud, Mr Irving.' Barnaby did not intend a rebuke, but he bridled at the headmaster's defensiveness.

'No, no, of course not. It's just that the whole thing is incomprehensible to me.' Irving's air of magisterial infallibility suddenly slipped. 'Merchet is not the sort of place you have a murder. To tell you the truth, the last twelve hours have been a complete nightmare.'

* * * * * *

Once Barnaby had settled into the Old Almonry drawing-room he had another session with Sergeant Taylor. It was a gracious room with antique furniture and expensive curtains, designed to impress potential parents. The two men sat opposite each other in comfortable armchairs, looking out at the abbey.

'No post-mortem report yet, but the first reaction last night was a close-range shot. It was so dark more or less anyone could have got close to her.'

'Is the excuse about moving her justified?'

'I think so. They knew she was dead, but no-one suspected she'd been shot until they got her inside. Cuthbertson's a highly reputable man – I've checked. Cardiologist from a teaching hospital. He thought it was a heart.' Taylor picked up a clipboard and put it on his knee. 'I've talked to a lot of people and I've got some initial statements. Mr Pilgrim has given me a list of boys on stage in the Somme scene, as well as those shifting props and so on. There's no reason to suspect the boys, of course, but they could have noticed something.'

'We can't rule them out. We keep calling them 'boys', but the seniors are seventeen and eighteen. They'd be prime suspects if we found a body after a pub fight on a Saturday night in Brighton.'

'That's true, sir. But this lot seem very respectable. They're all shocked by what's happened and they all want to help – or that's my impression so far. And they call me 'sir', as if I was one of the masters.'

'Make the most of it, Sergeant. We shall be back in the real world soon enough. Anything else?'

'I've spoken to Mr Wentworth. He's pretty cut up, I'd say – and he drinks. I saw empty whisky bottles around. There was something odd about his marriage, though I'm not sure what. I've been in their house and they had separate bedrooms. I've made a list of all the staff – masters, wives, matrons and so on. I've marked in red those who seemed to know the Wentworths better than the others. Charteris is letting me have the names of all the guests at the performance last night, together with seat numbers. One of the young constables is getting hold of the telephone numbers from the school secretariat, so we can chase anything up.'

'No other leads except your doubts about the Wentworth marriage?'

'I detect a bit of gossip about Mrs Wentworth, but it could be no more than that. Everyone's completely mystified.'

'Weapon?'

'Not a sniff of it so far. We went over the arena last night and we're doing it with more manpower this morning. It could be anywhere. The park's huge and there are ditches and hedges all over the place – not to mention the river over by the woods.'

'Time you got some sleep, Sergeant. I'll pick up the threads now, starting with Wentworth. Thanks for giving me an efficient start.'

Taylor was appreciative of the compliment and looked at Barnaby with new respect. He had a reputation for being hard to please. 'Strange place this. I hope it isn't going to take too long to get into. There's a formality here you don't get outside. I felt a closing of ranks this morning.'

'No-one likes a scandal, particularly on his five hundredth birthday. Merchet's a famous school. Have you seen the headlines in the press? But even schools like Merchet have to be aware of public opinion these days. Bad publicity turns off prospective parents. The independent school market's getting bigger all the time and if you pay fees of fifteen thousand pounds a year you call the tune.'

Taylor turned to go. As he reached the door he said: 'One odd thing. Mrs Wentworth had a dog, an alsation called Sabre. For some reason it's being looked after by Mr Calverley, the housemaster of Drydens. You would have thought her husband would have it, wouldn't you ? There's none so strange as folk. Oh yes, and one other little snippet. There's a woman on the staff called Pamela Baskerville – the men call her Mad Millie. One of the masters said he thought she was the one on the railing when the lights went up. The man he was talking to said he wished it had been.'

Chapter 17

The masters' room at Merchet had the air of an old-fashioned gentleman's club. It was oak-panelled, the walls were lined with oil paintings of former masters, and copies of *Country Life* and *The Field* dominated the tables. *The Times Literary Supplement* could be found by the more academic, the head of economics had recently added the *Investors Chronicle*, and from time to time the *Time Out* guide to London restaurants and bars was bought to satisfy some of the younger members. In general, however, the tone was dustily conservative and although, hidden away somewhere, discussion of current educational controversy was available in *The Times Educational Supplement*, no-one actually read it and anyone seen looking at it surreptitiously was assumed to be looking for a job elsewhere.

As masters lived in school property scattered round the estate or in Merchet Farthing, they often went home in free periods or for lunch; the masters' room only came alive at break when they gathered for coffee and biscuits and, in desultory fashion, discussed the issues of the day or picked teams for afternoon matches. Then, for twenty minutes, with some eighty gowned figures engaged in quiet conversation, it became the focal point of the school.

The day after the pageant the buzz of converse was notably higher than usual, but the room emptied at the usual time as masters went up to school and soon only Moncrieff and St. Leger, both having free periods, were left alone in leather armchairs at one end.

'I knew it would end in tears,' said Moncrieff.

'Don't be smug, Charles,' responded St. Leger with irritation. 'It involved a hell of a lot of work. What's more it was going well. Even you must admit that. The Somme was very moving – much better than in rehearsal. Much better than I imagined when I wrote it.'

'And then the lights went up.'

'As you say, "And then the lights went up". Who on earth would want to kill her? It's absurd.'

'I'm not a married man, Tristan, so I'm not going to pontificate about young women.' He paused, nodding his circle of white hair. 'But from all I hear sex is probably at the bottom of it.'

'It's easy to say that, but you can't point at an obvious motive. Can you *really* see James killing his wife – or anyone else for that matter? He's the one with the motive. Anyway, I always got the impression it was live and let live on both sides. No-one's going to convince me James is a murderer.'

Moncrieff took off his spectacles, polished them on the silk handkerchief protruding from his top pocket, then put them back on. 'I expect Dr Crippen's friends had a surprise, too.'

'The end of term's going to be a shambles.'

'Trinity always is.'

'Have you seen this Barnaby man?'

'Curious shape, but looks competent.'

'The Harrow match is still on. I'm surprised Harrow want to come.'

'They haven't much choice. You can't muck fixtures about at this stage of the term. Besides, it's one of the oldest in the cricketing calendar. They can hardly pull out just because we've got a body. They'll be curious anyway. There's nothing like a disaster in one institution to get the others flocking round.'

'Started your reports?'

'I've finished the Upper Sixth.'

'Are you going to the leavers' party at Denshams tonight?'

'Yes, but I'm going to pace myself this year. The end of Trinity is just a series of alcoholic hurdles.'

The conversation was discursive and trivial, both men skirting round the dominant subject. At length Moncrieff heaved himself out of his chair, breathing heavily. 'I still think it's sex,' he said, and left the room.

* * * * * *

Sylvester Ford was finishing his morning's teaching. It had been a strain. He had been off form, he knew that. As an experienced hand he had never had any trouble with discipline and any boy who overstepped the mark got short shrift. But this morning his mind was not on the job. The wretched Beaver annoyed him more than once and instead of freezing him with withering sarcasm he lost his temper. That, of course, was a mistake. In the subtle game of boys versus masters played out in every form-room a master's loss of temper meant points to the boys. Ford knew it – and so did Beaver.

He could not stop thinking about Jennifer. She had once been important to him, and not just because of their brief affair. Strange how far apart they had drifted. He knew he had never satisfied her in any sense, but she had once said that if a woman slept with a man there was always a bond. He had not felt that as the years passed. When they met on a social occasion they behaved like strangers.

Ford sniffed noisily, then sneezed. He took out a handkerchief and blew his nose.

It had been his fault rather then hers. He was ashamed of the way he had used her for his own purposes and nothing makes one withdraw from a relationship more rapidly than a sense of guilt. Beside, she *knew*. In a moment of alcohol induced garrulity he had told her. A cardinal folly: he had regretted it ever since. She knew the other thing, too. Not so important and she would never have told anyone. She had been strangely loyal.

How much would this gaunt policeman want to know? And how much would he have to reveal?

He thought back to the previous night and the moment he had held Jennifer's body. She had been so fragile, so light as he laid her on the ground. He had never loved her in the way he believed some men can love a woman; he was not that sort of man. He knew what it was to need a woman and he understood friendship; but he had never experienced the emotional peaks and troughs the poets celebrate. He counted himself fortunate.

He recalled his immediate emotions at the moment of discovery that Jennifer was dead. Pity, yes: she was young and beautiful and full of life. But something else. Relief. Yes, that was it: relief that a chapter in his life had closed.

He sniffed again and searched for his handkerchief. Another sneeze was imminent.

* * * * * *

St. Leger was lunching in Muchelney with Freddie Tichbourne.

He took off his gown and tossed it into a chair. 'Thank God *that* morning's over.'

'Sherry, Tristan? It's Tesco's, but dry and perfectly palatable.'

'Better not let Moncrieff hear you say that. He'll think standards are slipping even more than he suspects. Yes, please.'

'Seen the papers?' Tichbourne, tall, thin, wearing a gown so old it had a greenish tinge to it, put a *Daily Mail* on the table. A headline stood out in capitals over an inch high: MURDER AT MERCHET. A sub-heading added: KILLING AT TOP PUBLIC SCHOOL.

'I don't envy the head man handling the press. However much he helps them they'll still get things wrong. It's extraordinary but when you know the inside story about anything, nine times out of ten the press go astray. Reporters don't understand how public schools work anyway. For a start they don't grasp the relationship between the housemasters and the headmaster. They seem to think it's a sort of dictatorship at the centre; they don't see that individual houses can be relatively independent. I don't think Moncrieff's done anything Irving's wanted since he was appointed.

'The press will get hold of the gossip. Look at this bit. 'There was bafflement at Merchet last night over the killing. One source who didn't want to be named said: *Jennifer Wentworth was liked by everybody. She had many close friends, both among the staff and the boys.* Do you think they've got a whiff of the Treece business? Why should they mention the boys?'

'You say 'the Treece business', but that was only malicious gossip.'

'Are you sure? I don't think anyone knew the truth. Moncrieff had no idea, but some of the boys thought it was serious. I had one of my historians in for a drink last summer and he was very indiscreet. So much so I had to shut him up. The gist was that Treece was completely smitten – and near suicidal at one point.'

'Boys get things wrong.'

'Not that sort of thing. Remember, this was *their* side of the door. They usually know more than we do. Besides, the history of public schools shows it's not unknown for a master's wife to seduce a senior boy. Put seven hundred highly-sexed boys into monastic conditions and you're bound to get a scandal from time to time. At my place the 1st XV took turns with a Swedish *au pair* known as 'The Bicycle'. And there was a young matron at Theobalds during the war who was reckoned to have initiated three generations of sixth-formers.'

'But Jennifer... You're not thinking straight, Freddie.'

'All things are possible, Tristan. You're an idealist. As a house-master, I've learned one simple lesson. Never be surprised by anything.'

'She had a long list of admirers, but that's hardly a motive for murder. Who's going to help this Barnaby fellow pick up the internal vibes? We're a strange place at the best of times.'

'He'll do it if he's any good. After all, no-one has a motive to cover up unless he's the murderer. Or she, of course.'

'You sound like Mad Millie.'

'She wouldn't want the women to be left out.'

'Don't you believe it. She's the sort of feminist who thinks murder is a male preserve. I had an argument with her last term about male and female characteristics. Do you know, she wouldn't accept that some women actually enjoy being dominated. She went right over the top. Said I was fulfilling my own fantasies. Just for a moment last night I thought she was the one on the railing. It was only when I saw the auburn hair I realised it was Jennifer.'

'Perhaps Jennifer was killed by mistake. Has that occurred to you?'

A bell rang in the internal regions of the house.

'Lunch,' said Tichbourne, pulling off his gown. 'Let's go and see what the boys think.'

* * * * * *

Barnaby was making modest progress. Just before lunch a call from ballistics provided a piece of puzzling information. Jennifer had been killed by a .32 bullet, a single shot fired at close range. He was by no means an arms expert, but he knew a .32 was rare. Ballistics were equally baffled. 'It looks like something from the past,' said the expert. 'We haven't seen one like this for years. Do your best to find the gun.'

After lunch he interviewed Wentworth. They sat in the registrar's drawing-room, looking out over the abbey and the park. 'Best view in the school,' the registrar had said. 'Just the place to impress potential parents who haven't signed up. It looks idyllic and it doesn't overlook the places where the boys misbehave.' Today, with the warm weather continuing, the French windows were open. In the distance, above the woods, the Downs were hazy; nearer, in the valley, the 1st XI was on the Acre practising for the Harrow match.

Wentworth sat before Barnaby looking uncomfortable. Like so many bereaved individuals he had seen in the past it seemed events were moving too fast for him. He listened to Barnaby's questions, but was clearly struggling to concentrate on his answers. His expression, always serious and dominated by lines turning downwards, suggested abstraction; his grey suit was creased.

'It's difficult,' he said. 'Running the house and coping with all this.'

'Can you think of anyone at all who might have wanted to harm your wife?' Barnaby felt the question was trite and inadequate. He added: 'I think you should put your personal matters before your public ones for the moment.'

Wentworth's eyes moved distractedly. Then his whole being appeared to move into focus. His voice was harsh. 'I've no idea who wanted to kill her. But if you want it, I'll give you a list of the men she slept with. I think I'm up to date.'

'Had your wife been acting normally?'

'Perfectly normally. She'd even captured another young man. It never took long.'

'Nothing at all?' Barnaby pressed. He felt Wentworth was replying without thinking.

'I suppose...'

'Yes?'

'I suppose I should mention her grandfather. He died last term. He was her last relation.'

'Did he leave her anything? Please forgive the question.'

'Nothing much. He lived on a small pension and his cottage was leased from a local estate. Just a few books and odds and ends. Nothing valuable.'

'Had she any other money?'

'She had a certain amount. Getting on for £100,000. Insurance money when her parents were killed.'

'Has she left a Will?'

'Yes. We made Wills a couple of years ago. We left everything to each other. Strange, isn't it?'

'So you get it?'

'I suppose so.' Barnaby noticed the fleshiness round Wentworth's neck. The man seemed back on automatic pilot with his thought processes suspended. Then: 'For God's sake, you don't think I killed her for that?'

'As yet I don't think a great deal,' said Barnaby. 'I just want the facts.' He was aware he sounded like a B-movie detective.

Curiously the cliché stirred Wentworth. He became animated. 'The facts are simple. We led separate lives and Jennifer was woefully unfaithful. We lived together and there was a certain understanding, even a residual affection. We didn't hate each other and I would never have hurt her physically.'

'Do you mind talking about her...friends?'

'Lovers? No, not at all. I'm hardened to all that.'

'Go on.'

'The latest is Matthew Tawney, a young master who came last September. He doesn't know I know. She was still seeing Mark Calverley, but that had more or less fizzled out. Probably had finished. He was very upset. He'd committed himself much more than she had. Last summer there was a boy called Treece. I told her that was foolish and she agreed in the end. It didn't last long. Previous to that she'd had Ford.'

'And you didn't mind?' The words just slipped out.

'*Of course I minded!*' Wentworth looked at Barnaby as though at a notably dim pupil. 'But there wasn't much I could do about it short of a major upheaval. She didn't want to leave. She went on acting the dutiful wife in public and I never knew how much was public knowledge. I just threw myself into the job. I repeat, I didn't kill her.'

'Please, Mr Wentworth.' Barnaby held up a calming hand. 'Now I assume you attended the performance last night?'

'Yes.'

'And you were sitting in the audience from the time it began until...until you saw your wife's body?'

'No. I slipped out when it started getting dark – during Victoria's reign. I went back to the house to check that no boys were there. We'd agreed the boys either had to be in the pageant or in the audience. It was compulsory. I imagine most housemasters did the same, or sent one of their tutors.'

'But you were back in the audience when your wife was found?'

'Yes. But not in my original seat. I sat down at the edge of the stand so that I didn't have to disturb people by walking in front of them.'

'Do you know who you sat next to?'

'No. They were parents, but not of boys in my house. A big man with silver hair. His wife was small – a blonde – and much younger. I assume they would vouch for me.'

'That's very clear, Mr Wentworth. Just one last question. How can you be so specific about your wife's lovers?'

Wentworth looked straight at Barnaby with worried grey eyes. 'Because, Chief Inspector, in the long run *my wife always told me*.'

Chapter 18

Barnaby sat for some time after Wentworth had gone turning over his first impressions. It had not been difficult to detect the bitterness behind Wentworth's attitude to his wife. But he prided himself on picking up early signs of guilt and he had seen nothing to suggest he was a murderer. The one thing coming across strongly was his concern about the house and the boys; he seemed more interested in them than his wife.

He read the notes he had made and those given him by Sergeant Taylor. Nothing obvious struck him and he was acutely aware of how much of an outsider he felt. He needed to get into the culture of the school, to see how it worked, what the relationships were, what rumours were abroad.

He looked out of the window and saw two senior boys strolling away from the school towards the park. On the spur of the moment he went to the French window and called out: 'Excuse me. Could you spare a few minutes?'

The boys were surprised to be hailed and puzzled by the stranger. But when he had introduced himself they came in and sat down. He asked their names.

'Rupert Gibson, sir,' replied one, who was fair and thick-set.

'I'm Michael Parrish, sir,' said the other, a thin, bespectacled boy who looked erudite.

'Forgive me hijacking you like that,' said Barnaby, smiling. 'I just want to talk to someone to get the feel of the school. Are you happy about that? The headmaster has said I'm free to speak to anyone.'

The two boys nodded. The scholarly-looking Parrish took the lead: 'That's all right, sir. Sorry if we were suspicious. We thought you might be the press.'

'You're both sixth-formers, I take it?'

'Upper Sixth. We've finished A Levels and are having a slack time. Nothing to do now...' – he paused – 'now the pageant's over. Just a few leavers' dinners and parties and the term will be over too.'

'How's the school taking this business?'

The question was so general that Gibson and Parrish looked at each other vaguely. Again Parrish was the spokesman. 'A jolt to a well-oiled system,' he said. 'The place runs smoothly and copes with most things. We're used to being in the public eye. There's nothing new in that.'

'There's gossip, of course,' volunteered Gibson.

'Always plenty of that in a closed community like ours. Boys can be just as bad as girls,' said Parrish.

'Tell me about it.'

Again the open-ended nature of the question made the two boys turn to each other. They knew this was a serious police enquiry, but both felt loyalty to the institution they had attended for five years and neither wanted to speak out of turn.

'It's only talk,' said Gibson.

'I'll take it as that.'

Parrish adjusted his spectacles and coughed; he looked as though he was about to deliver a lecture. He said: 'The boys always know more about what's going on here than the masters. There are two levels of knowledge. The boys know all about their level and because one or two masters are indiscreet and talk to boys they also have a fair idea of what goes on in the masters' room. The masters know their gossip, but they don't know ours. It's a curious thing, but boys are generally more cagey about what they say. A master represents authority, authority means sanctions – and the ultimate sanction is expulsion. No boy wants to be responsible for that, hence the power of the traditional no-sneaking code. The masters who talk to boys think they're popular, but they just get taken for a ride.'

'So?'

Parrish, a bright classicist with an assured place at Oxford, was not to be hurried. 'So,' he said quietly, 'we know a good deal about Mrs Wentworth...' He stopped. 'I'm sure you realise, Inspector, that in an institution like Merchet where 17 and 18 year-old young men are meant to be chaste the business of sex becomes more significant than it ought to be. There's a lot of talk.'

'Just sex?'

'And drink – and drugs.'

'Are there drugs here?'

Parrish appeared on the brink of another lecture. 'No – Merchet's clean at present. There have been one or two cases in the time we've

144

been here. But any boy caught is immediately expelled. Everyone knows the score. Besides, the vast majority disapprove. Drugs only appeal to inadequate boys who haven't managed to make their mark in any other way.'

'You were talking about Mrs Wentworth and then you stopped.' 'There was a rumour that she had an affair with a boy – about a year ago. It wasn't common knowledge, but one or two of our year heard it. It may have been just talk.'

'Who was it?' Barnaby was blunt. He recognised a reliable source when he saw it and wanted to see how far the boy would go.

Gibson was looking at his feet, but Parrish spoke with the confidence of one who has made up his mind. 'Oliver Treece. I assume, Inspector, you will respect our anonymity on this.'

'Of course.' Barnaby's face registered nothing. He had long ago learnt to disguise shock or surprise. 'Is Mr Wentworth's house – Theobalds, is it called? – is it one of the houses where boys were expelled for drugs?'

The pause was more significant this time. 'Yes,' said Parrish.

Barnaby turned to Gibson and became more avuncular. 'Were you in the pageant, Rupert?'

'Yes, sir.'

'Which scenes?'

'I was in the main Corps scenes – Flodden, the Civil War and the battle of the Somme.'

Barnaby saw he was dealing with a more reserved boy, and probably a less intelligent one. 'So where were you when the lights went up?'

'Off stage, sir.' We were given a few moments of total darkness to get ourselves and all our kit away.'

'When did you first realise something was wrong?'

'We sensed it from the audience reaction. It was different from all the other scenes. Then Mr St. Leger called us all together – all the actors from our scene and those getting ready for the next one. And the stage gang as well. He told us there was a problem, though he wasn't very clear. He'd had a message on the phone from Mr Pilgrim. And Stephanie…er, that is Mr Higham, had heard something from the lighting box on his mobile. That would have been Mr Halstead.'

'Did you see Mrs Wentworth?'

'No. We were sent straight back to our houses. Some of the stage gang were kept back to do some tidying up – props and so on. There was a hell of a mess backstage. One or two of them saw Mrs Wentworth's body.'

'Why did no-one see her during the Somme scene?'

'It was too dark. I was on stage and saw nothing and I've spoken to other boys who say the same. There were flashes and bangs in no-man's land and flares in the park, but nothing over there. Any lights were on our side of the stage. They only made the other side darker.'

'How easy would it have been for someone to get to the railing unseen?'

'Very easy. There were people rushing all over the place and the noise was horrendous. Mr Pilgrim told us he wanted maximum contrast between the noise of the battle and the silence of the cross at the end. He's a brilliant producer.'

'Anyone could have moved about near the railing,' said Parrish. 'I was in the audience on that side and it was completely dark.'

'You didn't take part?'

'No, sir. I've been concentrating on my A Levels. I need my three As for Balliol.'

Barnaby had enough for the time being. He stood up, his bony frame moving in its characteristically jerky way. 'You've been very helpful. If you think of anything else, you know where I am.'

Parrish coughed in self-deprecation. 'There is one thing,' he said. 'And I must preface this by saying that my source is second hand – what you would call hearsay.'

Barnaby recognised the pedantry of the future academic. 'Go on.'

'There has been talk about Mrs Wentworth's. . .' – he searched for a word – '...conquests. One of the names mentioned is Mr Ford. That seems unlikely to me, but it's what some have said. Anyway, last night I was sitting near him with my parents. I expect you've been told he was one of the first to get up when the lights came on. He reached Mrs Wentworth and laid her on the ground.'

'Keep going.'

'I still hadn't taken in what was happening – it took time to adjust. After all the play-acting it was difficult to tell what was real and what wasn't. But I watched Mr Ford and I saw how he reacted when it was announced that she was dead. There's only one word to describe it.'

'And what's that?'

'Relief.' Parrish paused for effect. 'Sheer unalloyed relief.'

* * * * * *

The boys had gone. Barnaby stood at the open window looking out at blue sky and the high fleecy clouds of a warm June day.

He was thinking about the mechanics of the case, his thought processes random but leading to a coherent conclusion. Exactly when had the shooting taken place? At first he thought it must have been some time during the Somme scene – after all, there had been plenty of noise to cover a shot. Then, working on the principle that he who finds a body has often put it there, a principle that had served him well in the past, he wondered if Ford could have shot her at the end of the scene in the full glare of the floodlights. After all, he had dashed to the railing in an uncharacteristic way and might have done it while holding her. But this was out of court on two counts. First, there had been silence when the lights went up and there had been no sound of a shot. Second, because the more he thought about it, the more clearly he saw that Mrs Wentworth could not have died then. It must have been at the beginning of the Somme scene – indeed *before* the scene started.

The suffragettes had been shouting and banner waving and Mrs Wentworth had chained herself to the railing. But she hadn't really chained herself, had she? She had pretended to chain herself. Yes, there had been a chain and a padlock – it was all in Taylor's report – but she had just put her arms through the railing and created the illusion of being chained. There was no need to do it properly and, in any case, it might have caused problems in getting off the stage when speed was important.

So the moment the lights went down on the suffragette scene she would have been free to walk away, as all the rest did. Apparently there had been some confusion with the suffragettes going off and the soldiers coming on, but she would only have been at the railing for a moment or two when the lights went out. Whoever had killed her must have done it in that first period of darkness – before the shooting and noise of the Somme battle began.

Conclusions? No-one reported hearing a shot at that time, so it was likely the gun had a silencer. Furthermore, it was clear that whoever did it was familiar with the exact details of time and place in the pageant. He or she knew Mrs Wentworth would be at the railing when the lights went out but would have moved seconds afterwards. And identification in the sudden darkness would have been difficult. Was anyone else on the railing? Following a line of thought previously pursued by St. Leger and Tichbourne, he wondered whether it was possible that the wrong person had been killed.

Chapter 19

Barnaby had arranged for meals to be sent over to the Old Almonry and his supper arrived promptly at seven o'clock. It had been carried more than three hundred yards from the kitchens and was only lukewarm under the covers put over it. As he tackled the chicken casserole he considered his next step.

Reports were coming from various quarters, but nothing gave an obvious lead. No weapon had been found and interviews with masters, parents and boys merely confirmed known facts. One or two interesting snippets had emerged, but they were probably no more than that. Higham reported seeing Calverley behind the acting area at the end of the suffragette scene, a fact Calverley confirmed with the explanation that he had been to inspect his house and was taking the quickest way back to his seat. Likewise, Rathbone had been directing his troops in the critical area, and Higham himself had been there or thereabouts for much of the time. There was nothing to connect either Rathbone or Higham to Jennifer Wentworth.

He had also checked on the exact position of the women at the end of the suffragette scene and two interesting facts had emerged. Pamela Baskerville had been attached to the railings next to Jennifer and as far as anyone could tell in the darkness the last three women off the stage were Pamela herself, Miss Broad the matron, and the French girl Monique Ducatillon. All three assumed Jennifer Wentworth was immediately behind them, as she had been at rehearsals.

A parent in the front row who claimed not to have moved from the beginning of the performance until its unexpected conclusion reported seeing Calverley both going out and coming back. Alastair Munro had apparently also gone out along the gangway behind the front seats shortly after the lights went out at the end of the suffragettes. She recognised him by his beard. He was back in his seat when the lights went up after the Somme and had been one of the first on stage to help in the crisis. The only other thing she noticed was Matthew Tawney turning his torch on and off to look at his script during the Somme action. No prompting had been needed, but he was following the narration. When the shaded torch went on she could see his hunched outline sitting in the darkness. Tawney confirmed his use of the torch and said he had not moved from his seat.

Barnaby pushed his plate away and dabbed his lips on the immaculate white napkin sent up from the kitchen. He noticed that none of the early reports mentioned the Treece boy or his parents. Had they been there? He looked at his watch. He wanted Sergeant Taylor back as soon as possible. There were ill-formed ideas he wanted to discuss; and he foresaw some tedious legwork which he had no intention of doing on his own.

One thing worried him. Sex seemed an important issue and he anticipated some tricky interviews, notable the one with the boy Treece. But although he had frequently found sexual motives to be significant, a cautious voice told him to look for others before he got too hooked on one constantly dangled under his nose. What about money? Filthy lucre always looked attractive and Jennifer had some even if she wasn't rich. And why was Ford apparently relieved at her death? Just a boy with his imagination running away with him, or something more sinister? He needed to meet more of the *dramatis personae* face to face. So far most were just names on paper.

Instinct told him to go for Treece. At the same time a warning bell suggested he should set a firmer foot in the common room. What, for example, about Calverley? He had been close to Jennifer and Taylor had been impressed by his apparent reliability. He would see him when he had finished his supper.

* * * * * *

Drydens, a largely eighteenth-century house built of brick and flint, stood in a belt of trees at the edge of the estate. Calverley and his wife lived in the front while the boys' rooms were at the back. When Barnaby arrived the house was quiet as prep was still going on. Calverley ushered Barnaby into his study, a cool, book-lined room looking up the slope to the abbey tower, just visible above the trees.

'We'll go in here,' said Calverley. 'Mary's got a friend in the drawing-room. We shouldn't be disturbed here because the boys are working hard for end of term exams.'

'How are they taking it?' Barnaby enquired, studying the man in

150

the armchair opposite. He had already registered the air of cultured confidence, now he took in the humorous crinkles round the eyes and the warmth of a friendly personality.

'They're jumpy, Chief Inspector, after last night. Death is beyond the experience of most boys. They want reassurance.'

'Don't we all? Death is beyond most people's experience these days, Mr Calverley. Society has sanitised itself so efficiently that we're kept away from it until the last moment. Even then we try to fool ourselves. Evelyn Waugh saw it coming in *The Loved One*. Do you remember Mr Joyboy of Whispering Glades?'

Calverley looked at Barnaby with new respect. He had not met a literary policeman before. He laughed out loud. 'Certainly I do. I think Waugh's the funniest writer of the century, as long as you ignore the bleak moral landscape – and Waugh's own character.'

Barnaby had established his credentials. Now he was blunt. 'I'm glad to be able to speak to you privately, Mr Calverley. And I won't beat about the bush. I understand you and Mrs Wentworth were – were close.'

'Yes.' Calverley's emotions had been twisted and contorted over the past six months. He had just managed to come to terms with his rejection when he was faced with Jennifer's death. He had not yet had a calm moment to assess his feelings; he knew only that he had been drained before her murder. 'Yes,' he repeated. 'We were close. But it had come to an end, as it always did with Jennifer. I didn't want it to – and I thought it might be different this time. It wasn't, of course. Jennifer wasn't capable of a lasting relationship. She'd moved on.'

'But you knew her well.'

'Yes.'

'Probably as well as anyone?'

'Probably. Her husband – James – knew her in some ways, of course. You must if you live with someone. But she only discussed the daily round with him – assuming Jennifer told me the truth. They never got down to the things that really matter.'

'Simple question, Mr Calverley. Why would anyone kill her?'

Calverley smoothed back his hair, now silvering at the temples.

'We've all been puzzling, Chief Inspector. James had a motive of sorts, but he couldn't have done it. I don't think any of her ex-conquests felt sufficiently strongly to conjure up the jealousy. If anyone really loved her, it was me. And I knew she'd drifted away. My sense of loss is...what I feel...I can't talk about it. I couldn't have killed her.'

'What about your wife?'

'Mary?' Calverley looked as though he was considering the idea for the first time. 'You are blunt. Mary knew about us – but she seemed to have come to terms with it. We had a few major rows in the early days, but she was contemptuous of both of us. And she predicted it wouldn't last. She was right. I respect her, even if I don't love her. She couldn't kill anyone. The idea's laughable.'

'*Nor hell a fury like a woman scorned* ?'

'She's not capable of it.'

'That's what you keep saying about everyone, Mr Calverley.'

'She was sitting with our guests. She couldn't have got out of her seat without being noticed. The Sandbachs and the other parents will vouch for her. Apart from anything else she'd have had to climb over their feet to get out – like I did. I was the only one who moved throughout the whole performance. I've already made a statement about that to your sergeant.'

'Did Jennifer tell you about Treece?'

'She told me more or less everything. That's why I thought our relationship was different. I was wrong.' Calverley looked steadily at Barnaby, not hiding the sense of betrayal he felt. 'My turn to quote Congreve: *Man was by nature Woman's cully made, We never are but by ourselves betrayed.* Have you considered other motives, Chief Inspector?'

'Such as?'

'Money.'

'I always consider money.'

'Have you found the gun?'

'Not yet. A strange question, Mr Calverley.'

Calverley stood up suddenly. 'Forgive me, I'm forgetting my manners. We've all been shaken up. What can I get you. I've a nice bottle of Meursault open – or there's whisky. Perhaps you'd prefer coffee?'

'Thanks. A whisky, please. A small one.'

'Right.' Calverley crossed to a cupboard the other side of his desk, took out a decanter and poured two whiskies. With his back to Barnaby he said: 'The question about the gun wasn't just curiosity. I'm going to tell you a story – a remarkable story. As far as I know

I'm the only one who knows it now.' He returned to his seat and took a sip of whisky. 'Of course, if it becomes a motive for murder somebody else must have known.'

'Go on.'

'Jennifer had no close relations. Did you know that? Her parents were dead, she was an only child and the only family she was aware of was her grandfather. He died a few months ago.'

'She was upset?'

'She was. But that's not the point. You must let me tell this in my own way. You'll find it hard to believe.'

Barnaby sensed the rebuff, adjusted his legs clumsily and signified that he was listening.

'Some time last winter Jennifer got a telephone call from her grandfather. He was in his eighties and had decided to tell her something he had kept to himself for years. To be precise, since 1943.

'His name was John Trebilcock. During the war he worked for S.O.E. Does that mean anything to you?'

'Yes, Special Operations Executive. Spying in Europe, helping resistance groups in countries the Germans had overrun.'

'Right. Cloak and dagger stuff on the grand scale. Trebilcock had been brought up in France by a French mother. He spoke French fluently and early on in the war volunteered to work for S.O.E. when it was looking for people to link up with the French resistance. He was trained and eventually went over six or seven times, sometimes by parachute, sometimes landed by plane. It was dangerous, as you don't need me to tell you. The Germans often penetrated the resistance – and there were always unreliable Frenchmen ready to betray you. A lot of agents were caught and most were executed after torture by the Gestapo. Perhaps you saw the film 'Carve her name with pride', the story of the woman agent, Violette Szabo. She was shot in Ravensbruck.

So you had to know who you could trust and who you couldn't. Trebilcock became very friendly with a French family living on a farm in a remote part of Burgundy. It was one of the key areas of resistance and the farmer had a field where S.O.E. planes could land. Just as he trusted the family, so they trusted him. To cut a long story short, he fell in love with the daughter of the house, a girl called Chantal.'

Calverley paused for effect and watched Barnaby's reaction. He saw the concentration, the puzzlement about where the story was going, as well as the determination not to interrupt.

'On his last visit Trebilcock helped the resistance sabotage an arms factory in Dijon, then he went back to the farm to wait for the pick-up plane from England. On the night it came he had some time alone with Chantal and just as the plane was landing she gave him a small but heavy suitcase to take away with him. She told him not to open it until he was safely back in England. He took it without question and spent the last few minutes kissing her goodbye.'

Barnaby almost spoke, but restrained himself. At the same time, and wholly irrelevantly, he noticed the cut of Calverley's linen summer jacket. It was stylishly understated, clearly expensive, and somehow characteristic of the man.

'Once Trebilcock got back to the privacy of his London flat he opened the case. Inside were two leather bags, and in the bags, carefully wrapped in old newspaper, was a hoard of gold coins – English sovereigns and French Napoleons. Chantal had written a letter. It was short and to the point. Her family was a prosperous farming family that had never lost its peasant roots. It had always collected gold. She and her father suspected the German net was closing in on their area. There was no hard evidence, but recent arrests suggested a traitor within their organisation. Both felt their luck could run out at any time. She asked him to keep the gold for her family and said she would collect it after the war. Her trust in him was total.

'You can guess what happened, Chief Inspector. The net closed. Chantal's father was shot, she and her mother were deported to Belsen where rumour had it that both died. At the end of the war Trebilcock went back to France to find out what had happened. The Germans had burned down the farmhouse and the land had been disposed of to Vichy collaborators. As far as he could see the family had ceased to exist. Local resistants confirmed the death of the father – his name is now on a memorial at the side of the road between Avallon and Quarré-les-Tombes where he and half a dozen other members of the underground were shot, but there was no firm evidence of the fate of Chantal and her mother. The obvious infer-ence was that they had died with so many thousands of others in the Belsen camp. He followed up such records as there were, but found nothing.'

Barnaby's attention was total. Again he clumsily re-adjusted his long legs, but his deep-set eyes were motionless.

'Trebilcock was left with the gold. He was an honourable man who felt it was not his and that it should be kept in case a member of the family appeared. He was also something of a romantic who hoped Chantal might one day be restored to him. Nevertheless, after a while he married and had a daughter – Jennifer's mother. His wife died young, then his daughter was killed in a car crash with her husband. Trebilcock was left with his granddaughter, Jennifer, as his sole relation.'

'Did they all know about the gold?'

'No, he didn't tell anyone until he confided in Jennifer earlier this year when he felt ill. I imagine spies are good at keeping secrets.'

'Where did he keep it?'

'What would you have done with it?' Calverley did not resent the interruptions now.

'I would probably have buried it.'

'Exactly. That's what he did – under the water-butt in the garden. He told Jennifer where it was and said it would be hers when he died. He felt the trust would die with him. He had a heart attack in the spring and Jennifer saw him just before he died. He was still clear-headed and almost his last words to her were 'Don't forget the gold.'

'Jennifer loved the old man and was upset by his death, but she drove straight from the hospital to his cottage, made sure no-one was watching, then drained the water-butt and dug into the ground where it had been standing. In no time at all she found the leather bags about two feet down. She didn't open them at once – the cottage is isolated and she was nervous – but brought them back here and told me the whole story. She trusted me and, frankly, needed advice. We opened the bags together. As her grandfather had said, they were full of sovereigns, many from Victoria's reign, and smaller coins of Napoleon III – all gold.'

'Do you know how much they were worth?'

'Yes. Jennifer went to a coin dealer in London, taking a sample or two and without revealing her cache. Gold's gone down a lot recently, but even so this lot is worth getting on for £80,000. Difficult to believe.'

'Policemen hear many strange things. It's the nature of the job. Where is it now?'

'I don't know. At first she hid it in the attic. I can't be absolutely sure, but I don't think she told James about it at all. At the time I believe I was the only one she confided in, but she may have told others later – perhaps Matthew Tawney. It's a bizarre story, and the ending may be even more bizarre if no-one knows where it is now.'

'Or if someone did and decided to commit murder.' The romanticism of the story left Barnaby cold. 'Murder has been done for very much less.'

Calverley took a sip of whisky and looked out of the window. Hydrangeas, pink and blue, were coming into flower beyond the lawn; surrounding trees cast lengthening shadows and Jennifer's alsation, Sabre, was lying in a patch of late evening sun.

'There is more, Chief Inspector.'

'Yes?'

'There was also a gun.'

Barnaby was shrewd enough to see it was best to let Calverley get on with it in his own way. His interjections merely served to feed Calverley's sense of the dramatic.

'Trebilcock hadn't said anything to Jennifer, but when she dug up the gold she found a box as well – a box containing a gun and ammunition. She showed me and asked what she should do with it. It upset her. She wondered why her grandfather hadn't mentioned it – and she wondered why he had it. It worried her more than the gold. She didn't tell me about it when she first told me about the gold. Somehow she felt ashamed of it. It was only later, at the beginning of their term, she asked me what to do. I advised her to take it straight to the police. In fact, I offered to do it for her.'

'And did she?'

'I don't know. She certainly didn't do it immediately. She told me she still had it at half-term. She was worried that if she went to the police about the gun the whole business of the gold would come out. If I read her correctly, she got rid of part of the burden by telling me about it. In any case, we haven't seem much of each other this term As I said, she'd moved on.'

'What sort of gun was it?'

'An ugly one. I don't know about guns at all, but it was a hand pistol with a long fat barrel. It looked unbalanced.'

'And there was ammunition, you say?'

'Two or three small boxes. One had been opened, the others were sealed.'

'And that's it?'

'That's it. You see now why I asked if you'd found a gun.'

Barnaby finished his whisky, carefully put down the glass and stood up. His lean frame made him look tall as he bent towards Calverley.

'Thank you, Mr Calverley. A fascinating story. Which may or may not be relevant, of course.' He moved briskly to the door. 'Two things before I go. Tell me about the new French woman you have on the staff this term.'

'A delightful girl. One or two young masters are very smitten. And the boys think she's rather...rather 'cool' I believe the word is. Whether she's improving their French is a different matter. What's the other thing?'

'Why have you got Jennifer's dog?'

'Very simple. He got attached to me when Jennifer and I were seeing a lot of each other last term and he came away with us in the holiday. James has never had anything to do with him. It was natural for him to gravitate towards me. It was probably his fault my wife first got wind of our affair.'

'One supplementary, Mr Calverley. Where does the French girl come from?'

Calverley's air of confidence, born of education and an unconscious sense of social superiority, seemed to evaporate as he saw the way Barnaby was thinking. For an instant he paused, but this time it was not calculation.

'Burgundy,' he said.

157

Chapter 20

Irving had had a tiresome day. His large physical presence remained impressive to those round him, but his self-confidence felt diminished and almost for the first time in his career he wondered whether he was enjoying being a headmaster.

The telephone in his office had not stopped ringing and the school had been besieged by the press. Photographers had had a field day, crawling over all accessible areas. They could not get into Old Quad, which the police had sealed off, and the boys' houses were off limits, but everything else was fair game: lenses zoomed and shutters clicked, wielded by men in jeans with stubble-bedecked chins. Elsewhere reporters, local and national, sought out anyone who might have anything to say, however banal.

Irving's secretary did her best to stem the telephonic tide, but she could not be utterly ruthless and cut the link altogether because many of the calls were from parents anxious for reassurance. Further electronic communications arrived via the fax machine and E-mail. Not for the first time Irving cursed these media of instant and frequently thoughtless correspondence.

In the morning he had held another meeting of his senior management team to discuss the situation in a more considered way than had been possible the previous night and to confirm arrangements for the Harrow match. A quorum of governors had descended unexpectedly 'to keep a finger on the pulse', as one of them put it. Merchet might be a blameless victim, but they were worried by the publicity. The tabloids were already suggesting an undercurrent of wealth and sleaze as they lined up another ancient institution for attack. One or two unsavoury old boys, of whom every school has its quota, had been dug out to make critical comments. 'I snorted coke at Merchet,' said one, omitting to point out he had brought it in from home and been sacked on the spot.

Meanwhile the normal bric-a-brac of routine had to be dealt with. Irving had arranged to see Monique Ducatillon to consider the success or otherwise of her first term and whether she would come back in September. Tichbourne had sent one of his boys up to him for cheating in an end of term exam and as the boy was in serious trouble in other areas Irving had to contact his parents. Alastair Munro had asked to be fitted in before lunch for a chat about abbey services for the remainder of the term and a special service for Jennifer, while lunch itself was curtailed by the unexpected appearance of an architect wanting to review projected repairs to the library. This was followed by his normal weekly meeting with the bursar. In mid-afternoon he had an appointment with some Old Merchets who had come to discuss plans for the quincentenary dinner in the House of Lords.

Irving's secretary made sure that a host of minor matters did not reach him, but she could not stop a hand-delivered letter from Pamela Baskerville complaining about Paul Rathbone's behaviour backstage the previous night when troops had clashed with suffragettes. 'His attitude was outrageous,' she had written, 'but wholly characteristic of what occurs at Merchet. Male aggression in a male-dominated community is, of course, only to be anticipated, however...' Her diatribe continued over two sides. She would be expecting an apology in the fullest terms and the headmaster would no doubt ensure that she got it.

Irving narrowed his eyes and fingered his high-bridged nose as he read the missive. Aloud he breathed: 'The woman is plainly insane.'

* * * * * *

Barnaby had decided to follow up the Treece angle, but before he could do so Sergeant Taylor reappeared having caught up on some of his sleep.

'Modest progress, Sergeant. No gun yet – and we're still waiting for the forensic report.' He gave a quick résumé of the day's work.

'What do you want me to do?' Taylor's red hair was wiry, Barnaby noticed, and gave the impression of having drained all colour from his face.

'I'm going to see the Treece boy and then I'll finish for today unless something startling comes up. I'd like you to see how the weapon search is going, then check up on this French girl. Find out if there's any possible connection with Trebilcock and the S.O.E. She's probably a complete red herring, but she comes from the right part of France – and the gold interests me. Money always interests me.

Incidentally, keep all that under your hat. Calverley's the only one to mention it so far. I want to find out how widespread the knowledge is, but I'll do that in my own way.'

'Do you want me to see her tonight?'

'Up to you, Sergeant. It might be best if you went through the routine stuff with uniform and then got some more sleep. I want to see Treece now, but after that I suggest we both start afresh tomorrow. This Harrow match seems a big occasion.'

Taylor stood up. 'Right, sir. Just one thing. I've been looking back over the notes I made last night. This man Ford, Sylvester Ford – the artist. Something odd there. Considering what happened and the way he was first to her body, it's strange he didn't want to talk about her.'

'What did he talk about?'

'All sorts of things – mostly pictures. He made caustic remarks about the quincentenary celebrations, criticised the headmaster for waste of money on the pageant, and then complained about how he'd had to reorganise the pictures in some gallery and how inconvenient it had been. It was very self-centred and, frankly, pretty disloyal to the school. He's clever, but he didn't want to talk about Mrs Wentworth. He sheered off every time I mentioned her.'

'But he knew her.'

'Oh yes, he knew her well, I could tell that. He was downright evasive.' Taylor was pleased with the words. He repeated them with relish: 'Downright evasive.'

* * * * * *

Prep was still going on in Ryders when Barnaby rang at Moncrieff's front door. The house, largely Victorian at the rear but with an elegant Queen Anne façade on the private side, was silent. Wood opened the door and let him in.

'What exactly is your rank, sir?' Wood asked. He led him to Moncrieff's study and announced him formally: 'Detective Chief Inspector Barnaby, sir.'

'Good evening, Barnaby.' Moncrieff acknowledged the chief inspector with a curt nod of his white hair. 'I hope this won't take long. I've got to see some boys after prep and there's a pile of reports to start.'

'Not long, sir. I understand you have a boy called Treece in Ryders.'

160

'I have.'

'I should like to speak to him.'

Moncrieff peered over his half-moon spectacles. 'You mean you want to question him about this Wentworth business?'

'I believe they knew each other. It would be helpful if we could have a chat.' Barnaby did not usually suffer fools gladly, but he had been warned by Taylor not to be fooled by Moncrieff's old-bufferish exterior.

'I don't see what the boy can possibly tell you, but you can talk to him. I'll have to be present, of course, *in loco parentis*.'

'Very well, sir.'

Moncrieff picked up an internal 'phone that linked with his head of house. 'Get hold of Oliver Treece please, Simon. Send him over to the study straight away. Tell him Detective Chief Inspector Barnaby wants to have a word with him.'

When he had put down the 'phone, Barnaby asked: 'How much did you know about Treece's relationship with Jennifer Wentworth?'

'I don't know what you're talking about.'

'I have reason to believe they may have had an affair.'

'Rubbish.'

'It may be, but I don't think so. My sources were quite clear.'

'Sources?'

'Seemed reliable, but must remain anonymous.'

Moncrieff was uncomfortable. He prided himself on knowing more about his boys than most housemasters, but had had been taken off-guard. Now the events of last year looked different and he was irritated by Barnaby's confidence. 'He may not say much in front of me.'

'We'll see, sir, shall we?'

They sat in silence for a minute or two before a knock announced Treece's arrival. He was a tall blonde boy, solidly built, with intelligent eyes. He was still wearing cricket whites; the XI had been having a late net for the match next day. Barnaby felt he had already assessed the situation and decided exactly what he was going to say before he sat down. He crossed one leg over the other with careful nonchalance.

Moncrieff looked at him appraisingly, as though meeting him for the first time. He was already considering how best to deal with the boy's father. 'Detective Chief Inspector Barnaby wants to ask a few questions, Oliver. Just tell him the truth and try to imagine I'm not here.'

'I'll do my best, sir.' Treece looked at his housemaster with clear grey eyes. He knew he was going to be shocked. 'What would you like to know, Chief Inspector?'

'This won't take long, Oliver. I just want to verify a few facts. I understand you knew Mrs Wentworth?'

'I did, sir.'

'Better than most boys?'

'Better than most boys.'

'Is it true that you had an affair?'

Treece's eyes flickered briefly to his housemaster, then down to his shoes. 'Yes.'

'When?'

'Last year. Last summer term.'

Barnaby felt the tension in his words. The boy's exterior calm was concealing a much deeper emotion. 'How long did it last?'

'Seven weeks. Exactly seven weeks. I've counted the days.'

'And in that time you saw a great deal of each other?'

'Not really.'

'But you got to know her well?'

'I thought I did.'

'Forgive me, Oliver, I don't want to pry into something that seems painful for you, but I'm sure you see that I must find out as much as I can about Mrs Wentworth's background. When did the affair end?'

'The last day of the summer term.'

'Why did it end?'

'I don't know.'

'So it was Mrs Wentworth who stopped it. How did it end?'

'It just stopped.'

'Please, Oliver.' Barnaby was at his most persuasive. 'Try to answer a little more fully. What were the circumstances?'

Treece appeared to study the pattern on the carpet. 'I saw her in the afternoon of the last day. I was playing in a match against a South African touring team, but it was rained off at lunch. I rang her, said I was unexpectedly free and could see her. We went to – to our place and we made love. She said she'd write during the holidays and we agreed to meet in London. She was always very keen. She took the initiative in the first place. I would never have dared.'

He paused and quite suddenly the sophisticated young man

162

became a boy. His eyes filled with tears. 'She didn't write. We didn't see each other in the holidays. She didn't reply to my letters. I rang her hundreds of times, but she wouldn't listen. Either that or I got her husband. And when the Michaelmas term started she wouldn't see me at all.' Treece's words tumbled over each other. 'I caught her once after an abbey service when she couldn't get away from me. She told me it was over. No explanation, no goodbyes. Nothing.'

'And that was it?'

'Yes.'

'Who knew about it?'

'In the summer, when we were together, no-one knew, unless she told someone I didn't know about. When it stopped, I told a couple of close friends. I don't know how far it went round. Not far, but I expect some of the Upper Sixth knew. Her affair with Mr Calverley got to the boys quite quickly.'

'Did you tell your parents?'

'Not to begin with. I kept it to myself.'

Moncrieff leaned forward. 'But your father knew there was a problem, Oliver.'

'Oh yes, he knew there was a problem. I behaved badly. I wouldn't talk to anyone at home. I was upset and I didn't want to let Jenny – Mrs Wentworth – down. I still can't believe she's dead.'

'You said "not to begin with," said Barnaby. 'You told your parents later?'

'I told my father about a week ago. We're not close, but he came to watch some cricket and we started talking. Somehow I blurted it out.'

Barnaby thought he wasn't going to get much more. 'Have you any idea, Oliver, what might have happened last night?'

'No, sir, none at all.' Treece looked straight at Barnaby. 'I loved her, you know. But my feelings changed. I didn't speak a word to her last term- or this term for that matter. And for what it's worth there are no realistic theories in the Upper Sixth. Plenty of talk, but no more than that.'

'Your parents came to the pageant?'

'Yes. I wasn't taking part because I'm in the 1st XI and I've got to concentrate on my A Levels. Mr Moncrieff said he wouldn't let me do it even if I wanted to.'

'You sat with your parents?'

'Yes.'

'Did any of you move during the performance?'

'We had a picnic supper in the park beforehand. There was plenty of champagne – I probably drank too much – and I think we all went to the lavatory in the course of the evening. None of us was away for more than a few minutes. We were certainly all there when – when Mrs Wentworth was discovered.'

Barnaby stood up, his limbs moving in their uncoordinated way; Treece also stood up, with the smooth action of the natural games player: the contrast in motion could not have been greater.

'That's fine, Oliver. Just one more question. You say you didn't speak to Mrs Wentworth after Christmas. So she didn't ever say anything to you about the gold?'

'Gold?' Treece's face was blank.

'Gold.'

'I don't know what your talking about, sir.'

'Good. That's all I wanted to know. Thank you for being so frank about what was obviously painful for you. That'll do. Goodnight, Oliver.'

'Thank you, sir. Goodnight.' Treece had regained his equilibrium: he was once more a poised young man. But he left the room without looking at his housemaster.

* * * * * *

Sylvester Ford was drinking alone in his cottage in the village. He had once been married, but his placid wife had eventually walked out after suffering years of intellectual contempt as well as heavy drinking. The cottage reflected the lack of feminine presence. Books were scattered everywhere; an unfinished picture stood on an easel in the sitting-room, surrounded by paints and brushes; empty wine bottles and unwashed dishes competed for space in the kitchen; upstairs the bed was unmade.

Ford was a series of contradictions. On the one hand, he was a gifted artist and teacher whose standards gave his department its acknowledged reputation; on the other, his arrogant denigration of colleagues and regular criticism of Merchet values often led to something approaching social ostracism. Only a handful of sycophants, themselves risking isolation, followed with any enthu-

164

siasm.

Intellectually he was the epitome of rationality. For him emotion was a weakness. The irony was that while his arguments were always powerfully rational, his personal likes and dislikes were invariably emotional. As with Voltaire, reason marched in step with vindictive inconsistency. His round face, with its high forehead and ineffective beard, aroused hostility and he was a lonely man. In the privacy of his own home he faced the fact of his unpopularity and found his own compensations.

This evening he had already drunk a bottle of Côtes du Rhône. As darkness came he sat by the window giving onto the garden going over the previous night's events. Moths and other insects beat against the glass trying to reach the light.

Jennifer's death had left him cold. Their one-time relationship had been short and expedient. Looking back, he saw she had collected him like an intellectual trophy to put on the mantlepiece; he in turn had used her because she had connections in the art world. In any case his libido had never been more than modest and he realised early on that he could not match her appetite.

So on a personal level he had not been moved, even though he had been the first to reach her and had briefly held her in his arms. He remembered being gentle, but perhaps that was because it had all taken place before an audience; there was no feeling; it could have been anyone.

The heavy Rhône wine stripped away his inhibitions. The fact was that Jennifer's death was convenient. After all, she was the only person at Merchet who knew the truth about him. He looked for the corkscrew to open another bottle. And then he remembered he still had some of the other compensation upstairs.

Chapter 21

Sport is important at the old public schools. Such a truism is only worth stating because it might be thought that modern examinations, academic league tables and so on had destroyed traditional attitudes to games. True it is that much pressure has been exerted and sporting prowess no longer gives automatic support to an Oxford or Cambridge application – indeed, quite the opposite, a fact deplored by Moncrieff, who enjoyed writing recommendations to the admissions tutor of his old college ending: 'He is by no means an intellectual, but is an all-round games player and will undoubtedly be a good college man'- but distinction on the games field remains a goal eagerly sought by boys at all levels of the hierarchy. At Merchet clever boys were respected – membership of The Burke, a self-elective literary club for scholars which held dinners with black candles and circulating port, gave intellectuals a cachet well beyond the hoi polloi – but the average boy looked first to the Blood, the Merchet man with a reputation on the rugger or cricket field. Such gods strolled round the grounds in multi-coloured blazers, ties and caps, preening their feathers and exciting the envy of the less fortunate.

Cricket was the game with the greatest prestige, a fact duly reflected in the nineteenth-century pavilion on the Howard Acre, a building which said much about both Merchet and cricket. A grandiose construction of brick and flint, it contained a dining-room of extravagant proportions lined with the heads of animals shot by Old Merchets in the heyday of empire, together with fading photographs of long-dead teams and scorecards of long-forgotten matches. At the back was a dark but fully-equipped kitchen which produced teas for teams and visitors on match days. At one end was a billiard room and at the other a museum containing cricketing memorabilia, including a ball that had regrettably killed a new boy, loyally but myopically watching a match in 1872. Certain parts of the pavilion were out of bounds to all except capped members of the XI and curious rites of initiation attended the cap-awarding ceremony.

The annual match against Harrow was the climax of the season and had been played on the Acre for nearly two hundred years. On one occasion in the nineteenth century six future members of the cabinet had played, three on each side. Thus the edict that the match should go ahead was determined as much by the inexorable momentum of tradition as Irving's wish for routine to continue as normally as possible.

Certainly it would have been difficult to stop. Marquees for bars, lunches and teas had for some days been erected round the ground; invitations to parents, Old Boys, and various distinguished MCC guests had been sent out months ago; besides, the weather which had washed out the fixture in the two preceding years was set fair. It might be added that Jim Clode, master-in-charge of cricket, was aware of weaknesses in the Harrow team and the possibility of a Merchet victory. So, in spite of the blue and white police tapes surrounding the Old Quad and the mobile incident room, and police cars parked in the open space by the old monastic guest house, Harrow were informed the match would go ahead with the usual 11.30 a.m. start.

Barnaby sat at the open window of the Old Almonry and watched preparations. The marquees were being opened, with caterers' vans delivering food and wine; members of the XI, excused morning school, were having a quick net; the groundsman, whose beloved Acre had been cut and rolled in immaculate lines, was marking out the wicket. No-one would believe, Barnaby reflected, that a woman had been murdered here barely thirty-six hours ago. Not for the first time he marvelled at the ability of ancient institutions to take disasters in their stride.

He looked at the rough notes on the pad in front of him. Progress was not promising. The name Wentworth appeared over and over again amidst the scribbles and it went against the grain to dismiss the suspect with the most obvious motive; but the harsh fact was that his behaviour suggested nothing but innocence. Calverley had to be considered too, because he had been facing up to the imminent loss of his mistress, a mistress to whom he was clearly committed. But Barnaby prided himself on having a nose for the sort of man who could commit murder and Calverley did not fit the bill. A strong character, yes, opinionated, yes, but a man who assessed actions and consequences, a metaphorical chess player who saw through early

167

moves to the end play. He was not the type prepared to spend years in prison, whatever the provocation.

Through the window he saw Treece putting on his pads for a knock. Treece? Uncharted waters. He had been badly hurt, no doubt about that. And immature young men do strange things. Unmarried and having no children of his own, Barnaby, not for the first time, knew he was not at his best when assessing the young. What about the boy's father? He gathered father Treece was a go-getter, a man who was ruthless in his business dealings. He had attended the pageant and was coming to the match as well. Barnaby jotted a note against his name. He watched Treece play a polished forward defensive shot, head over the ball, left elbow cocked. 'The boy's a cricketer,' he mused.

Who knew about the gold? His instinct was to home in on the money. Too often in the past he had been led astray by fancy psychological theories when simple greed stared him in the face. The old man had kept the secret, but he was a spy and spies know the penalties of a loose tongue. Jennifer Wentworth was not a spy. How many people had she told? Barnaby was an unreconstructed male. To himself he said: 'She was a woman. Women talk.' She had told Calverley. Who else knew?

Again he scribbled on the pad, the words illegible to all but himself. 'Ford. Relief?' He still had to follow that up. Relief he had been successful? Or something else? Ford was an unknown quantity. From what he had seen so far he should not be ruled out.

He wrote again: 'Tawney.' Calverley had avoided talking about him, but if he read Calverley correctly he was a man with traditional attitudes who would not try to put the blame on someone else. Wentworth had said he was Jennifer's latest conquest – and Calverley's use of the Congreve quotation almost suggested he was the latest victim. Taylor had spoken to him on the first night and established his presence on the edge of the stage as prompter – a presence confirmed by the parent in the front row who saw him looking at his script with the aid of a torch. On the face of it Tawney looked no more than a naive young man. But he was the latest boy friend and it was conceivable Jennifer had told him about the gold. And what about the gun? Who else had she told about that?

Where *was* the gold? Had she buried it like her grandfather? If she'd sold it, where was the cash? There was no sign Wentworth knew anything about either the gold or the gun. Barnaby scribbled again.

He was still making notes when Taylor arrived. He was pleased to be interrupted and pushed the pad aside.

'I've seen the French girl. There'll be some checking to do, but I don't see a Trebilcock connection.'

'Tell me.'

'She comes from the right part of Burgundy -the Morvan. It's wooded and remote and one of the key areas of resistance during the war. But she has plenty of family. Parents and grandparents are still alive. No sign of any link with the resistance – or the war for that matter. The only possible interest is the town she comes from – Montsauche. It was burned down by the Germans in 1944 as a reprisal for attacks by the local maquis. She knows about that, but not much else. She didn't seem very interested and didn't understand why I kept asking the questions. Kept saying it was all a long time ago. I've done some homework on this and there's a museum of the resistance at St. Brissot in the Morvan. She says she's heard of it but never been there. I'll have to confirm what she says about her family, but I can't see anything to make a link with Trebilcock. They're shop owners not farmers.'

'What about the family Trebilcock knew?'

'The French police are working on them. The family name was Renard and it looks as though the Trebilcock story is confirmed. There are still some Renards in the area, but no sign of a connection with the Ducatillons.'

'Well done, Sergeant. We'll keep it all in mind – just get the details checked. I wish we could get the weapon.'

'Ten men still on the job, sir. But it could be anywhere – after all, we don't know that it wasn't disposed of miles away.'

'Right. I'd like you to get back to the seating plan. Go through it and telephone as many as you can get hold of. The bursar will have most of the numbers. Check everything we've got so far. Don't touch the Treeces for the time being – I'll deal with them. Meanwhile I'm going to see Tawney and Ford. You thought Ford was evasive. I'll try to find out why. One thing I've discovered about closed institutions is there are always people with something to hide. Sometimes it's relevant, sometimes not. The trouble is it all seems so respectable the secrets come as a surprise.'

'I don't suppose they're very different from the rest of us, sir.' Taylor had few illusions.

* * * * * *

Barnaby rang the headmaster's secretary to find Tawney's whereabouts. She said he was teaching a Lower Sixth but had two free periods coming up. Barnaby decided to see him in his form-room. He picked up the panama hat he wore in hot weather and set off towards the Fortescue Schools, part of the original school founded by Edward IV and named after one of his most loyal household men. The rooms had been modernised, but the building remained fundamentally medieval, with mullioned windows and dark stone corridors. No bells had been fitted and masters themselves decided when periods ended.

Barnaby arrived just as the boys were leaving, the younger ones tumbling down the steps like puppies, sixth formers strolling, files in hand, with casual dignity. He asked for directions to Tawney's room and found the young master standing behind a large oak desk on a dais at one end of the room. He was rearranging books on his desk.

'I thought you'd want to see me.' Tawney was guarded.

'Why don't we sit down?' Barnaby indicated one of the tables recently vacated by boys. Without appearing to, he eyed Tawney's firm features; he sensed his air of authority, although he was a much younger man.

'Right.' Tawney, who had taken off his gown to teach, picked it up, came down from the dais and sat beside Barnaby.

'A bit old-fashioned, isn't it?' said Barnaby, indicating the dais and the tables arranged in traditional ranks before it.

'We arrange things according to individual taste. One or two modernists do things more informally, but I like a clear line between teacher and taught. Establish that division and you can get something done. You can let your hair down later if you want to. Try to be too chummy at the beginning and you're lost. That's the basic rule of schoolmastering.'

'An interesting view for a young man. I should have thought your generation wanted more informality, more casualness.'

'Some do. But I remember the successful teachers at my school – and it wasn't a public school like this. They were the ones who stuck to traditional methods and were respected.' He paused, still wary. 'But I don't imagine you're here to discuss educational theory, Chief Inspector.'

170

'No, Mr Tawney.'

'I'm happy to discuss Mrs Wentworth – I suppose that's what you want – but although I've got a double free period I can only spare you the first one. I'm seeing a couple of my Oxbridge candidates in the second.'

'Let's be brisk, then. Tell me about your relationship with Mrs Wentworth.'

'Very simple really. I was the last one on her list. I imagine you have the picture. She was an unhappy woman.' Tawney's voice, Barnaby noticed, had moved into a monotone, as though he was distancing himself from emotion.

'You were having an affair.' Barnaby was blunt. 'How long had it been going on?'

'We'd been attracted to each other for some time, but we didn't sleep together until shortly after the beginning of this term.'

'You knew about the others – Mr Calverley, for example?'

'I loved her.' Barnaby saw honesty and pain in the grey eyes looking steadily at him. 'Yes, I knew about the others. I knew her reputation. One night I asked her to tell me about all of them. I wanted to – how can I put it? – I wanted to cleanse her.'

'All of them?'

'I believe so.'

'Including young Treece?'

'Including Treece. I found that hard to understand. She bitterly regretted it.'

'Did she tell you anything, about herself or anybody else, that might give a motive for her death?'

'No, nothing. She was very loving, very confiding. And very unhappy. I don't know if you'll see what I'm trying to say, but I wanted my love to make her whole again. I thought I could do it. She kept telling me she was hard and I kept contradicting her. She didn't really know herself.'

'I wonder. You saw her regularly?'

'Yes, and we had plans for a holiday.' Tawney looked away. 'We were going to spend the first week-end of the holiday at a hotel she knew in Dorset. In a village associated with Tess of the d'Urbervilles. She made the reservation the last time we were together.'

'She made the reservation?'

'Does it matter?' Tawney suddenly made contact with his

171

emotions; his voice reflected irritation and puzzlement.

'It might. It certainly tells me something about your relationship. What do you know about the gold, Mr Tawney?'

There was a pause, a long one. 'What gold?' he said.

Barnaby looked at him with a hint of sadness. He reflected on the power of the irrational emotion we call love. An impressive young man, in his judgement an honest man, had been turned into a liar.

* * * * * *

Barnaby went back to the Old Almonry by a roundabout route that took him past the cricket. The Merchet flag was flying on the flagpole by the pavilion and early arrivals were already prospecting the marquees for a drink.

He sat down on a wooden bench inscribed with the name of an Old Merchet killed at Dunkirk and watched the first overs. Harrow were in the field and the Merchet openers were having a torrid time against a couple of quick bowlers.

The Tawney interview had unsettled him. There had been an honesty about him, an idealism, that was disturbing. But he knew about the gold and had lied about it. Why? If he loved Jennifer – and he did not doubt that – he had every reason to want her murderer brought to justice. The only motive for concealing his knowledge of the gold was that it might in some way redound to her discredit. Or was he defending himself?'

A snick through the slips brought one of the Merchet openers a four, but the next ball uprooted his off stump. Barnaby shaded his eyes and studied the next batsman coming down the pavilion steps.

'Treece,' he breathed.

The young man reached the wicket, took guard, then stood back and surveyed the field with a confidence that might have been interpreted as arrogance. He gave the impression he intended to be there for some time. The first ball was fast and overpitched. Treece hardly seemed to move, but he timed his off-drive to perfection and the ball raced away through the covers to the boundary.

Barnaby leaned forward. This boy could bat. But he knew nothing about the gold, he was sure of that. Even as he enjoyed the spectacle of a talented young cricketer, the case nagged away. Treece was inexperienced and immature, and he had been badly hurt; but unless he was also a very gifted actor, mention of the gold meant nothing to him. Besides, if it was true he had had no links with Jennifer since the previous year, there was no reason why it should.

Treece leg-glanced for a single, then in the following over played a shot of real class: an on-drive that bisected the angle between the bowler and mid-on before reaching the boundary to the left of the sightscreen. In the seats between the main marquee and the pavilion Sir Roger and Lady Treece, who had just arrived, applauded their son. Barnaby watched as Charles Moncrieff, wearing a panama hat decorated with the colours of the MCC, strolled across to join them.

The sun was getting warm. Barnaby leaned back, surveying his legs stretching out in front of him, pulling his own rather plain panama down over his eyes. He enjoyed cricket and was looking forward to getting up to Lord's more frequently in retirement. But he continued to pick over the evidence and his eyes missed little. To his right St. Leger and Pilgrim were mixing socially with parents by the drinks marquee; to his left some members of the Upper Sixth, freed from the burden of A Levels and dressed casually in shirt-sleeve order, settled on a couple of benches; beyond them more food was being carried from a van to the luncheon tent by two waitresses in black mini-skirts. 'They do themselves well here,' he mused, not for the first time.

Then he saw Taylor approaching from the main school buildings. For one whose gait was not normally rapid he was moving briskly; even from a distance Barnaby detected the air of a man with something urgent to impart.

'The post-mortem,' he said. 'There's a surprise.'

'Well?'

'She was pregnant. Nearly two months.'

Barnaby did not give Taylor the satisfaction of seeing his own surprise. He turned back to the cricket where Treece had just executed a model defensive shot.

Chapter 22

Sylvester Ford did not like cricket; indeed, he did not like any sport. If there was one man who epitomised the division of interest between academics and sportsmen, it was Ford. In the masters' room he covertly lampooned those of his colleagues he identified as 'hearties'. His stated justification was a desire to raise academic standards; in fact, his motivation was a sour recognition of Merchet's infatuation with games together with the knowledge that his hostility was based on his own incompetence at them. At no point did he face the unpalatable truth that the games players, who spent day after day on the fields, in most cases worked harder than he did. So Ford did not gravitate down to the Howard Acre. Instead he went to the Dorter gallery where the Manners collection was on display. With so many visitors around he liked to keep an eye on things.

Barnaby, who had reluctantly left the cricket, found him standing in front of a watercolour by Cotman, a picture of the church at Swaffham. He introduced himself.

'I thought you'd want to see me, Chief Inspector.'

'Why is that?' Barnaby looked at the rotund outline of Ford, who had not yet had the courtesy to face him.

'Because it wouldn't have taken you long to discover my connections with Jennifer Wentworth. If the police don't make an arrest immediately – in other words, the murderer is obvious – everybody gets swept up in the search, even those with nothing to hide.'

'Did you know Mrs Wentworth well?'

'Very well – some time ago. Quite a long time ago.'

'Tell me about your relationship, Mr Ford. It's not mere prurient interest.'

'Of course. I'm sure you spend a lot of time turning over stones to see what unpleasantness you can discover underneath. There's plenty to find here at Merchet.'

'That's not a very loyal remark.'

'I'm not a very loyal person. I'm a cynic. I teach at Merchet because it pays me to and I'm left to get on with my own work. The twin

174

problems of the artist, Chief Inspector: money and time. Both solved here. I'm paid to teach and I teach well. Ask anybody about the reputation of my department. I don't have to be loyal as well.' He looked sideways at Barnaby. 'You asked me about Jennifer. We were lovers, very briefly, four years ago.'

Still without looking directly at Barnaby, Ford moved to the next picture, a Turner seascape of greys and yellows. 'Look at that colour and look at that light. A cold sunset on a lonely sea. An artist who could recapture Turner's light would make a fortune. I've tried often enough.'

'So you knew her well.?'

Ford laughed, the sort of laugh once described as 'hollow'; his wispy beard moved up and down, drawing attention to its inadequacy. He sniffed loudly.

'No-one got beneath the surface. She set her cap at someone, made him feel a million dollars and then dropped him. We were like a collector's butterflies stuck on a board.'

'And it all ended four years ago. No contact since?'

'We've talked several times. Merchet is a sociable community. We were put next to each other at dinner parties more than once. Some hosts didn't know about our relationship, others did and thought it would be amusing. She always took pleasure in keeping me up to date on her love life. And she was interested in painting. She used to work in a Bond Street gallery – that's what first brought us together. After all,' – he leaned confidentially towards Barnaby – 'the philistines are thick on the ground here.' The sneer was explicit.

Barnaby instinctively recoiled from Ford's attempt to create intellectual intimacy between them. He did not find Ford attractive and well understood how he had alienated so many of his colleagues. He probed with a loosely aimed arrow.

'Did Mrs Wentworth help to get your work shown in London?'

'Yes, as a matter of fact she did. My first exhibition, a small one, was at the Cellini Gallery where she used to work. I don't know whether you know the gallery scene, Chief Inspector,' – Barnaby felt the intellectual sympathy being subtly withdrawn – 'but most of them have an attractive young woman front of house, as it were. Lots of smiles and legs. Jennifer was good at that – and she was one of the more intelligent ones.'

'How did she help you?'

'She acted as a sort of middle-man between me and the management. They respected her judgement.'

'Did that all stop when you broke up?'

'Jennifer played no more part. But she left the Cellini soon after that. The governors don't like housemasters with working wives. In any case my work stands on its own merit. The gallery usually has one or two of my paintings for sale. They sold one of my oils last week.'

Barnaby changed tack. 'If I said to you 'Where did Jennifer put the gold?', would you know what I was talking about?'

Ford's round face was expressionless. He shook his head. 'No,' he replied, moving on to the next picture, a David Cox watercolour of a Welsh castle. He looked indifferent rather than puzzled, the indifference of the egocentric uninterested in other people and their problems unless they concern him directly. The picture seemed to have his entire attention.

Either that or he was a consummate actor.

* * * * * *

Barnaby left the gallery feeling obscurely dissatisfied. He did not take to Ford and was far from certain he had been told the truth; furthermore, he could see no reason for him to be relieved at Jennifer's death. Surely her links with the Cellini Gallery gave him a strong motive to keep her alive? And there was something else, something to do with the pictures. He could not put his finger on it, but an oddity had caught his attention and now he did not know what it was. Not a good morning.

He made his way back to the cricket. The midday heat slowed his pace and he kept to the shade of the trees lining the drive. Morning school was over and several boys were drifting down to the match. The crowd of parents and guests had grown, as had the clink of glasses and chatter of voices in the drinks tent. Merchet had advanced to 110 for the loss of 3 wickets; Treece was still batting.

Jennifer's pregnancy had come as a shock and one reason he felt dissatisfied with his handling of Ford was his puzzlement at Taylor's news. He had not anticipated it and it opened up a vista of motive he had not considered before. Calverley and Tawney moved into focus as possible fathers, but with Jennifer's track record it might be a mistake

176

to rule anyone out. Ford was a non-starter as a putative father if he was telling the truth about their relationship, but could he be trusted? Barnaby's instincts thought not. And the connection with the Cellini Gallery was definitely worth pursuing. Someone would have to go to Bond Street. Did he want to go himself, or should he send Taylor? And somewhere in his subconscious, overridden by the surprise of the pregnancy, was the detail he had noticed, the detail that did not fit. He would worry at it until he could drag it out.

There were still twenty minutes till lunch. Barnaby chose a seat under a chestnut tree and took off his jacket. He was on his own, well away from the main groups of spectators.

Treece was facing a left-arm spinner bowling from the pavilion end. The first two balls he played circumspectly into the ring of cover fielders; the third he lofted straight over the bowler's head for four, and the fourth, a shorter ball, he late-cut elegantly between slip and gully, a shot of some distinction for a schoolboy. The fifth ball was cleverly flighted, a shade slower. Treece, the adrenalin flowing after two classic strokes, played another aggressive shot, aimed in the direction of the long-on boundary. But this time he did not get to the pitch of the ball, it turned sharply and Treece only succeeded in playing it straight back to the bowler who caught it and threw it up delightedly. 'Good catch, injudicious shot,' mused Barnaby. He pulled a face of disapproval as the successful bowler was mobbed by his team mates. Professional sportsmen had much to answer for; he deplored the current vogue for individual triumphalism.

He watched Treece make his way back to the pavilion to alcohol-lubricated applause, his mind still sifting ideas. No leads on the gold; search warrants would be needed. How genuine was the Trebilcock story Calverley had told anyway ? It was far-fetched tale and might be a distraction, just the kind of red herring a clever man like Calverley would produce, particularly now the question of Jennifer's pregnancy had arisen. He must surely be in the frame as a possible father. On the other hand Tawney had acted as though he did know about the gold, so perhaps it did exist.

The watercolour problem would need another visit to the gallery. Barnaby would not have described himself as an intellectual, but he did know something about watercolours and over the years had acquired a small collection of genuine quality. What had caught his attention?

He watched two more overs, then went back to the Old Almonry for lunch.

* * * * * *

Taylor had already started eating; he was sitting in his shirt sleeves, tucking into pork pie and salad. Barnaby picked up the tray he had been sent and sat down on the opposite side of the table.

'Do we know who Mrs Wentworth's doctor was, Sergeant?'

'Yes. Most masters and their wives use the school doctor – a Dr Armstrong. The Wentworths are both on his list. Do you want me to follow up this pregnancy business?'

'No. I'll deal with that myself. I'll see him after lunch.'

'How are you getting on with the audience?'

'It's a slow job. The parents are a difficult lot. Some are important people, most are rich people. Several have gone abroad – business, holidays and so on. Fortunately the mobile phone makes it easier to track them down. We've drawn up a chart in the incident room and we're beginning to see who was where, who was moving and who wasn't. But there's a lot of crosschecking to do. Give us a bit longer and we'll have a reliable picture. No sign of anyone lying yet. Any joy from Ford?'

'Interesting – but nothing obvious. I've got a hunch about him and I may have to pay a visit to a gallery in London that sells his pictures. I don't take to him.'

* * * * * *

There was a time when every public school had its own sanatorium, with extensive accommodation for whatever epidemic might strike. Today, with the national health service dealing with emergencies, most of the old scourges beaten by antibiotics, and parents increasingly keen to nurse sick boys at home, the sanatoria have largely become surplus to requirements. All that is required now is a surgery for the doctor and a few beds where individual problems can be treated away from the house to give respite to the house matron.

The sanatorium at Merchet was an impressive eighteenth-century house with Doric pillars set in woodland about half a mile from the main school buildings. Part of it remained a medical centre, with a

178

surgery, several small dormitories for the sick, and two nurses in attendance. The east wing now provided comfortable sets of rooms for young bachelors, looked after by a daily help from the village. The west wing had been developed for a married man with a family; its high ceilings and beautifully proportioned rooms made it one of the most desirable residences on offer to the masters. The current occupant was Dr Armstrong himself, who had pressed his suit partly by virtue of long service and partly because as a thrice-married man he had a large number of children. There had been resentment from at least two masters and their wives whose claims had been overlooked and who considered Armstrong only a part-timer at the school as he also ran his own private practice in the village.

Immediately after lunch Barnaby made his way to the sanatorium and was directed to the Armstrongs' private entrance by one of the nurses. Armstrong let him in himself. He was a thick-set, grey-haired man in his early sixties, his face dominated by deeply moulded creases; his hollow bass voice, overhanging bushy eyebrows and hairs sprouting from his ears enhanced an impression of gloom.

'Come in. I was expecting you,' he said. 'I suppose you've found out Mrs Wentworth was pregnant?'

The two men went into the drawing-room and sat down by the open window. Through the trees they could see the distant cricket.

'Dr Armstrong, I've picked up a lot of threads about Mrs Wentworth, but so far they provide more questions than answers. How well did you know her?'

'I've been her doctor since she came to Merchet and our relationship was strictly professional. I meet a lot of the masters and their wives socially, but the Wentworths weren't among them. I know she led a colourful life here – it was difficult to avoid some of the talk.'

'You were supervising her pregnancy?'

'Of course.'

'Did she tell you who the father was? I understand it was unlikely to have been her husband.'

'No, she didn't say.'

'Did you ask?'

'Yes, as a matter of fact I did. You see,' – Armstrong stared directly at Barnaby – 'You see, in a sense it was none of my business, but this wasn't the first time Mrs Wentworth had been pregnant. She was pregnant this time last year.'

179

Barnaby registered the words, but did not speak.

'She was pregnant and she had an abortion. It wasn't her husband's child and he knew nothing about it. It was done privately in the summer holidays.'

'Do you know who the father was?

'Yes.'

'Did she tell you?'

'No. Munro – the chaplain – he told me. Mrs Wentworth had been to see him. She couldn't tell her husband and she wanted to tell someone. Munro came to discuss it with me – in complete confidence, you understand.'

'So who was it?'

'You're going to be shocked.'

'I doubt it. Policemen aren't easily shocked.'

'Well, you'll be surprised.' Armstrong was finding the revelation difficult. 'It was one of the boys. A real scandal if anything got out. I'm only telling you now because of the circumstances. In view of Mrs Wentworth's death I realise I can't hold anything back. Munro and I have discussed it and we agreed I should tell you.'

'Treece?'

'Yes.'

'You're certain Wentworth knew nothing?'

'As far as I know Munro and I are the only ones who knew. Wentworth was the complete cuckold.' Armstrong spoke with a hint of male contempt.

'And Treece?'

'Certainly not the boy.'

'His father?'

'No idea. Munro and I didn't say anything. And Treece's house-master – Moncrieff – knew nothing at all. He'd have been hopeless. He's totally out of touch with the modern world.'

'Did Mrs Wentworth discuss the possibility of another abortion?'

'She raised the issue, but said she would keep this child..'

'Any idea why?'

'Guilt. No mother really wants to lose a child. She felt awful over the first one. She discussed it quite frankly. I believe I was the only person she told this time – and that was simply because of the medical angle. She was a very independent woman.'

'No indication she'd told the father, whoever he was?'

180

'I can't be sure about that. I just got the feeling she hadn't.'

Barnaby looked out of the window towards the cricket. At a distance the small white figures were completely motionless. Nothing moved in the heat of the afternoon.

To himself Barnaby said: 'But suppose she had.'

Chapter 23

Tristan St. Leger had called a meeting of the history department immediately after lunch in the history library. He promised it would be brief in view of the match, but he needed to explain one or two changes for the coming academic year, including yet another alteration in the structure of the A-Level papers.

The historians had long ago annexed some of the older and more distinguished buildings as their prerogative and their library was housed in the scriptorium of the original abbey, a room with a groined roof and Gothic windows. The walls were lined with books and a dark refectory table stood in the centre. Six members of the department sat round the table, with St. Leger at its head; Clode was unable to come because of the match and they were still waiting for Tichbourne who, being a housemaster, was invariably late. Meetings were usually held before lunch with a glass of wine; today St. Leger had provided port. Conversation was random while they waited.

'The head man's picking up the pieces well,' said St. Leger. 'It's easy to be critical, but I take my hat off to him.'

'Years of experience,' responded Andrew Korn. 'Whatever Irving's faults – and I know I've been a critic – I'd rather have him than one of these managerial types who think they're running Tesco's and not a school. I hope the governors don't go for one of those when Irving goes. Frankly it's time we had another scholar.'

A young historian called Redpath chipped in: 'Did you hear about the spat between Rathbone and Millie before the Somme scene?'

'Millie's made sure the whole world knows about it,' said Korn. 'She's told everyone she's written to Irving demanding an apology. Extraordinary way to behave. And Rathbone's just as bad, of course. He's completely single minded as far as anything military is concerned.'

'A cross between Apthorpe and Widmerpool,' said St. Leger. 'And you could safely say that to him. He wouldn't get the allusion. He won't apologise either. Thinks it looks weak.'

Alastair Munro, who attended history meetings because he taught history to a lowly Shell form, said: 'It doesn't need a genius to work out it must have been round about the time of the row that Jennifer was killed.'

'So neither of them could have done it because they were both too busy,' said Redpath sarcastically.

St. Leger, his mind elsewhere, looked up and said: 'Barnaby's an interesting chap. He looks odd, but he impressed Mark Calverley. Knows his Evelyn Waugh apparently. I expect he knows about Apthorpe and the thunderbox even if Rathbone doesn't. What a frightful mess the whole thing is. I can't help feeling partly responsible for starting it off.'

Tichbourne had come in while St. Leger was speaking. 'Don't be daft, Tristan,' he said. 'If someone wanted to kill Jennifer he could have done it at any time. He or she chose the pageant because it was convenient.'

'Exactly.'

'I thought it was outstanding, Tristan,' said Redpath. 'The end of the Somme scene was a real *coup de théâtre.*'

'You can say that again.'

Munro studied the faces round the table and saw how detached they were from the drama they were commenting on. He wished he was. He knew he was involved whether he liked it or not. How relevant was the information given him as a priest? How could he judge? He looked at his colleagues and envied them.

'Time we started,' said Tristan. 'I'm sure you've all got better things to do than sit here. I want to get back to the cricket.'

'Typical Treece innings this morning,' said Tichbourne. 'Batted like a god for his fifty, then threw away a hundred with a dreadful cowshot. That boy's a problem.'

Treece was a problem all right, mused Munro. But Treece wasn't alone. What about the day Mark Calverley had, as he put it, 'come for a chat', and then stayed until three in the morning. He had always seen Calverley as one of the most principled and civilised men at Merchet, a model schoolmaster. That was not the picture now. In the privacy of his study layers of self-control peeled away and he saw the real man. The sophisticated veneer vanished; in its place was something totally different: a man of violent passion searching for the truths about his own distraught personality. Was he capable of murder?

'Right,' said St. Leger. 'Let's start by looking at the new type of question in the English history document paper. I had another circular from the board earlier this term.'

'God, what is it this time?' Tichbourne, a radical in so many areas but an arch-conservative within his own discipline, exploded. 'More emphasis on so-called skills and another watering down of knowledge? Another dose of empathy? We'll soon be lucky to find a board setting a decent history paper at all.' He waved a hand round the booklined walls. 'We can ditch this lot. The Goths and Vandals are among us. The quicker I get to my pension the better. No wonder Moncrieff and Spooner are glad to go.'

Munro was not listening. He could still hear Calverley's voice in his study, a voice rasping with emotion. 'I hate myself, I hate my wife – and I hate Jennifer Wentworth.' The following day, Munro recalled, Calverley's mask was back in place. He was as calm and controlled as ever.

* * * * * *

Barnaby left the sanatorium and walked through the trees towards the cricket. His mental processes, normally crystal clear and logical were for the moment foundering. Was he really investigating a case where an apparently respectable master's wife had conceived a child by a seventeen year-old boy? Stranger than fiction, perhaps. Or was it? Merchet provided a cloistered existence, but it was not immune to the changes in modern society. Fatherhood in a seventeen year-old in the outside world might be rare, but it was not abnormal. Why should he consider it so strange here just because he was surrounded by the academic trappings of an ancient institution? He had already noticed that whatever the formal uniform requirements were for the boys for most of the day, they relaxed into jeans, open-necked shirts and the ubiquitous baseball cap at the first opportunity. He wondered if he had chanced on a truth he had never previously considered: whereas the public school boy once wanted to show he was different from others less fortunate, he now wanted to be the same as everybody else, part of a youth culture embracing all classes.

There were more spectators on the Acre than before lunch and the atmosphere was soporific in the heat. The Merchet score had advanced to 165 for 6 wickets. The headmaster was talking to parents in the seats by the pavilion. Nearby Moncrieff was chatting to Pilgrim.

'I didn't anticipate murder during my last term,' Moncrieff was saying. 'It's cast a blight on everything. I've got a dinner or two lined up next week – White's and Pratt's – and the boys have organised a farewell for me in the great hall. Goodness knows whether I shall get to any of them.'

Pilgrim was aware Moncrieff blamed the pageant and all connected with it for the shadow over the end of term. An egocentric himself, he marvelled at Moncrieff's self-centred approach and concern for parochial matters. Typical of the man, of course. He realised that having put up with Moncrieff's outdated idiosyncracies for years he actively disliked him. The quicker he went, the better. 'Where are you going to live?' he asked.

'I've bought a flat in Chelsea. Quite small, but big enough for me. And there'll be room for Wood. He's coming too. Nowhere else to go. Besides, I shall need someone to look after me. Chelsea's central enough to keep in touch.'

'Keep in touch?'

'Yes. Clubs, Old Merchets in the City – that sort of thing. I should miss all that.'

At that moment Sir Roger Treece and his wife, both basking in the success of their son's innings, approached. Moncrieff turned towards them at once, completely ignoring Pilgrim.

Pilgrim stood up and walked away. 'Just keeping in touch,' he muttered. He did not know anyone as rude as Moncrieff.

* * * * * *

Barnaby lowered himself untidily into an old-fashioned deckchair near one of the sightscreens. Again he tipped his panama forward and appeared to be engrossed in the cricket; again appearances were deceptive.

The pregnancies needed attention. First, the sudden dropping of Treece the previous summer was now wholly understandable. How many people knew about it and who were they? But that was all a year ago. Was it as important as the new pregnancy? Possible fathers: Calverley? Tawney? Or someone else – a casual pick-up, perhaps?

And did whoever it was *know* ?

He looked round the ground at the quintessentially English scene. Parents were scattered in groups on the boundary, where many had had lunch parties. Their sons sat with them or in the tiered seats in front of the pavilion. Here and there he recognised a master being sociable. Could he really be thinking about teenage sex, abortion, adultery and murder behind this idyllic façade?

The pregnancies were important, he was certain of that. But as he watched one of the Merchet batsmen being run out going for a lunatic run he was aware of something else nagging away in the inner reaches of his mind. He went back to his interview with Ford in the gallery. To pick up Taylor's favoured word, Ford had been 'evasive'. He felt he could not trust anything he said. Suppose, for example, the affair with Jennifer had not ended when he said it did? That would open up all sorts of possibilities.

But that was not what was worrying him. The more he thought about it the more he realised it was something to do with the pictures. He could not pin it down, but there was something wrong, something out of place.

This would not do. He hoisted himself out of the chair and, regretfully turning away from the cricket, made his way back to the Dorter gallery. The door was open, but Ford was no longer there; indeed, the gallery was completely deserted apart from an elderly custodian, a woman with hair pulled back in a bun, wearing half-moon spectacles, who sat at a desk near the entrance. Barnaby introduced himself, then started to look at the pictures methodically.

He already realised it was a good collection; now he saw just how distinguished it was. Girtin, Turner, Cotman, Varley, De Wint, Cox – they were all there, a roll-call of the great names in the watercolour pantheon. Thinking of his own puny collection, he saw this was a treasure-house.

He moved slowly down the gallery. A Girtin showed Fountains Abbey in late evening sunlight, the stone of the abbey contrasting with the dark foreground already in shadow. An early work, he hazarded, before Girtin suppressed detail in favour of broader effects. Next came two De Wints, a summer scene on the Thames at Marlow and country folk haymaking in Lincolnshire. It was such a pleasure to see pictures of this quality he almost forgot why he was there. These were perfect. But somewhere something was wrong.

He went past a Copley Fielding and a Bonington and stopped at the place where he had held his conversation with Ford in the morning. In front of him was the Cotman painting of the market-place at Swaffham, with the church in the background. It was in Cotman's most detailed style, like *Street at scene at Alencon*, of which he had a reproduction in his study at home. Nothing wrong with that, but what about the one next to it? He leaned forward. Another Cotman: *The church at Buckenham Thorpe*, signed and dated 1832. He peered at it. What made him feel it was not quite right? The colours were fresh and in good condition, but no more so than any well-preserved picture of the same period; no doubt it was kept in a portfolio when not on display. And then he saw it. The spire. The spire on the church tower. That was what he had seen out of the corner of one eye while talking to Ford earlier.

Barnaby was a Norfolk boy. He had been born and brought up in Wymondham on the main road to Norwich. As a child he had led a carefree rural existence, walking and cycling with friends under the wide East Anglian sky. He knew places like Swaffham – and he certainly knew Buckenham Thorpe. He looked at the Cotman again. Yes, the church at Buckenham Thorpe looked just like that. *But it should not have a spire.* The Cotman date was clear: 1832. But in 1832 the church had only a simple tower. It was the Victorians in the 1860s who had decided to improve their medieval heritage by adding a spire. *In 1832 there had been no spire for Cotman to paint.* Ergo, either someone had made an addition to the Cotman, or it was not a Cotman at all.

Chapter 24

Barnaby looked down the length of the gallery. On each side the pictures were hanging in lighted cases. With the realisation that one picture was not as genuine as it appeared, his professional scepticism cast a doubt over the whole collection. He moved on, looking closely at two Welsh castles, one by Varley the other by Cox. The self-congratulation he had allowed himself at unmasking the apparently spurious Cotman gave way to irritation that he was not a real expert. He did not know exactly what he was looking for, but an idea was germinating.

He looked at a Samuel Palmer: *Wood at dusk*. It had the strange simplicity of a Palmer and the characteristic russet colour. But why did the paint look so fresh? Or was that his imagination? His excitement was rising; it looked as though his amateurish knowledge of an esoteric subject might for the first time in his career prove useful. If his suspicions were right, he had a new motive for murder.

He went to the next picture: a Constable view of London from Hampstead Heath. The mackerel sky was attractive, but were the colours a bit insipid? What about the two Parisian scenes by Bonington? They looked all right, and he approved the almost acid green of the Père Lachaise cemetery in one of them. He moved on. A Copley Fielding: *Brighton Beach*. A lovely picture. It looked perfect. But his critical faculties would not lie down. Too perfect?

Next came an undistinguished Mediterranean scene by W.J.Caparn, whom he had never heard of. Then another De Wint. He stood back and looked at it. Yes, that was another oddity. Here was a gallery packed with gems and then, quite suddenly, for no obvious reason, a third-rate painting sandwiched between two masterpieces. It stood out like a gap in a set of otherwise faultless teeth. Something odd was going on here.

He went back to the desk where the elderly custodian was reading.

'Is Mr Ford still around anywhere, please?'

'No, I'm afraid not. He stayed for a while talking to one of the parents, but he left some time ago.' The clipped precision of her speech was in tune with her trim appearance.

'How long will the gallery be open?'

'Until 5 o'clock. We wouldn't normally be open today, but there are a lot of visitors here for the cricket and we always open on special occasions. After all' – she smiled a tight little smile – 'a lot of the paintings were given by old boys and they like to be able to see them.'

'Well, I'm sorry, Mrs...?'

'Miss, Chief Inspector – Miss Bingham.'

'I'm sorry, Miss Bingham, but I must ask you to close the gallery now. Ring Mr Ford if you can get hold of him' – Barnaby saw the telephone on her desk – 'and tell him I should like to see him as soon as possible. Please make it sound urgent. I shall be in the Old Almonry.'

Miss Bingham's precision did not desert her. She took off her spectacles, folded them and put them in a case. She closed the book she was reading and placed it with care on top of another book on her desk. 'Very well, Chief Inspector,' she said.

She made no further comment. She looked, Barnaby thought, a bit like the popular view of Miss Marple.

* * * * * *

Back in the Old Almonry Barnaby found Taylor drinking tea and eating cake. 'The cake's good,' he said.

Barnaby, a light eater himself, was beginning to be irritated by Taylor's capacity for food. He ignored the cake, but poured himself some tea.

He said: 'No joy with the gun?'

'No – but I've been talking to Wentworth.'

'Go on.'

'I've checked the account of his movements during the pageant. Nothing inconsistent and, like you, I don't see him as a murderer. He's obviously upset by his wife's death – probably more than he's letting on. The drink's getting to him.'

'I had that impression, too.'

'He'd been drinking with parents at lunch and he'd overdone it.'

'You didn't tell him his wife was pregnant?'

'No.'

'Good. I want to use that when I see Calverley and I want it to be a

189

surprise. Right, I've got some telephoning to do. There's something going on in the art gallery. You can get back to the movements during the pageant. Check Calverley and Ford particularly. I'm getting more interested in both of them. And while you're at it, see if Jennifer Wentworth had a mobile 'phone. If she did, she probably used it for private calls.'

Taylor picked up the last piece of cake and left the room. When he had gone, Barnaby rang directory enquiries and got the number of the Cellini Gallery. After suffering the inevitable Vivaldi on the holding tape, he eventually spoke to a Mr Fanshawe, one of the partners.

'I believe you've had dealings with a Mr Sylvester Ford?'

Fanshawe was courteous, but guarded: 'Yes, Chief Inspector. We've exhibited some of his work.'

'And sold it?'

'And sold several items.' Fanshawe coughed self-deprecatingly. 'I am, of course, always happy to help the constabulary, Chief Inspector, but I'm sure you will understand that I not like discussing my clients' affairs over the telephone.'

Barnaby ignored this. 'Does his work fetch high prices?'

'Oh, no. Barely into four figures. I'm sure he would tell you that himself. To be honest, he's one of our lesser lights, but we've always managed to sell anything he's given us. Nothing inspired, but his technique's good.'

Barnaby paused. He was moving into unknown territory, so was purposefully vague. 'Have you had any other dealings with Mr Ford?'

'Other dealings?'

'Have you ever sold anything for him other than his own work?'

'Look, Chief Inspector, I really must insist that if you want any more information you must come up here to see me. I'm not at all sure what you're asking. I'm happy to help, but I must respect my clients.'

'And I'm investigating a case of murder, Mr Fanshawe. I shall expect a full disclosure of anything that may be relevant when I see you.'

Barnaby put the 'phone down. A visit to London was tedious but necessary. It looked as though his theory was being confirmed.

Through the window a ripple of applause drifted up from the cricket.

* * * * * *

Barnaby went down to the Acre again. Apart from his own interest in cricket, he sensed the match was the centre of school activity for the day. He wanted to see Ford, who had not yet responded to his message, and Calverley.

He looked at the scoreboard. Merchet were all out for 201 and Harrow were opening their innings. It was still hot. Round the ground many parties were still eating tea; others were already into an early gin and tonic. The whole occasion seemed merely an excuse for eating and drinking. He suspected he had seen more of the cricket than most of the parents. Ford was not there, but he spotted Calverley standing on his own by one of the sightscreens. He was smartly dressed in a linen suit; as usual he looked cool and controlled.

'Mr Calverley, I'm glad to have caught you.'

'Hullo, Chief Inspector.' Calverley looked towards Barnaby, whose unathletic progress he had followed round the boundary. Though not anxious to speak to him, he was relieved he was not the father of the boy he had in the XI, a dreary, self-important man to whom he would have to be sociable at some stage and whom he had been subconsciously avoiding all afternoon. 'Any progress?'

'In a way, Mr Calverley, in a way. We've had the post-mortem. There's one question I must ask you. Did you know Mrs Wentworth was pregnant?'

Calverley's face betrayed no emotion. He said, foolishly as it seemed to him: 'Pregnant? How could she be pregnant? No, of course I didn't know.' He paused. 'No, she didn't tell me.'

Barnaby looked at the puzzled face in front of him. 'No,' he said. 'I can see she didn't.'

Chapter 25

Smoking is not allowed at public schools and this has for years given it the allure of forbidden fruit. Generations of boys have sought quiet places where a furtive cigarette may be enjoyed out of the eye of authority, the whole operation made more attractive by the flouting of rules and the scoring of bravado points in the eyes of conformist contemporaries. Today, of course, the tobacco temptation has been joined by alcohol and drugs and a conspiratorial cigarette is a relatively mild peccadillo in the league table of offences open to those seeking notoriety. Neverthless, smoking remains forbidden and most housemasters work on the principle that if you clamp down on smoking you are less likely to end up with more serious disorders.

James Wentworth had worked hard to limit smoking in Theobalds. He knew which boys smoked and he made life so difficult for them that they rarely tried to smoke in their rooms. He prided himself that Theobalds was a smoke-free zone and believed any boy fancying a cigarette would go either to a friend's room in another house where the regime was less efficient or find somewhere in the park. Such complacency was asking for trouble. As one old housemaster said: 'It doesn't matter how tight a ship you run, the boys will do you in the end.'

The boys had in truth 'done' Wentworth. Harassed by regular visitations to their side of the house, two or three adventurous souls discovered that the connecting door between the disused coal cellar on their side and the cellar beneath Wentworth's private side was not locked. Wentworth used his cellar for coal – he still relished an open fire – for furniture surplus to requirements, and for wine storage. The adventurers soon realised that as long as they kept relatively quiet and had some idea of their housemaster's whereabouts, they had a den in which to enjoy a surreptitious cigarette, comfortable chairs to sit in and, if they were not too greedy, the occasional bottle of wine.

Thus it was that on the afternoon of the Harrow match, having seen Wentworth on his way to the cricket, Beaver and Skirmish, neither of whom had any interest in sport, opened the connecting door and settled down for a quiet afternoon with a packet of Benson and Hedges. It was not to be as uneventful an afternoon as they imagined.

They found the two chairs they had long ago decided were the most comfortable, lit up their cigarettes, and got out a couple of top-shelf magazines hired from an entrepreneurial boy who specialised in importing such material.

'Shall we risk a bottle?' asked Beaver.

'We had one last week.'

'I don't think he counts. And he's probably got some new ones in for the end of term. Besides, he's pretty occupied at the moment.' A twinge of guilt touched Beaver. 'Perhaps we ought not to, after all... It would look pretty bad...'

'Let's just look. You're right, he may have restocked. I've got my torch.'

Holding their cigarettes with affected maturity, the two boys crossed to the darkened corner where Wentworth kept his wine. Ranks of dusty bottles were just visible lying on their sides in the gloom.

'New cardboard boxes. He's had a delivery. Shine the torch.'

Skirmish flashed his torch over the racks and boxes stacked in disorganised fashion against the wall.

'That's the gap we left last time,' said Beaver.

'Pity there's no gin. I don't like wine much.'

'Chassagne-Montrachet,' said Beaver in a passable French accent, peering at a bottle. Then in a voice of mimicry: '1987, old boy. Is that a good year?'

'It's all the same to me. He won't miss it. He's drinking heavily this term himself. I went to see him the other day to get my options sorted out and I thought he was plastered.'

Beaver put out a hand and got hold of the neck of the bottle. As he did so, he realised it was in some way wedged. He pulled vigorously and the bottle came out. At the same time something was dislodged and fell heavily at the back of the rack, something making a metallic jingling noise. Almost without thinking Beaver stuck in his free hand to see what it was.

'What is it?' asked Skirmish.

'Shine the torch.' Beaver was kneeling now, his hand searching the floor at the base of the rack. 'Hey, I say...' For one who was normally sophisticated well beyond his years, he reverted to the immaturity of a young boy. His eyes were wide. 'I say,' he repeated, 'look what I've found.'

* * * * * *

As a Scotsman, Alastair Munro was not greatly interested in cricket; however, as chaplain he felt it his duty to appear on public occasions. Accordingly, at the end of an interview with a policeman who had taken him through his view of events at the pageant in some detail, he set off for the match with the intention of getting a cup of tea and possibly catching parents whose sons had expressed an interest in being confirmed the following term. He was taking a short cut past the library when he became aware of a boy at his side who had caught him up.

'Sir,' he began. 'Have you got a moment?'

'Hullo, Beaver. Yes, of course.' Munro knew his austere appearance could be off-putting to the younger boys and he always made a conscious effort to be avuncular. 'What can I do for you?'

'It's difficult, sir.'

Munro looked at the puzzled face beside him. He knew something of Beaver's reputation, but intuition told him this was an occasion to listen. 'Do you want to talk out here, or would you rather come back to my study?'

'It's fine out here, sir.'

'Come down to the Acre. We'll find a quiet spot.' They walked in silence until they found two chairs on the side of the ground furthest from the pavilion and marquees. 'Now what's up?'

'Sir, I'm telling you because I don't think I can talk to anyone else.'

'Is it just your problem, or is anyone else involved?'

'Skirmish knows, sir. He was with me.'

Munro nodded. He might have guessed.

'He didn't think we should say anything.'

'But you did.' Munro leaned towards the boy confidentially. 'Just tell me what the problem is in your own way.'

'Well, sir, it's like this.' Beaver arranged his thoughts and then set off on an edited account of the afternoon's escapade. 'We were just

194

smoking, sir, nothing worse than that.'

'So why are you telling me? I'll bet Mr Wentworth knows you smoke.'

'Oh yes, sir, but he doesn't know we do it in his cellar.' Beaver looked embarrassed. 'Besides, after... after all that's happened we felt we ought not to be there.' He struggled for words. 'We didn't really know Mrs Wentworth – though we had tea with her when we were new boys – but it almost seemed we were taking advantage of Mr Wentworth when he must be very upset.'

'But that's not the problem.'

'No, it's what happened next. You see, sir,' – he had decided to leave out the Chassagne-Montrachet on the grounds of irrelevance – 'we were poking about down in the cellar and quite by chance we found hundreds of coins.' He paused for effect. Like many troublesome boys, he was something of an actor. 'Gold coins. There really are lots of them. They're in bags, but one of them has tipped over and they were spilling everywhere. They must be worth *thousands*.'

Munro looked carefully at the boy. He was dark-haired with an energetic, mobile face. He was clearly telling the truth. 'So why are you telling me?'

'It seemed to us, sir, that they'd been hidden. And look at what's happened... I don't know whether Mr Wentworth knows they're there or not. And I could hardly ask him, could I? I couldn't say 'I've been smoking in your cellar, sir, and I've found some gold.' Besides,' – he looked up at Munro and smiled mischievously – 'Besides, sir, we might want to go there again.'

Munro was heartened the boy could confide in him. 'Nothing worse than smoking, Beaver? You know what I mean.'

'Certainly not, sir. We've sometimes had a drink, but that's the lot.' He was indignant. 'We don't have anything to do with drugs – if that's what you mean, sir. I don't know anyone who does.'

'Good, I'm relieved to hear it. Now, Beaver, you're not the fool you sometimes try to make out. Are you telling me all this because you think it may have something to do with Mrs Wentworth's death?'

Beaver looked at him with clear eyes. 'It did occur to us, sir, that with Mrs Wentworth's death and police crawling all over the place it's a bit strange to find a fortune in her cellar.' He repeated: 'They must be worth *thousands*.'

* * * * * *

195

Harrow were recovering. After losing two early wickets they made steady progress and were 90 for 2 when they resumed after tea. The game was well balanced.

Calverley watched one of his boys bowling, but his mind was elsewhere. The news of Jennifer's pregnancy was a terrible shock. It was a double murder: mother and child. Could it have been his child? Almost certainly not. Jennifer had been with Tawney for most of the term and although he had seen her from time to time there had been no sex since the first fortnight. Most of the time they had talked about the problems caused by her grandfather's death.

Why hadn't she told him about the child when she'd been so frank about everything else? Because she didn't know who the father was? Or was she frightened to tell him? She would have told him once, in the early stages of their relationship. But recently? Doubtful. She'd been drifting away for weeks. The jealousy he recognised only too well stirred in him again. He actually liked the young man, but jealousy is unreasoning, beyond control. He found himself a prey to emotions he had previously only read about, only considered in an intellectual way. Suppose Tawney was the father. Had she told him? And if she had, had she also told him about the gold...and the gun?

He realised he was posing the same questions which must be exercising Barnaby. But he was driven on by his jealousy; he was surprised to find it so potent even though Jennifer was dead. He would ask Tawney.

He looked round the ground. The torpor of the afternoon was still apparent. Some visitors were lying on their backs basking in the sunshine, making no pretence of watching the cricket; others were carrying trays of drinks. Irving, glass in hand, was sitting with a pair of governors in the pavilion seats. Moncrieff was as prominent as he had been throughout the day; he had cornered an Old Merchet he had once taught, now a stockbroker with a reputation in the market. Munro was sitting with a boy on the far side of the ground. Here and there other masters were being sociable. There was no sign of Tawney.

Calverley watched another ball, then set off back to the school.

* * * * * *

Barnaby had gone to the mobile incident room where Taylor was collating material with a couple of constables.

'We've got a mountain of paper work and we're getting a clearer picture of movements,' said Taylor. 'And forensics have come back.'

'Yes?' Barnaby still considered himself fit, but was getting his breath back after walking briskly up the slope from the Acre. He looked at the plan of the amphitheatre seating pinned up on a board.

'They're not at all sure about the gun. The ballistics man said something called a Welrod is a possibility. He says it's rare – I've never heard of it, have you? It was a very close shot. No more than a couple of feet and it might have been closer.'

'Never heard of a Welrod. Couple of feet? Close enough to be sure you won't miss. But it was pitch black. Difficult to be sure you were close to the right person.'

'It might depend where you were starting from.'

'Movements?'

'Nothing really new, sir,' said the young constable plotting movements on the seating plan. 'Calverley, Ford and Tawney were near enough. Rathbone and St. Leger were in the right area – though by all accounts Rathbone was having a right old barney with Miss Baskerville. More difficult for Wentworth. I'd say well-nigh impossible without being seen getting down to the stage. There is just one thing, sir.'

'Yes?'

'The Treece family were in the front row – and they weren't meant to be. You asked me to check them particularly, sir. Sir Roger Treece is a crusty so-and-so. He didn't like the seats he'd been given. He got here early, made a fuss with Mr Charteris and got his seats moved.'

'How did he manage that?'

'I asked the same question, sir. Mr Charteris says he left some flexibility in the seating plan because he knows how awkward one or two parents can be. Merchet fathers are wealthy and powerful men used to getting their own way. He knew someone would complain.'

'Which side were they?'

'The side nearest the murder.' The constable pointed at the seating plan. 'Up here, sir. Five seats down from Mr Ford and six away from the Wentworth party.'

'Did they move once they got there?'

'They went out during one of the natural breaks early on, but father Treece says none of them moved after the Victorian scene.'

Taylor said: 'I've got a print-out of Mrs Wentworth's calls on her mobile coming soon. Her husband's quite happy for us to poke about among her things.'

Barnaby was looking at the seating again when the telephone rang. It was Ford, who had received his message and was waiting at the Old Almonry. He promised to be with him shortly. To Taylor he said: 'Get hold of Sir Roger Treece. He's down at the cricket. Tell him I want to see him this evening when the match finishes. And don't worry about him being wealthy and powerful. Just say he's wanted.'

Barnaby was gruff and peremptory. Anyone who knew him would have recognised the mood. The case was near breaking point; he did not want a slip now.

* * * * * *

Sylvester Ford was frowning. The genial presence conveyed at their earlier meeting had gone. Barnaby noticed the bow tie under the beard: immaculately tied, but greasy.

'Miss Bingham said you wanted to see me. And I understand you've given instructions for the gallery to be closed.'

'There's a problem.'

Ford sniffed in a way Barnaby had come to recognise as character-istic. 'Look here, Chief Inspector, I haven't got long. Please be brief.'

Ford was showing the side of his personality that alienated so many of his colleagues: an arrogance based on assumed intellectual super-iority. Barnaby ignored the change of mood. Experience told him it was a good sign, an indication of someone on the defensive.

'I went back to the gallery, Mr Ford, and had an instructive time looking at the collection.'

'I told you it was good.' Again the hint of truculence.

'I'm particularly interested in the Cotmans. Are you certain they're genuine? Have you a full record of provenance?'

Ford frowned again, as though dealing with a recalcitrant junior boy in the Shells. 'Of course they're genuine and of course we have a record. This a private gallery, but it's open to the public. You don't imagine we're totally unprofessional. Merchet has a reputation. We can't afford mistakes.'

'Of course not. Nevertheless, one of the Cotmans is, as I say, inter-esting. I should like to know the provenance of his *Church at Buckenham Thorpe*. And I should like to look more closely at the

198

picture itself.'

'I can arrange that. When?'

'It would be helpful if we could do it now, Mr Ford.'

Ford's brusqueness evaporated. 'I'm busy, Inspector, as I said before, but I'm happy to satisfy your curiosity. I'll put off the boys I was going to see and I'll bring the picture and any paper work back here in a few minutes.'

Barnaby noted the change of mood; it was as though Ford had decided a conciliatory attitude was more politic. His confidence remained undented.

Ten minutes later Ford returned. He was carrying the picture and a box file.

'Do you know Buckenham Thorpe?' asked Barnaby.

'I've been there once, but I'm not a Norfolk man.' He was almost jocular. 'All too rural and puritanical for me. I'm an urban animal.'

'I was born in East Anglia.' Barnaby took the picture and held it out in front of him, his fingers gripping the gold frame with care. 'And I did the first ten years of my service there. Tell me, how did Merchet get this?'

Ford opened the file. 'We've got four Cotmans, all gifts of Old Merchets at various times. They weren't part of the original Manners collection, but we added them to it and hang them together. Let's see who gave this one.' He leafed through the papers slowly. 'That's strange. There's nothing here on Buckenham Thorpe – all the others are here. I could have sworn we had documentation of every picture.'

'I don't think it's strange, Mr Ford.'

'Why not?'

'Because it's not a Cotman, whatever the signature says.'

'Not a Cotman?' Ford's voice rose in the querulous manner Barnaby had remarked previously, the style that placed a question mark over the intellectual credentials of the person he was addressing. 'No-one's queried it before. I'm sure we've got the paperwork somewhere even if it's not in this file. It's possible Miss Bingham moved it for some reason. I'll speak to her.'

'It's a fake, Mr Ford, and I'll tell you why. Look at the spire on the church tower. I know that was added by Gilbert Scott in the second half of the nineteenth century. Cotman couldn't possibly have painted this in 1832 – the date given here. There was no spire in 1832 and he died in 1842. Whoever painted this didn't do his homework.'

'Oh dear,' said Ford, his large head nodding forward. 'It rather looks as though an Old Merchet has deceived us and made us think he was bequeathing something more valuable than it is. But perhaps he was fooled too. Perhaps he gave it in good faith and didn't know any more than we did.'

'Perhaps.' Barnaby was brisk. 'Leave the painting with me. I want a closer look at it. In the meanwhile, please tell the headmaster I've closed the gallery. It should be cordoned off already.'

'I thought that was temporary.' Ford's plump face, normally rubicund, had acquired an unusual pallor. He sniffed again. 'I'm sure...'

'The gallery will remain closed. There's something wrong there, a problem which may not be unconnected with the murder of Jennifer Wentworth.'

* * * * * *

Arriving back at his office, Barnaby found the telephone ringing. It was Taylor. His normally phlegmatic voice betrayed a hint of excitement.

'We've got Mrs Wentworth's mobile 'phone print out. Calverley's on it, Tawney's there – you'd expect them. But there are three unexpected ones. Pamela Baskerville's there, so is Ford, and then the one I don't think either of us anticipated: Sir Roger Treece – just three days before the pageant.'

Chapter 26

The match was moving to a climax. Merchet took wickets regularly, but Harrow kept the scoreboard beneath the sycamore trees ticking over and soon needed 24 to win with 2 wickets remaining. News of the approaching dénouement had filtered round the school and more boys were drifting down to watch.

Jim Clode sat in front of the pavilion with his Harrow opposite number; they were old friends and had each played a few games for Sussex.

'If there were more matches like this, John, there wouldn't be so much of this limited over nonsense. You just need two captains prepared to take a risk.'

'We've certainly collected an audience. I haven't seen any parents leave yet.'

'Most of them have started on the gin again. Which reminds me : I'm being remiss. What do you fancy? We'd better have something to steady our nerves.'

'I'll have a spot of that Sancerre we had at lunch, if there's any left.'

'So shall I.' Clode stood up. 'We've even got the chaplain down here.' He pointed across to the trees on the far side where Munro was standing on his own. 'I don't think he knows what a cricket bat is.'

Munro was not concentrating on the cricket, indeed he was barely aware he was watching it. He was considering what to do about Beaver's confidences and at the same time marvelling at the way Jennifer had managed to cause problems for him over the past year.

What was he to do now? Clearly he had to tell someone about Beaver's find in the cellar, but should it be Wentworth himself – after all, it was his house – or the police? And how was he to keep Beaver out of it? His loyalty to the boy's confidence was paramount.

Behind it all lurked his own twisted feelings about Jennifer, unfulfilled and unexpressed, together with his jealousy of those who had become her lovers. He tried to be honest with himself and did not like what he saw. 'Sin,' he muttered. 'The Calvinist tradition has much to answer for.'

He was so preoccupied he did not notice the balance of the match swinging towards Harrow. Without losing another wicket, they now needed only eight runs, with time for one more over. They had just taken ten from a loose over by an unintelligent fast bowler whose response to a crisis was to bowl faster and more wildly than usual. The Merchet captain now brought back Treece with his medium-pace outswingers for the final over. He calculated the experienced Treece was more likely to hold his nerve than a tyro leg-spinner only recently promoted from the Colts.

In his deckchair beneath the oaks to the right of the pavilion Sir Roger Treece sat forward, his head hunched into his shoulders; his wife, whose interest in cricket and her son was marginal, continued talking to another mother on her right. Treece had received the message that Barnaby wanted to see him, but had no intention of moving before the match was over. It was still very warm; the abbey tower, visible above the trees, was bathed in evening sunlight.

Around the ground parents stood up or emerged from the drinks marquee for the final over. Groups of boys lined the boundary nearest the school. Clode and his opposite number were joined by the coaching professionals of both sides. The Merchet pro, an ex-county cricketer, nut-brown after years in the open air, a pessimist with little confidence in his own team and a long career in betting, said: 'Ten to one Harrow make it.'

The Harrow batsman took two from Treece's first ball, but the second delivery was a shade slower and he was comprehensively bowled. The boys on the boundary cheered, as did many parents. There had not been so much excitement on the Acre for years.

'Good boy, good boy!' exclaimed father Treece. Then to his wife: 'Watch this, Margaret. The boy's going to win the game.'

His wife put a hand over eyes to shade them from the evening sun and looked out to the wicket.

'Is he bowling?'

Treece was used to his wife's indifference. She had only been persuaded to come because it was an opportunity to show off her new Versace dress.

Six to win, four balls to come and one wicket to fall. The last Harrow batsman, a bespectacled boy who had wrought havoc as a spin bowler but had hoped not to bat, peered myopically down the wicket.

202

'Come on, my boy, come on!' breathed father Treece.

The next ball was far too good for the batsman. He played late, the ball took the outside edge before bisecting the angle between first slip and the wicket-keeper and running away for four. The home crowd – for that is what it now was – groaned. Three balls to go, two runs to win.

Barnaby appeared through the trees and stood next to Munro. 'You couldn't ask for a tighter finish,' he said.

Munro ignored the comment, seemingly oblivious to events on the field.

'There's something I must tell you. A boy says he has found a great number of gold coins in the cellar of Wentworth's house. It was a confidence, you understand, so I depend on your discretion. I've decided to tell you in case it's relevant.'

Barnaby kept his eyes on the cricket where Treece was walking back to his mark.

'Thank you, Mr Munro. That's information I've been waiting for. You've saved me a lot of time. Don't worry, I'll be discreet.'

Oliver Treece turned, ran up to the wicket with obvious determination and bowled a brisk, good-length ball.

Again the batsman edged it, but this time the ball went as a sharp catch to first slip, who caught it and threw it up in delight. The match was over and Merchet had won. Again a cheer went up, this time louder and more excited. Treece and first slip were submerged under the congratulations of their team mates. Some of the younger boys ran onto the field as their heroes made for the pavilion.

Barnaby turned to the chaplain. 'A good match, Mr Munro – though I should like to go back to the days when a player who'd done something outstanding had the grace to look mildly embarrassed. Not much chance of that with all this high-five nonsense. They only do it because they see it on television in every test match. Now tell me about this gold.'

Sir Roger Treece was out of his seat and beaming. 'Well done, Oliver!' he said to anyone prepared to listen. 'Well done, my boy!'

From across the field Barnaby, listening to the saga of Beaver and Skirmish's smoking afternoon, watched Sir Roger. 'I wonder,' he said under his breath.

* * * * * *

Treece congratulated his son as he went into the pavilion, then strolled across towards Barnaby and Munro.

Munro was telling Barnaby about a memorial service for Jennifer he was arranging for the following evening.

'Something very short and simple, Chief Inspector. Just an opportunity for the school community to remember her and express its sadness before the end of term. You'll be very welcome if you would like to come – and any of your men, of course.'

Barnaby thanked him and said he might well attend. Then Munro saw Sir Roger Treece approaching and, hastily making his excuses, slipped away.

Treece was smiling expansively; he spoke in his best board-room manner, exuding confidence.

'You wanted to see me, Chief Inspector. I hope you'll forgive me for waiting till the match was over. I couldn't leave while Oliver was still performing. Have you got any sons?'

'No, Sir Roger, I'm not married. But I think I can understand something of what you feel. Oliver played well today. His innings this morning was first class and he kept his nerve in that last over.'

'Thank you. It's kind of you to say so. Now let's not beat about the bush. What do you want to see me about? I've already made a statement to one of your men about the evening of the pageant.'

'I see you appreciate straight talking, Sir Roger. Tell me how much you know about your son's relationship with Mrs Wentworth.'

'Until a few weeks ago nothing at all. I could see something was wrong with the boy and I suspected it was connected with last summer term, but he wouldn't say anything about it. His house-master didn't have a clue what was wrong. A good chap in many ways, Moncrieff, but not exactly tuned in to modern youth.'

'So when did you find out?'

'It came out bit by bit this term. I made it my business to come to one or two of Oliver's matches. He began to tell me some of it while he was waiting to bat during the Winchester game. I didn't press for the whole story because he was opening up of his own accord.' Treece's creased, leathery features almost relaxed into a smile. 'Probably the first time in my life I've shown any sensitivity.'

'When did he tell you who it was?'

Treece's expression changed again: the heavily moulded face looked like granite.

'Three days before the pageant. He'd held back because he was doing his A Levels and he knew I'd play merry hell. He rang up to tell me when he couldn't keep it to himself any longer. You see, once she had ditched him he was bitterly jealous and he made sure he knew who the new lovers were. He told me it was Mrs Wentworth – and he also told me about Calverley and Tawney.'

'How did he know?'

'Young men aren't daft, Chief Inspector. By the beginning of this term some of the senior boys had a good idea what was going on. I suspect Oliver was one of the last to realise.'

Barnaby accepted the rebuke. He noted the cut of Treece's suit, the expensive Jermyn Street shirt and silk tie. Over his shoulder he saw parents drifting back to their cars. Human nature being what it is, he was looking forward to his next question.

'When did Oliver find out about the abortion?'

'Abortion?'

'Last summer. Mrs Wentworth.'

Treece thrust his head forward. For an instant he looked, thought Barnaby, like a malign toad. A vein pulsed angrily in his temple. He did not speak.

Barnaby went on: 'There is every reason to believe Oliver was the father. What did he know about it?'

Treece recovered his equilibrium. 'I'm staggered, Chief Inspector. I knew nothing of it – and I'm sure you'll find Oliver has no idea. I believe that once he opened up – which took long enough, heaven knows! – he told me the whole truth as he knows it. Frankly, I find it very hard to believe. Are you sure it's true?'

Barnaby ignored the question. He had the initiative and years of experience told him not to lose it when dealing with a man like Treece.

'Did you ever meet Mrs Wentworth?'

'No.'

'But you spoke to her.'

'How do you know that?'

'You spoke on the telephone – three days before the pageant.'

'Yes, I rang her. She wasn't in. I spoke to her husband. He said she'd ring me back. She did.'

'Your number's recorded on her mobile 'phone. What did you say to her?'

Treece's eyes, small and sharp, flicked sideways and then straight back at Barnaby.

'What do you *think* I said?' he barked. 'I told her exactly what I thought of her, that I wanted to see her when we came down for the pageant – and that I would be taking the matter up with the headmaster.'

'Did you see her?'

'We'd arranged to meet the morning after the pageant. She was coming to our hotel in Lewes.'

'So you didn't meet. Not even briefly before the pageant?'

'No. Oliver pointed her out to me when she appeared on stage. A good-looking woman,' he said grudgingly, 'but a complete bitch.'

Barnaby changed tack abruptly: 'One thing, Sir Roger. Why did you change seats to get into the front row?'

For the first time a line of humour moved over Treece's face. 'Because we'd been given bloody awful seats at the back. I never put up with that, at Merchet or anywhere else. You'd have done the same.'

Treece had relaxed. He plainly did not see why Barnaby asked the question.

* * * * * *

Barnaby walked back to the school. The trees lining the main drive cast lengthening shadows; it felt cooler. Most parents had left and the boys were back in their houses. For once he walked slowly.

He had got to start sorting the wheat from the chaff. So far he had been seduced by the lure of motive: sexual jealousy, the lust for gold and the greed he suspected to be the basis of whatever was going on in the gallery: after all, that was why he was going to London to visit the Cellini Gallery in the morning. But motives lie in the human psyche; human beings are unpredictable and certainly not always rational. How else explain heroes and martyrs?

What about the mechanics of what had actually happened? He could see the seating plan in his mind's eye; imagination conjured up possible movements in the darkness. By chance he had already seen one of the boys on stage during the Somme scene, but he was only one boy. What about the others? And Rathbone? And the suffragettes? They had all been through initial interviews with Taylor or one of his team, but he ought to see them himself. What about – his heart sank at the prospect – Pamela Baskerville?

Back at the Old Almonry he was relieved to find himself alone. Taylor and his minions were combing through the statements still coming in to the incident room; uniform were continuing the search for the gun in far-flung areas of the park.

Paul Rathbone responded promptly to a telephone call and collected up the six boys who had been on stage at the critical time. Barnaby recognised Rupert Gibson, whom he had already met, as they sat round him in a circle.

'These were the only ones actually on stage,' said Rathbone. A tall man with prominent ears, he constantly pulled his shoulders back as though on parade; it gave the impression of an unfortunate physical disability. 'I had half a dozen others letting off thunderflashes, firing blanks and so on, but they were behind the acting area and went nowhere near the railing.' He spoke in a clipped way, with a precision he considered military.

'What I don't understand, Mr Rathbone,' said Barnaby, 'is why no-one actually saw Mrs Wentworth before the lights went up. There must have been some light or the audience wouldn't have seen what was happening at all.'

'Quite right, Chief Inspector, quite right. There were spotlights at various times – for example, on the Bristol Fighter that flew over at the end – and we sent up flares in the park behind the action so that soldiers could be seen creeping about in outline. But we only illuminated part of the acting area – the British side – and that made the edges even darker.'

'That's what I said,' volunteered Gibson, anxious to capitalise on his earlier interview with Barnaby.

'And there were piles of sandbags on the other side representing the German front line,' said another boy with tousled hair. 'We spent most of our time on our faces crawling into no-man's land. We've talked about it and none of us saw anything.'

'It was all we could do to see each other,' said another. 'If you remember, sir,' – he turned to Rathbone – 'you originally gave us fixed bayonets, but you scrapped them when I skewered Gibson's backside in the first rehearsal. You thought I'd done it on purpose, sir, but I couldn't see him.'

Barnaby looked at the six fresh faces and thought of the Merchet war memorial he had seen earlier in the day with its endless lists of young men killed in two world wars. If this had been 1914 they would probably all have been dead within four years.

'So everything went according to plan on the night? No mistakes, nothing different? Nothing that might help me?'

The boy with tousled hair spoke: 'It went better than any of the rehearsals.' He hesitated. 'There was one thing, but it's probably nothing at all. I haven't given it a thought till now.'

'Yes?'

'Right at the beginning, when everything was totally dark, before we got out of our trench to go into no-man's land. I heard a sort of pop. Mr Pilgrim's commentary had started and we were ready to move. I heard this sound over on the other side, beyond the sandbags.' He looked down at his hands, then back at Barnaby, with the sort of open expression Barnaby's experience had taught him to trust. 'I can't really describe it – yes, I can – it was like a champagne cork coming out of a bottle.'

* * * * * *

Barnaby had just rung Pamela Baskerville and arranged an interview later in the evening when Sergeant Taylor returned. He arrived opportunely with supper, carried on a tray by a waitress from the masters' dining-room.

'There's a bottle of claret this evening, gentlemen,' she said. 'With the compliments of the masters' room steward.'

'They want us on their side,' said Taylor when she had gone. He was a cynic who did not understand the Merchet culture and felt alienated by it. 'I'd rather have a bottle of beer.'

'We're making progress, Sergeant. I'm beginning to see who the runners and riders are in this one. The pregnancy is important, Ford's up to something dodgy in the gallery – and I think we've found the gold. I'm going to see Wentworth in a minute. I don't think he knows it's in his cellar. I'm sorry for that man.'

'The gold must have something to do with it. I'd back cash against lust any day.'

'You're a middle-aged man, Sergeant. Think back to your younger days. I'd back lust. Anyway, I'm not ruling it out. And when I've finished with Wentworth and Baskerville tonight I'm catching a late train to London for a visit to the Cellini Gallery first thing in the morning. You can hold the fort here.'

After supper Barnaby went round to Theobalds. He found Wentworth closeted with Clode discussing one or two house problems. Clode, ebullient after his cricketing success, immediately withdrew. Wentworth, he noticed, was drinking whisky.

Reluctantly, because he wanted Wentworth's confidence, he intended to protect the source of his information. 'This is going to be a shock,' he began.

'Nothing about Jennifer will surprise me now. I realise I hardly knew her, in spite of the confidences we shared.'

'She inherited something from her grandfather.'

'What?'

'Some gold – a lot of gold. In many people's terms a small fortune.'

'Gold?'

'Gold – and a gun. I can probably tell you the whole story when this is all cleared up. At the moment just take it from me that she brought them back with her after the old man died. I believe the gold's in this house – and the gun may be.'

Wentworth, pale, puzzled, said nothing; his face was devoid of emotion. He emptied his glass and poured himself another whisky.

'We need to go to the cellar,' said Barnaby.

Wentworth led the way into the hall. He opened a door at the far end and descended a narrow staircase. 'There's nothing much here. Just junk we've collected.'

'Where's your wine?'

'Over here.' Wentworth went past an old table-tennis table and various pieces of furniture. 'One or two nice bottles and a lot of plonk.' His voice was expressionless.

There was no sign of Beaver and Skirmish's earlier visit. The smell of tobacco had dissipated, bottles had been restored and chairs returned to their usual positions.

'Is there a light?'

Wentworth turned on a light. Barnaby went to the stacked wine bottles and moved a couple of them. Immediately there was the sound of falling coins. Beaver and Skirmish's attempt to restore order had been only a modest success. As Barnaby moved more bottles, more coins fell onto the floor, some rolling out into the open. Eventually he pulled two bags from the back of the rack; one, more or less full, had remained upright, the other, which had fallen over, had spilled half its contents.

'Where did the old man get it from?' asked Wentworth.

'France. It's a long story.'

'And you think someone killed Jennifer for it? I didn't even know about it.'

'We mustn't jump to conclusions. It may not have anything to do with her death at all.'

Wentworth stooped and picked up two of the coins. They lay in the palm of his hand.

'Sovereigns – both Victoria. It's not possible. And a gun, you say? What sort of gun?' Only now was he catching up on the implications of what Barnaby had said. His pallor was striking. Barnaby could see bafflement and anger struggling for mastery. 'Who knew about this?' he asked.

'That's just what I want to know, Mr Wentworth.'

The bags were made of leather, soft, dark brown and stained, with leather draw strings to close the mouth. Barnaby took hold of the one which was still full and looked inside. Some coins were loose; others were wrapped in what looked like yellowing newspaper. Sheer curiosity made him open the mouth wider. A small piece of paper, clearly more recent, was rolled up and held together by a rubber band.

He opened it. The words, written in an educated but shaky hand, were clear. *For Jenny. Veteris vestigia flammae.* It was signed *John Trebilcock.*

He looked at it blankly. Then somewhere in the recesses of his mind a memory stirred. He was not a Latin scholar, but he had been educated at a genuinely academic old-style grammar school. The phrase was familiar.

Chapter 27

Barnaby, never at his best dealing with women, anticipated his interview with Pamela Baskerville with some apprehension. In the event she was in mellow mood when she came to see him and he was surprised to find she did not fit the stereotype he had been led to imagine.

'I'm sorry to have to drag you over, Miss Baskerville. I know you've seen one of my men and made a statement, but I need to concentrate on a few key moments. You were in the middle of everything at the crucial time.'

Pamela Baskerville was wearing a simple white blouse with a full-length black skirt. She looked cool and feminine; her face, with its strong bone structure and striking eyes, was not made up, but her smile was genuinely friendly.

'I'm glad to come, Chief Inspector. I hope I can help. It was a dreadful night for everybody.'

Barnaby, still not at ease, looked at the notes in front of him. 'If I go through the main outline, perhaps you'll correct me if I go wrong – or if you remember something else?'

Baskerville inclined her head. Her hair, usually unruly, was carefully groomed; her high cheekbones seemed attractive rather than aggressive.

'According to this, the suffragette scene revolved around you and Mrs Wentworth. I understand that you were meant to be the Pankhursts, mother and daughter, and you were the ones who chained yourselves to the railings.'

'Yes – we had a jokey argument about who should be mother and daughter. I told Jennifer she had to be Emmeline – the mother – because she was older than me. She agreed, but said she had no intention of making herself look older. As usual she looked a million dollars and I probably looked older than she did. We both wore one of those luscious Edwardian hats. On her it looked chic, on me it was like a pancake.'

'You chained yourselves to the railing – but you didn't really do that, did you?'

'No, we just stuck our hands through. We needed to get off stage

211

smartly when the lights went down.'

'How close together were you on the railing?'

'A couple of yards apart. The other women were round us shouting and cheering. Jennifer and I had the main speaking parts, so we were in the front.'

'Then the lights went down and you all went off. I gather it was very silent and disciplined until there was a...' – Barnaby searched for a word – 'until there was a slight contretemps off stage when you met the troops coming on.'

Baskerville's face darkened, but she said nothing.

'Had you any idea that Jennifer was still back on the railing? Had you, perhaps, expected to go off stage with her?'

'No. She was nearer the audience than I was. I was conscious of Miss Broad behind me. I had no idea she wasn't with us until we got back to the changing rooms. Besides,' – she paused – 'besides, by that time I was concerned with Paul Rathbone's impossible behaviour.'

For a moment Barnaby thought she was going to launch into a tirade, but she refrained. She pointed at the notes in front of him. 'It's all in my statement.'

'You say Jennifer was nearer the audience than you were. Were any of the other women between her and the audience?'

'There were during the shouting and so on, but John Pilgrim had told us to get into some sort of order before the lights went off, so we could get away quickly. We'd rehearsed that and we all knew Jennifer would be last off because she was on the end. When the lights went down, she was nearest the seating.'

'Apart from the suffragettes themselves, and Mr Pilgrim, who else would have known she would be last off?'

'Anyone who attended the rehearsals. Most of the staff looked in at one time or another – and lots of boys, too. All the stage gang, all those dealing with the lighting – the list is endless.'

'Forgive me asking this, Miss Baskerville. If what you say is accurate, it is most unlikely that anyone mistook Jennifer Wentworth for you. Would you agree?'

Pamela Baskerville was surprised; she had plainly not considered the possibility. 'Don't tell me someone's suggested I was intended to be the victim. I may be a thorn in the flesh of this old-fashioned male institution – Mad Millie and all that – but I don't think anyone wants to murder me.' Momentarily the idea appealed to her. 'Except, perhaps, Paul Rathbone. But then I want to murder him, too. Sorry, Chief Inspector, I'm being flippant.'

* * * * * *

Housemasters are aware that unexpected problems can occur at any time and they become inured to the disruption of their private lives. Calverley returned to Drydens with the intention of talking to Tawney about Jennifer's pregnancy immediately, but was faced with just such a situation.

First, there was a note on his desk from his head of house. *Sorry to bother you, sir, but the Desai business has blown up again. Can I see you this evening? Paul.* More pressing, however, was his matron, who arrived at the same time as he did. One of the junior boys had been having a shower before prep and, fooling around with a friend and some soap, had slipped and hurt his leg. She didn't know how serious it was, but it clearly needed attention. Unfortunately the doctor was unavailable and the matron did not drive. Calverley had little choice but to take the boy to the local Accident and Emergency department himself. Accordingly, he rang the house tutor to tell him to look after the house, left a message for Paul Sandbach saying he would contact him as soon as he got back, told his wife he would not be in for supper, and set off for Brighton with the damaged boy.

As luck would have it, Calverley's arrival at the hospital coincided with the appearance of a group of pensioners suffering from shock after a mishap to their coach during a day's outing from London, so it was nearly eleven before he got back to Drydens. Investigation revealed the boy's leg to be bruised but not broken and he received the rough edge of his housemaster's tongue for daft behaviour before being dispatched to bed.

With that problem out of the way, Calverley got his head of house round to discuss the bullying of Desai. He produced beer, Sandbach relaxed, and it was well past midnight before they finally broke up.

They decided that two bullies required firmer treatment than they had received so far, while Desai himself, the victim of a sedulously over-protective mother, needed to be taught how to stand on his own feet.

Calverley went to the kitchen where his wife had left out a cold

213

supper. As he picked at it and drank a whisky he had brought down from the study, he realised his own problems had faded into the background; he had almost forgotten he intended to speak to Tawney.

* * * * * *

The Cellini Gallery is one of those discreet art galleries in Bond Street which appear to defy economic logic. Although seemingly devoid of customers and often displaying second-rate pictures at astronomical prices, they present a glossy face to the world and radiate confidence.

Barnaby took a late train to London after seeing Pamela Baskerville, spent the night with a police friend, and was on the doorstep when the gallery opened at nine in the morning. He was greeted by an immaculately dressed young man with a yellow tie, pointed features and crinkly hair curling over his collar.

'Chief Inspector Barnaby? Ah, we were expecting you. Please come in.' The young man enunciated as precisely as he dressed. His voice managed to convey a form of welcome, yet at the same time to question the presence of a policeman in the artistic emporium he guarded.

Barnaby looked round the walls. The main salon had an exhibition of oils by an artist apparently influenced by Monet but whose preferred dominant colour was orange. Few had been sold.

'They go down very well in Canary Wharf, Chief Inspector,' volunteered the young man. 'All that minimalism needs cheering up.'

'An acquired taste,' said Barnaby. He had already noticed a pretty young woman sitting at a desk in an inner room. She was dressed in a navy suit: short skirt and high heels suggested she occupied the post once held by Jennifer Wentworth.

'Mr Fanshawe will be down in a moment,' said the young man. 'He had an early appointment with an American, but he knows you're here.'

Mr Fanshawe did indeed materialise within minutes. He was tall, grey-haired and distinguished in a rather weather-beaten way; he wore a bow tie, a blue one. Barnaby saw that the dressing of the staff was as important as choosing pictures for the walls.

Fanshawe clearly did not want to discuss what might be difficult business publicly. He invited Barnaby into an inner sanctum, a

214

comfortable room with expensive antique furniture and two notable pictures, a Pissaro and a Matisse.

'I like the Pissaro,' said Barnaby.

'I've not met an artistic policeman before.' Fanshawe eyed Barnaby with respect. 'Now tell me exactly what you want to know. I am, of course, aware of the...' – he coughed – 'of the problems at Merchet. They have been exploited to the full by the national press.'

'To start with I should like you to tell me what you know of Jennifer Wentworth.'

'She worked here both before and after her marriage. Most galleries like to find a decorative girl for the front of house, as it were, and she filled the role perfectly because she was intelligent and knowledgeable as well. She was with us for six years in all.' He lowered his voice. 'I only wish the present incumbent was as well qualified. Pretty legs and face, but a bird brain. Can't tell a Pissaro from a Picasso.'

'Honest?'

'Completely. From time to time she handled substantial sums of money. There was never any reason to doubt her integrity. Quite the contrary.'

'Boy friends?'

'Oh, yes. She had plenty of followers, mostly intellectuals of one sort and another. There was an Oxford don I thought she might marry and she had a fling with a surgeon from St. Thomas's – before she finally settled for Wentworth. I didn't think that would last.'

'Why not?'

'He didn't look as though he had enough...' – he looked embarrassed – 'enough stamina.'

'You were probably right. Now how did you first have dealings with Sylvester Ford?'

'Jennifer introduced him. She thought we might be able to sell some of his work and I respected her judgement. We gave him a small exhibition. He doesn't go for high prices, but he sells. He has a good technique. I have records, of course, if you want to see them.'

'Yes, I shall want to do that. But I want to know something else first. Did you ever sell anything else for him?'

Fanshawe was guarded. 'Yes, as a matter of fact we did. He'd inherited one or two good nineteenth-century watercolours. His grandfather was a scholar and collector – one of those gentlemen polymaths we've lost. He wrote a notable monograph on Thomas Girtin.'

'One or two?'

'A few more than that.'

'Good ones?'

'Yes. There was a David Cox, I recall, and a De Wint.'

'Cotman?'

'Possibly. I should have to check.'

'And you sold them here?'

'Yes, but if they didn't sell quickly we put them into Sotheby's for him.'

'And you're certain they were all genuine? You checked the provenance?'

A shadow passed over Fanshawe's face. Art dealers are sensitive if either their expertise or integrity is questioned.

'I had no reason to doubt them. I'm a Renaissance specialist myself, but my watercolour man gave them a clean bill of health. We can all make mistakes from time to time, but I would back his judgement any day. As for provenance, Ford's grandfather was a well-known collector with a genuine reputation. The details all fitted. They weren't dodgy pictures appearing out of the blue.'

'Details can be faked, like pictures.'

'Are you suggesting we've been selling fakes?' For the first time Barnaby noticed a slight tic by Fanshawe's right eye. 'I don't think so, Chief Inspector, I don't think so. If you know anything at all about art, you must know that the Cellini Gallery has a reputation it cannot afford to lose.'

'But you can't be sure?'

The shadow passed; Fanshawe smiled. 'You can't be absolutely *certain* of anything in the art world, Mr Barnaby. We don't like to admit we're wrong but, sadly, we are all deceived from time to time. We were once completely fooled by a Breughel – Breughel the Elder, that is. But you have to have a certain expertise to survive and we don't make mistakes very often. I believe all the paintings Ford brought me were the genuine article.'

Barnaby smiled in turn. 'I accept that, Mr Fanshawe. Just for the moment suppose they were not. Do you think Ford could have painted them himself?'

'His technique is excellent, as I've said, but most of his work has been in oil. If I tell the truth, he didn't seem greatly interested when we sold his grandfather's watercolours. I have to say he was more interested in the money – if that doesn't sound too crude.' Fanshawe seemed shocked to have uttered such a sentiment about an artist with whom he was associated. Again the tic was active.

'Not at all, Mr Fanshawe. I can well believe that. I'm sure we all think about money from time to time.'

'Policemen are professional cynics.' Fanshawe was smiling again and plainly felt he was counter-attacking.

'Only because we deal with the underside of society, Mr Fanshawe, on behalf of those who don't want to dirty their hands. To misquote Wilde: 'It's difficult to see the stars if one is constantly looking in the gutter.'

* * * * * *

The Brighton line always seemed one of the most uncomfortable in the country to Barnaby. The train was fast, but the rolling stock was not yet modernised and the permanent way gave a rough ride. He sat in a corner seat feeling every jolt, yet managing to detach his mind to mull over the case.

There were too many things missing. For a start, there were several possible motives but nothing that stood out as obvious. Then there was the gun: the connection with Trebilcock was attractive, but where was it? And if that was the gun he wanted, it immediately pulled the gold back into focus – and it was difficult to see a realistic motive there. Could there possibly be any link with Ford and whatever was going on in the gallery? Perhaps there had been a development while he had been away.

A mobile 'phone rang – inevitably – and a man sitting several seats behind him began a loud conversation laced with the usual banalities. 'I'm on the train...'

It broke Barnaby's line of thought and his mind wandered. Where had he heard the Latin phrase *Veteris vestigia flammae* ? He was familiar with it, but he didn't know why and he couldn't remember what it meant. He'd done Latin up to a modest level, but he knew that wasn't the context. He'd met the phrase somewhere else – and if he could

217

recall where that was he would know what it meant. It probably didn't matter anyway, but he had a tidy mind and disliked loose ends.

The man on the 'phone was excelling himself: 'We've just been in a tunnel...I shan't have time for lunch, so I'm eating a Mars bar...'

Then Barnaby remembered. He might not have been good at Latin, but he had always done well at English and Thomas Hardy had fascinated him in the Sixth Form. He had devoured all the novels before leaving school. To begin with he had not realised Hardy was a poet as well, but once he did, he gave the poetry the same dedication. Now he remembered the poems Hardy wrote shortly after his wife died, an outpouring of passion for a woman from whom he had been estranged in their later years. He headed the poems *Veteris vestigia flammae* – and Barnaby remembered the meaning being rendered as: 'Ashes of an old flame', or 'Traces of an old love.'

The train swayed and rattled noisily over a rough set of points.

So Trebilcock's note to his grand-daughter was simply a reminder of where the gold had come from – a confirmation of the wartime love affair. That was tidy. Released from its immediate preoccupation, his mind wandered off through the Hardy canon. The case had Hardyesque angles. Jennifer Wentworth reminded him of Arabella in *Jude* – the scheming girl who first seduced the academically ambitious Jude. He thought of Hardy's preoccupation with Fate striking down good intentions. Tess's confessional letter to Angel Clare, which he didn't find because it had slipped under the carpet; the rain on the day of Michael Henchard's public entertainment in *The Mayor of Casterbridge*; the tragic irony of the water gushing from the gargoyle to destroy Fanny Robin's grave in *Far from the Madding Crowd*. What of the irony that it might be Trebilcock's gun which had killed his grand-daughter? Were there other ironies to come?

The train arrived in Brighton before lunch. Barnaby was met by a police car and was surprised to see Taylor driving it.

'We've got something,' said Taylor, as he pulled away from the station.

'The gun?'

'Next best thing. The cartridge. Rathbone produced it this morning. Says he found it in the armoury.'

'Explain.'

'The boys in the Somme scene were firing blanks – .303. If you remember, there were cartridges lying all over the place when the

218

forensic boys arrived. They checked them to make sure they were normal and when they'd finished Rathbone collected them all up and put them back in the armoury. He did it himself. Apparently he returns used cartridges when he applies for the next live ones; it's part of the routine. He's quite certain they were all .303, and forensic back that up. But this morning he was looking in the box – 'Just checking,' as he put it – and he found a .32. He brought it straight to me.'

'So either a mistake was made the first time or it was put in the box later.'

'Exactly.' Taylor accelerated through the traffic, the satisfied expression on his face suggesting more information to come. 'The forensic team would have found the .32 on the ground if it had been there. So I'm sure Rathbone didn't make a mistake. It must have been put in the cartridge box later by someone with access to the armoury.'

'Many possibilities there?'

'No. You've seen what an enthusiast Rathbone is about the Corps. He's as proud of his security system as he is of everything else. Only a handful of people can get in.'

'Who?'

'Rathbone controls the keys. The sergeant-major has one, but he's been off duty this term with a stomach ulcer and was actually in hospital the night of the murder. His wife is sure his key hasn't left the house while he's been away. Two young masters who are officers – a Mr Ritchie and a Mr Parry – have keys for an emergency. But I've spoken to them and they say they've not used their keys for over a year. There's no connection between them and the case anyway. They helped with certain scenes done by the Corps in the pageant, but they're adamant their keys never left their houses either.'

Taylor's face, topped by its frizz of red hair, was unusually mobile. He looked sideways at Barnaby as they drew clear of the last houses and headed for a gap in the Downs. 'There is just one boy who has a key. It's a privilege given to the Senior Under-Officer. This whole place works on privileges of one sort or another.'

'And who's that? Have we met him?'

'Oh yes, we've met him all right. It's Oliver Treece.'

Chapter 28

The mood of the school was sombre. The euphoria generated the previous day by the unexpected victory over Harrow had evaporated and reality now held sway. There had been a murder, the police were investigating, the tabloids were enjoying themselves at Merchet's expense; and the abbey service for Jennifer was to take place in the evening.

As far as it was possible Merchet was working normally. That meant five periods in the morning and, as it was not a half-holiday, two more in the afternoon. Calverley had a heavy teaching programme and when not in the form-room was busy with house matters, so he had not yet had a chance to speak to Tawney. Tawney himself taught every period. As a perfectionist, he felt his teaching was not up to standard. Every emotion in him seemed as dead as the crumpled body he had seen on stage. He wanted to weep, but fought back the tears. He had successfully avoided both Calverley and Wentworth; for different reasons he could not face either of them. He was still debating whether to go to the service.

Munro taught three periods in the morning and spent the afternoon preparing the service. It would be a tense occasion and he intended choosing his words with care. After working in his study he went to the abbey, where he was joined by Jasper Hillyard and the choir for a rehearsal of the music.

Moncrieff had been disturbed by the revelations Oliver Treece had made to Barnaby in his presence. Now he had had time to come to terms with them he invited Oliver for a discussion over coffee after lunch. Although an old-fashioned housemaster who believed in a stiff upper lip rather than soul-searching therapy, he felt he should have known of Treece's problems. He had no doubt the whole unfortunate business was Jennifer Wentworth's fault, as he had told the boy's parents the day before. He would have to go to the service, of course, but he was still hoping he might get away in time for one of his London dinners.

Irving's day was disjointed. The press continued to pester him and he was spectacularly rude to a reporter caught in Theobalds trying to talk to boys. He realised that was probably a mistake, but it made him feel better. He had at last made his own statement to the police about the pageant. They did not seem greatly interested; he had the impression he was merely repeating things they had been told many times already. Before lunch he began to redraft the newsletter he sent to parents at the end of term. He had started the original before the pageant: it would need subtle manipulation to get the tone right now.

Sylvester Ford was spending a tense day. He realised he had a problem and he suspected Barnaby knew more than he said. But Ford was intelligent: he saw no reason to reveal more than he had so far. How many cases, he wondered, had come to court because a suspect spoke too freely when the police were simply probing? After all, what evidence had they got? Barnaby had torpedoed the legitimacy of a Cotman, but his gallery would not be the only one in the country to have a doubtful exhibit. He was more concerned by the irritation in his nose, with its constant sniffing and sneezing. He wondered whether it would be wise to visit the doctor.

James Wentworth was trying, unsuccessfully, to fill his time. His teaching was being covered by sympathetic colleagues, Clode was dealing with the house, and he was left in a limbo where he had nothing to do but think. The business of the gold had stupefied him: he saw he had been wrong to imagine he had any real understanding of Jennifer. The truth was he had never known her. His self-esteem, not high at the best of times, had collapsed completely.

In his search for occupation, he had had the gold valued. Prices had fallen recently, he was told; gold was not what it was. Even so, the pile of coins in the cellar was still worth a small fortune. He supposed it was now his. Alone in his study, looking out at the sunlit downs, he laughed aloud. He recognised, as if from a distance, the harsh sound he had heard many times during the years of his marriage.

* * * * * *

Barnaby and Taylor were back in the Old Almonry. A pile of sandwiches stood on a side-table, but they had not touched it.

Barnaby picked up the watercolour of Buckenham Thorpe and held it at arm's length; then he did the same with Samuel Palmer's *Wood at dusk*, which he had also taken from the gallery.

'I'm sorry, Arthur,' – he had discovered Taylor's Christian name during their recent drive – 'I want you to go back to Brighton with these. There's a shop in The Lanes called Hathaways. It deals in antiques of one sort and another. The owner's a man called White. He's an authority on watercolours. Ask him to look at these and give me an opinion. He's sharp, and he's got a criminal record, but I trust his judgement before the fancy boys in Bond Street. He owes me, but you can tell him he'll get a fee. Grab a sandwich and eat it in the car. Get back as soon as you can.'

Taylor looked at Barnaby's strained face. For the first time in the case he sensed urgency.

* * * * * *

Once Taylor had gone, Barnaby tried to get hold of Rathbone. He was teaching a Remove which could not be left on its own, but he promised to come at the end of afternoon school. While waiting for him, Barnaby went to the incident room, where a constable was collating information. One or two members of the audience were only now responding to police enquiries.

'Nothing new, sir,' said the young officer, 'but we've got confirmation of the seating plan. One of the American parents was using a camcorder. He concentrated on the scene his son was in – the colonial scene with the Red Indians – but he shot bits of the others as well. And he took one picture of the audience from the front. There are no discrepancies with the details we've got. They all seem to be telling the truth about where they were.'

'Did he take the suffragettes?'

'Unfortunately not, sir. Nor the Somme. He'd more or less run out of film and was keeping the rest for the fireworks. You've heard about the cartridge?'

'Yes. When can we expect the ballistic check?'

'They promised something this afternoon.'

'Let me know the moment it comes through.'

Back in his office Barnaby found Rathbone waiting. He had sent his Remove back to their houses five minutes early. 'I judged this was more important,' he said. He managed to convey the impression that anything connected with his military activities took priority.

'I know about the keys,' said Barnaby. 'But I want to check the

222

details. Your own armoury key has not been out of your possession and no-one could have got hold of it?'

'Certainly not.'

'Is Mr Calverley anything to do with the Corps?'

'He did a stint when he first came. Those were the days when it was assumed every new master would automatically do about five years. A hangover from the time when young masters had all done National Service. Even Moncrieff did his bit. It's very different today. They can choose whether they want to join or not.'

'Mr Wentworth?'

'No, he's never been in the Corps. But he supports it. He persuades most of his boys to join.'

'Mr Tawney?'

Rathbone raised a finger. 'Not yet, Chief Inspector. I'm optimistic though. He's a good man, very good man indeed. Good with the troops, know what I mean? He said he wouldn't join in his first year. Said he wanted to find his feet in the school before he took on too many responsibilities. Very sensible. But he asked to be shown the ropes and I think he'll come in next term. I had him in only yesterday, going through the sort of things he'd have to do, the courses he'd have to go on and so on. My impression is that he'll sign up. I told the head man so. He's not a skiver like some of the others.'

'What about this key young Treece has got?'

'Symbolic, Chief Inspector. Mark of trust. Senior Under-Officer and all that. First-class boy – in my view the outstanding boy of his year. He could easily have been head of school. Fine cricketer – I think you saw that – and lined up for Oxford if the A Levels go well. I made him Senior Under-Officer without hesitation.'

'And you're quite sure no-one else has a key apart from Mr Ritchie and Mr Parry?'

'Absolutely certain. Tight ship, y'know. Even the head man doesn't qualify.' He laughed, showing a set of irregular teeth. 'The armoury is inspected regularly by the army. Always gets a clean bill of health. No scrimshankers here.'

'How did the cartridge get in there?' Barnaby found Rathbone's pseudo-military style wearing.

'Difficult to say. In theory not possible.'

'Exactly, Mr Rathbone. So which of your men is not as reliable as you think?'

* * * * * *

Merchet Abbey was originally founded in the tenth century during the period of religious reform associated with St Dunstan, but it remained a modest creation until the thirteenth century, when an energetic abbot embarked on a building programme designed to rival the recent Cluniac foundation at Lewes. Much of the abbot's work was destroyed at the Dissolution and various houses in Merchet Farthing bore testimony to the energy of villagers in carrying away stones; the abbey church, however, survived intact and remained the spiritual centre of the school. Widely recognised as one of the finest examples of Gothic architecture in the south of England, it had a west front almost rivalling the splendour of the cathedral at Wells. It was here that St. Leger conceived the pageant; here Jennifer Wentworth was to be remembered.

A public school is a relatively closed community and a death at any level is disturbing. Munro decided from the first that there should be a service for Jennifer. In view of the circumstances, it could not yet be a funeral service, nor a fully-fledged memorial service: it would be a simple recognition that a familiar figure, for some close, for others more distant, was no longer among them; an opportunity for the community to express its sadness.

The service was due to start at 5.15 pm, but much of the congregation had gathered by 5.00 pm. It was a formal occasion – the Usher stood at the west door in his top hat and tails – and boys wishing to attend had been told to revert from shirt-sleeve order to jacket and tie; masters wore gowns. The service was voluntary, but all the boys from Theobalds were there, as were sizeable numbers from other houses. Jennifer Wentworth was a well-known figure and many had a nodding acquaintance with her. Monitors were ushering people to their seats.

Barnaby's initial instinct was to avoid the occasion; he did not want to be an interloper at a private grief. Second thoughts, however, suggested otherwise. It might be an opportunity to observe the Merchet scene to his advantage. He might, for example, see how individuals reacted to each other. He was not to know how important those second thoughts were to be.

'Good evening, sir.' A monitor approached him at the door. 'Would you care to sit at the front of the nave on the left hand side? You'll be with the masters and their families.'

Barnaby had seen boys behaving in various ways since his arrival, not always unimpeachably; but there could be no doubt about Merchet courtesy and confidence when they were on public display. He walked the length of the nave and was shown to a seat near the front.

He settled himself into his pew and looked round the congregation. Irving was in his usual stall near the lectern, his wife beside him. The masters' stalls were full. He recognised some faces, but others he was seeing for the first time. The Calverleys were next to Tawney, with the St. Legers and Pilgrims beyond. Rathbone was next to Ford, who had Jane Osprey on his right. Charteris was with Spooner, while Moncrieff had his matron, Miss Broad, on his left. Beyond her Pamela Baskerville was next to the Clodes. Looking at the numbers, he guessed that most of the eighty-odd members of the masters' room had turned out.

Elsewhere social groups had drifted together. Members of the works department were in the south transept with the ground-staff; secretaries and other personnel from the bursar's office were in the north transept with visiting music staff. Around him, in the front two rows of the nave were other masters and their families. The boys filled the main body of the nave, together with various visitors who knew the Wentworths.

The organist, a boy who had already captured an organ scholarship to Cambridge, improvised on a Handelian theme. Jasper Hillyard looked at his watch, then checked that the whole choir had turned up. Monitors continued to show latecomers to seats. The abbey was nearly full.

* * * * * *

Calverley had engineered his seat next to Tawney. He leaned towards him and whispered: 'Neither of us thought it would end like this.'

'No.'

'You were the one she wanted. She'd made that clear to me.'

'She still talked to you.'

'She trusted me. I take it she told you about the gold.'

'Yes.' Tawney was monosyllabic. This was a conversation he had tried to avoid. He hoped the service would start.

'And the gun?'

'Yes.'

'She ignored my advice. I told her to get rid of it right at the start.'

Tawney said nothing. The organist, previously wandering aimlessly in the upper register, reverted to his main theme and increased the volume.

* * * * * *

Barnaby subconsciously noted the exchange between Calverley and Tawney. His mind was elsewhere. Ballistics had confirmed the cartridge as the one responsible for the murder bullet and he was looking for the flaw in Rathbone's security arrangements. Presumably it would have been possible for someone to break into the armoury, in spite of Rathbone's protestations, but there was no evidence of illegal entry. Which took him back to the keys. Treece might be a high-minded boy, but that had not stopped his seduction. Suppose his father had played some part. How might he have reacted to paternal pressure? Alternatively there was no problem at all if Rathbone himself was involved. But what possible motive could he have?

What about Ford? He did not like the man and hoped his own feelings were not influencing him unduly. He was an established figure at Merchet, albeit a controversial one. Was it within the realms of possibility he had used his seniority and authority to get hold of a key? Far-fetched. He looked at the dome of Ford's head glinting in a shaft of sunlight beyond the choir. He wondered how Taylor was getting on in Brighton.

And at the back of his mind, uninvited but persistent, lurked the Shakespearean quotation from *King Lear*, a quotation Thomas Hardy used to show he was by no means the first to blame to blame the gods for Man's misfortunes: 'As flies to wanton boys are we to the gods; they kill us for their sport.'

* * * * * *

Calverley leaned towards Tawney again. The service was about to start, but he had one more question, the crucial one.

'Did she tell you she was pregnant?'

'Pregnant?'

226

'So she didn't tell you either?'

Tawney's face was drawn and expressionless. 'It's rubbish.'

'Post-mortem. Barnaby told me.'

Alastair Munro and the assistant chaplain came into the chancel from the vestry. The organ played a few more bars before concluding on a sustained chord.

Tawney was ashen. 'It's not possible,' he whispered, the sibilants crossing the narrow divide between the stalls..

The congregation, many of whom had been holding quiet conversations, fell silent. Munro advanced to the chancel steps; he waited until he felt the silence envelop him. Then he spoke.

'We are here today for a short while to mourn the death of Jennifer Wentworth. As I say, it will be a short service and I'm sure most of us will be concerned with our private thoughts and prayers. But it will also mark a moment of memory for our community as a whole. Some of us knew Jennifer well, some hardly at all, simply as the housemaster's wife who walked her dog in the park. But her presence was amongst us and we shall all of us in our various ways miss her.

'The service will be very simple. The choir start by singing Mozart's *Ave verum corpus*; I shall give a short address and lead some prayers; the choir will then sing an extract from Mozart's *Requiem* – the *Lacrimosa dies illa*; and finally there will be the opportunity for anyone who so wishes to light a candle and place it up here by the altar in Jennifer's memory.'

Barnaby was watching faces. Most were mask-like, betraying nothing of the thoughts behind them. Bruce Irving looked stern, as though recent events were an affront to a well-run institution. Moncrieff's circle of white hair bobbed as he inspected the congregation; he seemed to be checking who was, and who was not, present. Stephen Higham was fiddling with the shoulder of his gown as if he found the occasion embarrassing. Barnaby looked round at the boys massed behind him. He could not see Treece.

The choir sang *Ave verum corpus*, Jasper Hillyard conducting from one side of the chancel. Mozart's brief, poignant masterpiece echoed round the ribbed vaulting, impressing even the most unmusical of boys with the solemnity of the occasion.

Wentworth was crying openly. His matron, a kindly middle-aged woman put her hand on his arm in a comforting way. Calverley's head was bowed; Barnaby could not see his face. Ford was staring fixedly at a stained-glass window depicting St.Michael with a flaming sword; the contrast between his impressive forehead and insignificant beard was more marked than usual. The evening sun, still warm, streamed through the glass, throwing red, purple and yellow onto the wall opposite.

The Mozart ended and Hillyard motioned for the choir to sit. Munro stood up and moved towards the pulpit for his address.

Before he could reach it there was a disturbance. Matthew Tawney, whose face had been in his hands since his whispered conversation with Calverley, stood up, pushed past the Pilgrims and St. Legers and made for the door in the south transept. His movement was not as disturbing as it would have been if he had gone down the nave to the main door, but his central position in the masters' stalls ensured that most people saw him go.

Calverley turned to his wife. 'Stay here,' he said firmly. 'I'm going after him.' He, too, pushed past the Pilgrims and St. Legers and went to the transept door.

Barnaby, who had been moved by the Mozart and had closed his eyes, was instantly alert. He looked at the reactions on the faces of other masters, but saw nothing except surprise and, in one or two cases, irritation. Munro paused, one foot on the bottom step of the pulpit stairs. Ford continued to stare at St. Michael as though nothing had happened. Barnaby's instinct for crisis, honed by years of experience, took over. He stood up, apologised to those he pushed past, crossed the nave and went to the door through which Tawney and Calverley had disappeared. Heads turned to follow him.

Outside the school seemed completely deserted. Boys had been told to stay in their houses if they were not attending the service and no-one was about at all. A police car was parked by the library. The school flag, hanging at half-mast, was limp in the windless air. Beyond the Mathematics School, towards the west, a black head of cloud, piled ridge upon ridge, suggested a coming storm. The sunlight radiated downwards in clearly defined beams. The only sound was the drone of a small petrol-engined aircraft flying high over the sea to the south.

Tawney and Calverley were nowhere to be seen.

Chapter 29

Calverley had caught up with Tawney immediately outside the abbey. The younger man was weeping uncontrollably.

'Come back to Drydens, Matthew.' Calverley took him by the arm and steered him into the cloisters on the quickest route to his house. He looked at the grey face with a pity he could not understand. He was acutely aware of the irony of the situation. 'I'm sorry you had to find out like that. I thought they'd told you.'

'No.'

'I expect Barnaby was going to take you off guard, like he did me.'

Tawney was not listening. He said: 'It wouldn't have lasted.'

'How do you know?'

'It never did. She told me.' Tawney turned his tear-stained face to Calverley. 'Was it yours?'

'It couldn't have been.'

'So it must have been mine.' Tawney's monotone was as grey as his face.

Calverley said nothing. The two men, walking slowly, reached Drydens and went in. They sat down in the book-lined study. Calverley tried to keep communication going.

'I was jealous of you. I loved Jennifer as I never loved another woman. I love Mary – in a way. Mary's comfortable and kind. But Jenny was different. She made me throw away all restraint – I became obsessed. I discovered what love really means. I didn't know before.'

Tawney looked at the older man. He said nothing.

Calverley went on: 'I was less realistic than you. I thought I could make it last. She said she was hard and I didn't believe her.'

'What did she tell you about me?'

'Enough to let me know our relationship was reverting to friendship and nothing more. She was blunt. She didn't deceive me.'

'Were you jealous?'

'Of course I was. At first I could have ki...' Calverley stopped. 'No, that's silly. I was very angry. And I suppose I felt a middle-aged fool lured up the garden by a pretty woman. Strangely I was still grateful for being shown what love is.'

Tawney was not listening. He was looking out of the window. 'She didn't tell me about the child. Why didn't she? It was my child.'

'Perhaps she was waiting for the right moment.'

'Don't defend her.' Tawney spoke fiercely. 'It was my child.'

Calverley felt the need to keep talking. 'My marriage will never be the same again. It's all a terrible mess. I had to let her go to you. It reminded me of the last act of *Der Rosenkavalier* – with sexes reversed. I was the Marschallin handing over Octavian to Sophie. In spite of the jealousy, I almost felt generous.'

Calverley did not think Tawney had heard. He was looking out of the window again. Then, unexpectedly, he said: 'One of the great moments. Probably the best music Strauss ever wrote.' He spoke automatically, his real thoughts elsewhere.

'It doesn't explain what happened – that night. I still don't know what she did with the gun.'

'I do,' said Tawney. 'I know exactly what happened.' The bitterness of his tone was unmistakable. 'I must go. Thank you for telling me about the child.'

Calverley was nonplussed. Tawney crossed to the door and went through it without speaking. Out of the window Calverley watched him crossing the quad towards his rooms. Emotionally in turmoil himself, he was surprised to find himself pitying the younger man.

He had barely taken in his final words: 'I know exactly what happened.'

* * * * * *

Barnaby had already been to the Abbot's House looking for Tawney. Not finding him there, he retraced his steps to the abbey, where the service had ended and the remnants of the congregation were drifting away. He saw he might be button-holed and that was the last thing he wanted, so he went quickly back to the Old Almonry. Taylor was waiting for him, having just got back from Brighton with the pictures.

Barnaby's contact, White, had been quite explicit. A small man with gimlet eyes and a blood-red complexion, he hopped about with pleasure. 'Fakes,' he said. 'Bloody good fakes, mind you. But

230

absolutely dud.'

'Can you prove it?' asked Taylor.

'Oh, yes. Look at this.' He took the Cotman out of its frame and held it up to the light. 'Whatman paper. Watermarked 1903. Probably taken from an old book or atlas. The Palmer's dated 1910. Our chappie knows what he's doing and his technique's pretty good. But he can't fool me. Cotman and Palmer were dead and gone to the painters' Valhalla when this paper was made.' He put the picture down. 'Now, Sergeant, did you say something about a fee?'

Barnaby laughed. He knew White's sense of humour and Taylor's report of the interview lost something of its flavour.

'Could there be others?' asked Taylor.

'I'm sure there are. There were several I felt were 'wrong', but I couldn't pin anything down. That wraps up the case against Ford. Open and shut. Fraud and theft.'

'Theft?'

'Oh, yes, theft. What do you think he was selling at the Cellini Gallery?'

'Fakes.'

'No, he was too clever for that. He took genuine pictures from the gallery here and replaced them with his reproductions. His fakes would soon have been found out in the London salerooms. The fact his grandfather was a well-known collector gave him the opportunity to create a credible provenance. Down here there was a lower risk of discovery – a risk he was prepared to take. Most of the pictures were from the Manners collection, given just after the war, and some of the others were bequeathed to the school before the war. Most of the donors are dead now and unless anyone with particular expertise came along and looked too closely he stood a good chance of getting away with it. I understand he often found excuses not to put the watercolours on display as well. But he became too complacent – the usual story. He started painting his own pictures to fill some of the gaps. That's what happened with *The church at Buckenham Thorpe*. I'm sure he actually went up to Norfolk to paint it. It was sheer chance I happen to know about the spire. His luck held till then.'

'How much did Jennifer Wentworth know?'

'That's what I'm going to ask him.'

'Fraud, theft – and murder?'

'Possible – even probable. I want his rooms searched. You get onto that now while I see Tawney. There's something odd going on with him too. I went to his room twenty minutes ago, but he wasn't there. Give me the school telephone card. I'll try him again.'

Barnaby picked up the 'phone and tried his number. It rang for so long he thought Tawney was still out. Then Tawney answered. His voice was barely recognisable.

'Hullo?'

'Mr Tawney, I'd like to speak to you. Is it convenient now? It must be this evening.'

There was a lengthy pause; Barnaby wondered if he was still there. Then: 'Yes, it's convenient.'

Barnaby's intuitive responses came into play again. All round him he detected urgency. There was no time to be lost. He turned to Taylor.

'Get hold of Ford. Keep him with you while you search his place. I want to see him again tonight anyway. You can be as tough as you like. Make sure he stays put and doesn't leave the premises. Whatever happens, I don't want him off the hook. Right, I'm going to see Tawney.'

* * * * *

Looking back at it later, Barnaby could see why he was so depressed as he made his way to Tawney's rooms. He did not know for certain, but subconsciously he suspected the truth; and subconsciously he wondered if he would be too late.

Personal thoughts intruded. His approaching retirement seemed more attractive than it had for some time. His juniors saw him as a workaholic, but he knew his energies were flagging. He had enjoyed watching the cricket with his panama over his eyes. But old instincts were strong. The sense of impending crisis meant he had to act, to stay in control. His intuition was not infallible, but it had served him well in the past.

He crossed the quad, threaded the cloisters and came out beyond the abbey. The heat of the day had left a breathless, heavy atmosphere. The threatened storm had not materialised, but the sky was now overcast and grey.

232

He walked quickly, his thin body bent forward, his mind preoccupied. He registered certain vignettes as he passed. Stephen Higham talking to a boy outside the library, his arms waving about characteristically; a group of sixth-formers in coloured blazers strolling down to the Dacre Club; a couple of young masters he did not know going off for a game of tennis; Alastair Munro, still in his cassock, talking to James Wentworth on the steps outside Theobalds. Again he marvelled at Merchet's capacity to seem normal. He hoped it would cope with whatever shocks were still in store.

He reached the Abbot's House. As he climbed the stairs – Tawney's rooms were on the first floor – he heard the music. He recognised it: the trio from the last act of *Der Rosenkavalier*. He stopped on the half-landing to listen.

As he paused, a boy came down the stairs. It was Oliver Treece. 'Good evening, sir,' he said politely.

'Hullo, Oliver. Been seeing Mr Tawney?' hazarded Barnaby.

'No, sir. Mr Rathbone – his flat's on the same landing.' Treece looked puzzled. 'He was asking about my armoury key.'

'What did he want to know?'

'Whether I'd used it or lent it to anyone, or whether anyone could have got hold of it.'

'And you said?'

'I didn't use it and I didn't lend it. It's a sort of ceremonial key and I'm not even sure which lock it fits. And I don't suppose anyone else could get at it because no-one knows where I keep it. In any case my room is locked. As you probably know, sir, senior boys are allowed a weekly ration of beer. We certainly don't want the juniors getting in and nicking it.' He was smiling. 'We can't trust them an inch.'

'That sounds secure enough.' Barnaby looked at the fresh-faced young man. He seemed absolutely normal, just as he imagined a clean-cut public schoolboy. It was difficult to relate him to the problems of the past year. He could only think of one thing to say: 'Well played yesterday. A good knock – and you kept your nerve in that last over.'

'Thank you, Mr Barnaby.' He almost blushed. 'It was touch and go.'

'Well done, anyway. Goodnight.'

It was an agreeable exchange, if not an easy one for either of them. Even as he spoke the final pleasantry, Barnaby's questioning mind wondered whether the boy was telling the truth, whether it was strange to find him coming down from the rooms belonging to Rathbone and Tawney.

He continued up the stairs and knocked on Tawney's door. The strains of the Strauss trio had given way to the final duet between Octavian and Sophie. Their voices carried through the door onto the staircase.

Then he heard it. He'd never heard the sound before, but he knew exactly what it was and it galvanized him into action. Without knocking again he grabbed the handle of Tawney's door and turned it. The door was locked. Simultaneously he shouted, 'Tawney.' He tried the door with his shoulder, but it refused to budge. He shouted again, and this time Paul Rathbone appeared at the door opposite in his shirt sleeves.

'Problems?' he said.

Barnaby wasted no time with explanations or courtesies. 'Ring Tawney on your 'phone,' he said curtly. 'If you don't get an answer, I've got to get through that door.'

Rathbone, who preferred to give orders, recognised the voice of authority, as well as the air of crisis. He rang Tawney's number. 'No reply.'

'Who's got a key?'

'The Usher's got a key to everything, but he won't be in his office now. He'll be at home in the village. Let me try the door.'

Barnaby stood aside and Rathbone threw his shoulder against the door. It refused to give way. Rathbone rubbed his shoulder. The last bars of *Der Rosenkavalier* worked through to their bitter-sweet ending.

'I've got something that will smash a panel if it's urgent,' said Rathbone.

'It's urgent.'

Rathbone disappeared into his flat and re-emerged carrying a heavy brass artillery shell. 'It's all right,' he said, seeing Barnaby's alarm. 'It's quite dead. Purely ornamental – but heavy. I use it as a doorstop.'

Rathbone raised the shell and crashed it against the door panel. At the second attempt the panel splintered. Barnaby pushed his arm through the hole. The key was in the lock on the far side and he opened the door. 'I'll go first,' he said.

The music had come to an end and after the battering of the door there was silence. The two sash windows were wide open. They looked out onto a small orchard; beyond was a larger field with sheep in it. The room itself was long and high-ceilinged; books dominated two of its walls. A large mahogany desk faced the door. A red light on a stack of audio equipment between the two windows showed the source of *Der Rosenkavalier.*

Barnaby took it in swiftly. Then he saw what he feared. Protruding from behind an easy chair was a trousered leg ending with a black male shoe. Half a dozen steps forward and he confirmed his worst expectation. Lying on his back with blood over one side of his face was Matthew Tawney. There was more blood on the carpet by his head. In his hand was an ugly-looking pistol of a type he had not seen before.

He knelt to feel for a pulse, but the staring eyes and bloody mess by the temple told him enough. Tawney was dead

Rathbone was paralysed with shock. 'Christ!' he exclaimed. He had never seen a dead body before.

Barnaby reacted with the efficiency born of experience. For a start he wanted to be on his own, so he got rid of Rathbone.

'Go back to your flat please, Mr Rathbone, and call the school doctor. Tell him it's an emergency and get him here as fast as you can. Don't give him any details – say you're speaking on my behalf. Then please stay in your flat for the time being. I may need you again. Tell no-one about this – that means no-one. I'm sealing the whole area and I'll tell you when you can leave.'

Rathbone's military façade crumbled; he was shaking. 'Right,' he said. 'Right, I think I've got that. I'll get Armstrong.' He gave a final glance at Tawney's body and left.

Barnaby waited for the door to close, then picked up the 'phone on Tawney's desk and rang the incident room, where he knew there was a man on duty. He was curt. 'We've got another body. Now listen carefully. First, ring Brighton. I want the full murder squad back here as fast as possible. The Abbot's House – first floor. Is the other constable with you? What's his name – Bray?'

'Yes, sir.'

'Good. Tell him to arrest Sylvester Ford at once. The charge is theft – for the time being anyway. I don't want any slip-ups with him. We'll get one in the bag. Then I want Sergeant Taylor over here just as soon as you can get hold of him. He should be with Ford. Have you got all that?'

'Yes, sir. I think so.'

'Right – get going. And stay by the 'phone. Report back to me as soon as everything's under control. I'm in Tawney's flat – that's internal Merchet number 432.'

Barnaby looked down at the body with its staring eyes. The expression on the face was one of surprise. Suicide? The gun was still in Tawney's hand and he had heard that sound when he was on the landing outside the door. How had the boy described it? Like a champagne cork – yes, that was it. But he remembered the Claydon Court case years ago – oddly another school – and the man found with a gun in his hand. That had been murder.

Had that sound been the moment of death? He mustn't jump to conclusions. As always he felt guilty when a case produced a second corpse. And he was thinking about Hardy again: was this the final irony?

Chapter 30

Barnaby averted his eyes from the body. He had reacted automatically to the events of the last few minutes. Now he needed to be reflective.

He looked round the room. A door in the corner led into a bedroom and beyond that was a bathroom; the bathroom was entirely internal and had no window. He opened the door of the large wardrobe in the bedroom: it was full of clothes and there was no room for anyone to hide. As in the study, the bedroom windows were open. They, too, looked out onto the orchard and the field. He leaned out. It would have been impossible for someone to have jumped from the study windows, but there was a fire escape outside the bedroom. This was the back of the house and had been substantially rebuilt in the nineteenth century. Between the two windows was a small iron platform, with vertical ladder rungs running to the ground. An exit was possible here.

Beyond the orchard and the field the main school drive curled round to the gates of the estate. He watched a car pull out of the parking area behind Drydens and set off into the trees towards the London road. He hoped Ford was secure.

He did not touch it, but he looked at the gun again. He was in no sense a firearm specialist, but he knew it was unusual. The butt was squat, the barrel long and fat; it clearly incorporated a silencer. As the agency of the death before him it had an innate ugliness; its physical proportions and lack of aesthetic balance increased its repulsion.

It had to be the gun that had also killed Jennifer Wentworth. He knew where it came from if Calverley was telling the truth. But who had been keeping it since Jennifer's death? Tawney? Calverley? They were the two closest to her in the last weeks of her life. Ford? A liar and a fraud, but there was no evidence of a connection with Jennifer since she collected the gun from Monks Risborough. Niggling away was the memory of his encounter with Treece on the stairs only moments ago. Mere chance, or something more sinister?

He looked at Tawney's body again. He was a young man and he

237

looked even younger in death. His eyes, staring blankly at the window, were a self-imposed indictment for Barnaby. So far he had touched nothing except the 'phone, which he had handled with a handkerchief. He noticed the light on the amplifier of the audio system again. To one side was the empty C.D. jewel case of *Der Rosenkavalier*, the Karajan version. Somewhere in the recesses of his memory he recalled a woman at a dinner party saying that if she had to die she would like to do it accompanied by the last act of *Rosenkavalier*. Was this stage management? But stage management implied care, thought, time. Why was there no note, no explanation?

He examined the desk again. There was no note there, nor on the floor. He did not want to start opening drawers or turning things over before the forensic team arrived, but his impression of Tawney was of a meticulous man, a man of order. Unless he was woefully awry, he believed he would have left an explanation of suicide. Or was that too rational? Suicide meant desperation. Desperation might destroy all character traits in a final act of nihilism.

The arrival of Dr Armstrong, lugubrious as ever, broke his reverie. The deep creases of his face and heavy jowls reminded Barnaby, bizarrely, of a bloodhound. He seemed unsurprised by the appearance of another body. He confirmed Tawney's death in a matter of fact way, distancing himself from any emotion.

'Looks instantaneous. One shot, I would say, without cleaning him up.' He looked up at Barnaby from his position on one knee by the body. 'Merchet will find this difficult. Linked with Jennifer Wentworth, I suppose?'

Barnaby was non-committal. 'Thank you for coming. That's all for the moment. Please say absolutely nothing about this for the time being. I don't want to go public until I've had the police team here. I'll let you know.'

As Armstrong left, Taylor arrived. He was breathless and had obviously run up the stairs. He looked at the body dispassionately.

'Suicide?'

'It looks like it.'

'Is he our man?'

'Could be.' Barnaby was laconic. 'What about Ford?'

'I was just going to tell you. Ford wasn't at home, so I haven't seen him yet. But I've been over his place. There's a surprise.'

Barnaby was irritated. 'Don't play guessing games.'

'Cocaine. In his bedroom. It'll need to be tested, but it's cocaine or I'm a Dutchman.'

'That explains a lot. The sniffing and sneezing – and the need for money. I felt that man didn't fit here. He's got a few intellectual cronies, but he's an isolated figure. I hope Bray's picked him up. We don't want any loose ends there.'

'He was still looking for him when I left the cottage. Has this chap any links with Ford? Or has the picture business been a wild-goose chase?'

Barnaby was not listening. He was registering the fact that Ford had been at large somewhere in the school at the time he had been trying to get into Tawney's room. What possibilities did that open up? He tried to imagine the unathletic, pot-bellied Ford climbing out of the window onto the Victorian fire-escape. Absurd.

'We've caught a thief and a fraudster, whatever else happens. No obvious link with this. I suspect Jennifer Wentworth was more valuable to him alive than dead.'

'And the gold? That would have helped fund Ford's addiction – if that's what it was.'

'We're not certain who knew about it. No evidence Ford did. It could be just Calverley and Tawney. It may not be relevant at all.'

'If this is suicide,' said Taylor, indicating Tawney's body, 'why now?'

'I don't know. It might be something that went on between him and Calverley in the service. They were talking and Tawney suddenly walked out.'

Taylor moved circumspectly round the body. Dr Armstrong had put a white napkin over Tawney's face and blood was beginning to seep through. 'So we don't know why he killed himself. And if we assume he killed Mrs Wentworth we don't know why he did that either. After all, she'd dropped Calverley and gone to him.'

'Difficult to fault that summary, Sergeant. I can't answer either question. But I'm beginning to understand Tawney. If I've got him right, he was a man of principle, a man of ideals. Everyone I've spoken to stresses what an upright fellow he was – and what a successful schoolmaster. The clue may lie there.'

'A man of ideals,' said Taylor sarcastically, 'so he murders someone.'

The telephone rang. It was Constable Bray. He was succinct: 'Ford's gone, sir.'

'What do you mean, gone?' Barnaby was uncharacteristically

brusque; he was also aware his response sounded obtuse.

'He wasn't at his cottage and no-one's seen him in the school since the service. I spoke to the man who lives in the cottage next door and he says he saw him driving off. About half an hour ago.'

'Which direction?'

'Coast road, sir. He says he had suitcases with him.'

'Who is this man?'

'A chap called Hayward. He's head groundsman here. Says he particularly noticed the cases because he couldn't understand a master going off during term time.'

Barnaby turned to Taylor. 'You stay here and deal with the forensic lot. They'll be here any minute. I'm going after Ford.'

'At least this one won't move,' said Taylor.

* * * * * *

Barnaby went back to the incident room and set things in motion for the pursuit of Ford. Adjacent police forces were contacted, details of the car circulated, and ports along the coast alerted. He even arranged for local airfields to be watched. It all seemed very dramatic, but he had no intention of being blamed for half measures. He looked at his watch. It was getting late, but there was a lot to do before he could consider bed.

He rang Taylor to check the forensic team had arrived. They had and were still hard at it. Then he telephoned the headmaster. Irving had been dining with one of the governors and was not pleased to be interrupted.

'What is it?' he asked testily.

'I must apologise for disturbing you so late, Mr Irving, but I have two pieces of bad news and it is a courtesy that you should be told at once.'

'Go on.'

'First, I am very sorry to have to tell you that Mr Tawney is dead. I found his body earlier this evening.'

'Tawney?' Irving, normally in command of a situation, was off-balance. 'Dead? How?'

'Shot.' Barnaby fell into the monosyllabic dialogue.

'Who by?'

'I don't know. It could be suicide. No proof yet.'

240

'You said you had two pieces of news.'

'Yes. Your head of art – Mr Ford – appears to have left the premises. I've initiated a hue and cry for him. I'm not sure of the full extent of the charges yet, but they will certainly include fraud and theft. He's been selling pictures from the Dorter gallery and he's been faking others. He knows we're onto him and I don't think he'll get far.'

Barnaby felt the tension he had created at the other end of the line.

'I'll come over,' Irving said.

The session with Irving was short and to the point. The headmaster wanted to know the details of Tawney's death, as well as chapter and verse for the charges against Ford. Barnaby did not mention the cocaine suspicion. Irving did not probe further into the possible murderer of Jennifer Wentworth or Tawney; as a good administrator he merely wanted to ensure he was master of the facts as they were known. The drama of the situation had not entirely escaped him, but he was concerned with immediate problems. What would he say to the School in the morning? Who would cover vacant periods? And how, at this late stage, would he set about finding satisfactory replacements for two key members of staff in time for the new academic year starting in September?

When Irving had gone, Barnaby yawned and looked at his watch again. He levered himself out of his chair and set off back to Tawney's flat.

The forensic team was packing up. The photographer was taking his final shots. A police doctor, a man who was totally bald and looked bored, was writing notes at the desk. He said: 'Not much doubt about suicide in my book.'

'The gun's interesting,' said the firearm specialist. 'I haven't seen one of these for years.' He pointed at the weapon, now encased in a plastic bag on the desk.

'What is it?' asked Barnaby.

'A Welrod. A bit of an antique. Used during the Second World War.'

'Who by? It doesn't look like any normal military pistol I've seen.'

'Special operations – people like S.O.E. Single shot, silenced. Used for assassination jobs by allied agents in Europe. Nasty looking thing. Very rare. Strange to see it crop up here. We'll have to test it, but I'd lay odds it goes with the cartridge and is the gun that killed the woman. Who is this chap?' He indicated Tawney's body, now enclosed in a body-bag on a stretcher.

'A young schoolmaster,' replied Barnaby. 'Now,' – he turned to Taylor, who was standing by the open window – 'anything new?'

'Yes, they found this under the body when they moved it. It's a personal tape-recorder. The sort of thing you talk into when you want to record something and it's easier than writing it down.' He picked up another plastic bag from the desk.

Barnaby took the package eagerly. 'We must hear this. There was no written note. He might have used this instead. I want to play it now. Any problem?'

The fingerprint man signalled agreement. 'It's covered in prints. Just be careful.'

Barnaby held the recorder in a handkerchief and ran the tape back to the beginning. The forensic team, now packed up, stood round expectantly. Hardened and cynical though they were, they could not disguise their interest.

Barnaby pressed the play button.

Chapter 31

The machine crackled, as though with a loose connection. Then came a voice, thin and tinny, but recognisably Tawney. He was speaking German. At first it was not clear what was going on, but when he spoke in English it became apparent he was preparing a lesson on Schiller. He talked about the plays, particularly *Wallenstein*, and then he concentrated on the *Ode to Joy*. He was planning to link it with Beethoven's setting of it in the Ninth Symphony. He referred to the Furtwängler recording made at the re-opening of Bayreuth after the war and took the opportunity to discuss the problem of musicians like Furtwängler and Strauss who continued to perform in Nazi Germany.

Barnaby was impressed. Tawney's ability as a schoolmaster was immediately apparent. Eventually his voice stopped. The tape continued to roll silently.

Taylor was bored. He said: 'Glad I didn't have to go to *that*. Nothing much there. I was hoping...'

'Listen.' Barnaby held up a hand.

The tape crackled into life again. Tawney's voice had changed: it was brittle and breathless; his delivery was staccato.

'I expect you'll find this. I hope you'll find this. I want to explain myself. I don't want pity or sympathy – I want to be understood.'

The mood in the room changed. Barnaby and Taylor looked at each other. The photographer stopped fiddling with his equipment. The voice continued, punctuated by pauses.

'I've no choice now. I've got the gun and I know what I'm going to do.' Pause. 'I expect you realise I killed Jennifer. If you don't now, you soon will. But do you know why? I loved her... No-one can say I didn't love her. I loved her too much. I killed her because I knew it couldn't last. I was jealous of her past – that was bad enough. But I was jealous of the future. I knew she wouldn't stay with me. She couldn't be faithful – she told me so.' A long pause. 'She was good at sex, and that's what she wanted, but she didn't begin to understand love. She had no idea of the effect she had on men, no idea of the way she damaged them.

'I'm a fool. I was lonely – and I had a notion of romantic love. She was everything to me – I would have done anything for her. I spent every waking hour thinking about her. She was matter of fact. She wanted a man in bed. 'None of this pedestal nonsense,' she said when I tried to explain my feelings.' Another long pause. 'And she made demands, sexual demands...'

The tape went silent again. The tension relaxed. It seemed to have finished.

Another crackle. Then: 'She gave me the gun to get rid of. She kept it because at one time she talked about finding out what her grandfather had done in the war. She thought it might help her track down his activities if she had some evidence to show the authorities. Mark had told her to hand it to the police. She ignored him, but now she was with me she asked me to do it. I said I would. But she gave it to me at the wrong time. I loved her, God knows I loved her. But I wasn't going to lose her like all the others. She was going to be *mine*.'

The voice sounded normal, almost banal; the sense of the words froze the attention of all in the room.

'It wasn't difficult. Anyone in the front row could have done it. No prompting was needed in the Somme scene, so I could go anywhere. It was dark, totally dark after the brightness. I knew exactly where she would be – at the end of the railing and last off. She knew it was me. I wanted her to know it was me. I was right behind her. I told her 'No-one else is going to have you.' There was another long pause. 'Just one shot. I was very close. I could have missed, but I didn't. I wasn't going to be just one more. She wrecked lives. She was beautiful...'

The breathlessness increased. 'She told me about all of them – even the boy. *How could she?* You may not understand me, but I understand myself. Love is possessive, jealous. Love wants everything, the whole being.'

The disembodied voice had risen in pitch. After another pause it returned flat and calm. 'This evening in the abbey Calverley told me she was pregnant. It was *my* child – it must have been my child. She didn't tell me. I killed my child as well...' The voice trailed off and was followed by another silence.

'You will understand the rest. I have no alternative.'

Tawney's final words seemed to hang in the room as they waited

244

to see if there was any more. The recorder crackled again; the tape went on turning silently.

'So that's that,' said Barnaby. 'I should have known. I should have been able to stop him. It's pure Hardy. The final irony is the killing of his own child. I should have foreseen what would happen once he knew the truth.'

'Poor bugger,' said Taylor. 'Poor lonely bugger.'

'A vulnerable man, a voracious woman. Disaster more or less inevitable.'

'It saves a lot of work,' said Taylor. 'Thank God for that.'

* * * * * *

Barnaby telephoned Irving again. He was in bed, but not asleep.

'It's all over, Mr Irving. I'll tell you the worst and then I think I can guarantee there won't be any more. We're still after Ford.'

The headmaster was not normally a good listener; however, on this occasion he was silent while Barnaby explained the evening's events. When he had finished, Irving said, in a masterpiece of understatement: 'It raises problems. Have you told Tawney's family yet?'

'It's in hand.'

'I've no sympathy for Ford. He'll be sacked, of course. Treece could be tricky. I don't think the boy will come to any harm in the long run, but in these litigious days its conceivable his father might sue us. On the other hand, I suspect he'll keep quiet while we try to get him into Oxford.'

'I'm going to bed, Mr Irving.' Barnaby felt it was his turn to be tetchy.

'Of course, Chief Inspector, of course.' Irving diplomatic antennae readily detected the need to keep the police on his side now that so much was to become public: his tone became solicitous. 'You certainly deserve a good night's sleep. But I'd be grateful if you would come to my house first thing tomorrow morning. In view of what's happened, I shall be calling a meeting of my senior management team before I address the School. That will be at eight o'clock. It will be helpful to have you there to deal with any questions.'

Barnaby sighed inwardly. 'Very well, Headmaster,' he said.

* * * * * *

Barnaby was staying in one of Merchet's guest rooms, a small, black-beamed room over the old monastic warming-room. The night was short and he slept badly. The case was more or less wound up and there was satisfaction in that; but he blamed himself for Tawney's death and something was niggling away at the back of his mind which he felt should have warned him of Tawney's guilt and the possible outcome. If he could have pinned it down earlier, he might have taken preventive action.

He shifted his feet – for once the bed was long enough for a man of his size – and found a cool area of sheet. Tawney had the gun and the ammunition: no problem about that. But how did he manage to put the used cartridge into the armoury without a key? Then suddenly, it was clear. He sat up and looked out of the window at the fields lying silent in the moonlight. He remembered the conversation with Rathbone about the Corps. What had he said? He was optimistic about Tawney joining the Corps next year. The words came back; he could hear them clearly now: 'I had him in only yesterday, going through the sort of things he'd have to do...' He had imagined Tawney going across from his flat to Rathbone's; after all, they were on the same landing. But he had not meant that. He meant Tawney had gone to the armoury. He was showing him 'the courses he'd have to go on and so on.' Rathbone had not seen it any more than he had. Tawney was bright. For all he knew he had arranged the visit. He knew where the box of empty cartridges was kept. All he had to do was slip the incriminating .32 cartridge in with the others when Rathbone wasn't looking.

He lay down and managed a couple of hours of uninterrupted sleep.

He was up at 6.30 and in the middle of shaving when Taylor rang.

'They've got Ford. He was on the car ferry to Calais. Travelling on a forged passport. He's more of a con artist than we gave him credit for.'

'I suspect he's sold things abroad as well. We may find the Merchet thefts are only part of the story. The cloak of public school respectability could cover a multitude of sins. Anyway, get him back to Brighton. That's the end of the story as far as he's concerned.'

Barnaby looked at his bleary eyes and the white beard of shaving soap round his face. Time for a holiday, he thought. Once he had imagined his energy, fabled in the CID, would be everlasting. Now he was beginning to feel mortal like everyone else.

* * * * * *

Barnaby made himself a cup of coffee, spruced himself up, and arrived at the headmaster's house in time for the eight o'clock meeting. Irving sat behind his desk; St. Leger, Pilgrim, Moncrieff and Killigrew sat in a half-circle before him: all were gowned and suited. Irving waved Barnaby towards an empty chair and said: 'I'd like you to go through everything you told me last night, Chief Inspector, and anything else, of course, that has happened since. Then we'll be in a position to judge how to handle the School.'

Barnaby looked at the serious faces around him, assembled his thoughts and outlined the case. He omitted personal details he felt not relevant and said nothing of Ford's probable drug habit because it was not yet proved. He concluded with his assessment of Tawney.

'He was a lonely man in a strange environment. When Mrs Wentworth befriended him, he felt loved and accepted. But he had an idealistic view of her that was' – he looked for the words – 'inconsistent with the facts. He wanted her to be perfect and to be completely his. He soon saw he could not change her and she would never belong to anyone.' He glanced round as if to reassure himself his audience was entirely male. 'She was one of those women who enjoy the chase of a man but want to move on when the prey is caught. Usually considered a male characteristic,' he added didactically, 'but not as uncommon in women as you might think...

There was an element of self-disgust, too. He saw how his own desires had made him a victim like all the others. Killing her was the act of a desperate and unbalanced man. He was a perfectionist in all he did – Oxford First, outstanding schoolmaster, conscientious to a degree. You should hear the tape of his lesson preparation; he'd thought through every detail. But the relationship with Mrs Wentworth was a failure. And then he found he'd killed his child as well. Suicide was the only logical conclusion.'

'Very sad,' said St. Leger, who felt he should say something. 'Sorry to be so trite.'

'So Ford and Treece had nothing to do with it?' said Irving.

'No. Just names on the Wentworth list. Ford tried to get away

247

because he saw his particular game was up.'

'And the gold?'

'Totally irrelevant. Except that it was buried with the gun.'

'Why didn't she tell her husband?' Pilgrim asked.

'I've no idea. She told him about the men, I suspect, because that was part of the sexual thrill. The gold and the gun were different. Besides,' – again Barnaby looked round the gowned figures – 'who knows what really goes on inside a marriage?'

There was silence. Irving joined his hands before him as if in prayer. At length he spoke.

'Let me sum up. In our quincentenary year, at the height of our celebrations, we have a murder, a suicide, a head of department who is a forger and a thief, a boy in our charge who has been seduced by a housemaster's wife, a secret abortion, and the revelation of affairs involving senior masters.' He looked at his management team with an air of despondency. 'Gentlemen, it will not look well to the outside world.'

The masters looked at their feet. There was little to say.

Tristan St. Leger, who tried to see the funny side of any situation, allowed the hint of a smile to flit like a shadow across his face. He said: 'But no drugs, Headmaster, no drugs.'

Irving looked at him seriously. The idea had plainly not occurred to him.

'No, that's quite true, Tristan. No drugs.' His face radiated relief. He repeated: 'No drugs.'

St. Leger looked down again. He had always known the headmaster had a limited sense of humour.

Barnaby also looked at his feet. He wondered when he would have to reveal the truth.